# OUT OF THE DEEP

## BOOK ONE
## THE RESURRECTION INITIATIVE

# MICHAEL F. GUIDRY

ARCHWAY
PUBLISHING

Archway Publishing books may be ordered through booksellers or by contacting:

Archway Publishing
1663 Liberty Drive
Bloomington, IN 47403
www.archwaypublishing.com
1 (888) 242-5904

ISBN: 978-1-4808-5753-7 (sc)
ISBN: 978-1-4808-5754-4 (e)

Library of Congress Control Number: 2018900865

Print information available on the last page.

Archway Publishing rev. date: 02/25/2018

# PROLOGUE

Dr. David Keats looked at the woman lying at his feet. He'd tried to stop her from bleeding, but nothing he'd tried had worked. He turned his head to the side and looked back at the other woman. Woman number two was sprawled in a pile of seaweed and debris not fifty feet from where he was standing. She was already dead.

Keats examined his hands. Both were saturated with blood. He knelt, took a piece of the dying woman's blouse, used it to wipe his hands then pulled his cell phone out of his shirt pocket. It was almost dark now and he knew the phone's light could bring big trouble. So he used the tail of his shirt to hide the light while he typed a three word text message. He typed *Elizabeth, call me*. He studied the text for two or three seconds then pressed send. After about a minute the cell's screen went dim then dark. He waited another five minutes. He got no response.

For all he knew Elizabeth could be dead by now. He typed a second text message. *I'll try you again when I get to the house*. This time he pressed send immediately. What he'd typed was a lie. An intentional deception. He wasn't on his way home. He'd only typed that because he knew there could be unwanted eyes looking at Elizabeth's phone.

Keats checked the time. It was almost 7:00 pm. He thought about the last words of Elizabeth's friend. The woman had told him the absolute truth. He was in grave danger. As a matter of fact he was convinced he'd be next to die if he didn't get away from Follett's Beach. But where could he go? He certainly couldn't go home. He couldn't go back to the University either. Not with Linda Cunningham on the loose. Campus Security had no idea where the woman had gone, and for all he knew, she could still be on Campus, hiding somewhere, waiting to kill him. He thought about

Cunningham's bizarre reaction to the assignment he'd given the Interns at the end of the class period. The woman had to be insane. Had she somehow followed him here and then shot these two women? Given where he'd been and where he was now, that didn't seem feasible. So if she hadn't done this...who had?

"People should learn to see and so avoid all danger.
Just as a wise man keeps away from wild horses and mad dogs,
So one should not make friends with evil men.
Nor should he go to places that wise men avoid."
—Budda

# PART ONE

# MIND GAMES

# CHAPTER ONE

**University of Texas Medical Branch Galveston
Department of Clinical Psychology
Same Day, 2:00 PM**

*She could be carrying a weapon,* thought Keats. He immediately stopped staring at the woman. Knowing what he did about her, he couldn't afford to take the gamble. So he telegraphed nothing. In other words, his body language gave her no indication he was thinking what he was thinking. He simply looked down at his briefcase which was sitting on the floor next to the lectern, bent over, casually shoved all his stuff into it then picked it up and headed for the door. She followed him. He stepped to one side and let her walk through the doorway first. She immediately turned and scurried down the corridor toward the elevators. He hurried and went the other way.

With random acts of violence occurring on College Campuses and Universities, year in year out, and most of it lethal, the moment Keats reached his office he called Campus Security. He told the Security Officer who answered the phone who he was and what he needed to report. All he got was silence on the other end of the line. Keats repeated himself and this time he was much more succinct. He also put special emphasis on the *'Dr.'* part.

There was more silence. Finally the Security Officer told him he had to look him up in faculty roster before he could discuss anything with him. It took the Officer two or three minutes just to find the roster and another minute or so to find his name.

"I see here you're a Psychiatrist," said the Officer.

That'd been a statement, not a question. Keats corrected the man.

He said, "I'm not an MD. I'm a Clinical Psychologist. I have a PhD."

"OK," said the Officer. More silence.

Finally the Officer said, "Go ahead. I'm listening."

Keats told the Security Officer what he suspected. Gave him an adequate description of the woman and told him when and where he'd last seen her. The Security Officer thanked him then abruptly hung up. Keats placed the telephone receiver back in its base. By then it was almost 3:00 pm.

The woman's name was Linda Cunningham. Keats removed her folder from the filing cabinet. He opened it. Spread her documents out his desk. She was a transfer student, new to the Program this semester. Keats had leafed through her folder at the very beginning of the semester, but this time he took a more thorough look.

She looked really good on paper, had more than adequate recommendations. He thought about what he'd just witnessed. None of it fit what he was reading. She was a Psychopath. In Keats professional opinion, the documentation almost had to be bogus. It was either that, or she wasn't actually Linda Cunningham. He decided he'd have her removed from the Program first thing Monday morning and barred from coming back on Campus. He placed her folder in the middle of his desk, got up and left.

He intentionally took a circuitous route to get to the faculty parking lot then left campus as quickly as he could. After he cleared the faculty lot he started breathing a little easier. For the next two days he needed be with his equals. Kick back and relax. But is that what was about to happen? No. Keats had no way of knowing there'd been a bizarre shit storm brewing for several months. This thing with Linda Cunningham was only the first indication the storm had made land-fall earlier that week.

# CHAPTER TWO

## Old Town Galveston

After Keats left the University he'd driven around in Old Town for about an hour and during that hour he'd called Campus Security three times. The last time he called he was told Linda Cunningham had managed to leave Campus without being confronted. That didn't really surprise him. The same Security Officer had answered the phone every time he called. The man was a joke.

When he'd questioned the Officer, asked him if he was going to do anything else. The man had told him *no*. Told him he'd notified the Galveston P.D. Said he'd provided the authorities with everything they needed. He assured Keats the local authorities would keep an eye out for Cunningham and pick her up if she was spotted. Keats thought about what the man really meant when he'd said he provided the authorities with *'everything they needed'*. *'Nothing'* was probably a much better fit. In the back of Keats mind he felt like neither this man nor the local authorities understood the gravity of the situation. He decided if that's the way it was, there wasn't a damn thing he could do about it. He headed straight for The Strand.

By 4:10 pm Keats was seated at his usual table in front of a sidewalk café on Strand Street. He had a standing Friday afternoon dinner date with a woman named Elizabeth Davenport. Davenport was a local Plastic Surgeon. For some reason she was running late. When she did show up she was across the street and approaching the café from the wrong direction. She spotted Keats about the same time he saw her. She'd looked him right in the face. Sustained eye contact for maybe four or five seconds then quickly looked away like she didn't know him. Keats couldn't understand why she'd done that.

He watched her veer toward the street. Then he watched her take a seat on a concrete bench near the curb. She was directly in front of him now, but still on the far side of the street, and still pretending not to know him. This was definitely a different twist to their usual Friday afternoon routine. After the Linda Cunningham fiasco back at the University, he was in no mood for games.

More than just a little irritated, he started ignoring Elizabeth completely. He picked up the half empty water glass sitting on the table in front of him, fished out a piece of ice with his teaspoon, and put the ice into his mouth. Then he looked up and down the street, looking first at one thing and then another. He avoided looking directly at Elizabeth, but he was still able to see what she was doing. And after maybe ten seconds he could tell things were changing. He looked directly at her again. She had her eyes locked on him now. He spit the piece of ice back into the glass and set the glass on the table.

This was strange. Keats ignored the waiter who was refilling his glass with water and focused entirely on Elizabeth, nothing else. The waiter left quickly and another ten, maybe even fifteen seconds passed.

Evidently Elizabeth could read the vacant look on his face, because her demeanor began to evolve. She started clenching and unclenching her right fist, pumping the hand, like she had a cramp in it or something. He watched the muscles in her jaws began to torque. She crossed her legs. Then she leaned forward and started using her right hand to adjust the strap on one of her sandals. She tucked the front of her skirt between her legs with her other hand and began massaging the calf of her left leg. After a moment or two the massage migrated to her thigh. The look on her face was really strange.

Keats tossed his napkin onto the table and stood. Evidently standing up was the wrong thing for him to do, because Elizabeth started shaking her head violently from side-to-side. He settled back into his chair. Her head shaking stopped as soon as he was sitting down again. Now she was holding her head perfectly still. He watched her cut her eyes sharply to the right, twice. He followed her line of sight, looked to his left and across the street.

That's when he spotted her problem. A large shabby-looking man was standing not more than sixty feet from where she was sitting. The guy was near the end of the block, leaning against the brick wall of a vacant building, and had a dead stare fixed on Elizabeth. Keats best guess, the son-of-a-bitch was stalking her.

Suddenly the guy stopped staring at Elizabeth and shifted his attention across the street to him. Keats looked back at Elizabeth. He could tell from the look on her face she'd not wanted the guy to know about him. Keats looked back at Elizabeth's pursuer.

This was a big guy. He was wrapped really tight. Obviously he knew he'd been found out and appeared to be extremely pissed about that. Keats reflected for a moment. Anybody with any sense at all would know better than to mess with this guy. But what choice did he have? It was entirely too late to practice good sense.

Keats sized the guy up. He was maybe six-foot-seven, a bit overfed, but still powerfully built. He had dirty-looking brown hair and his complexion was splotchy. The shirt he was wearing was a nondescript tan. It was all rumpled up and wet with perspiration at the armpit. The creaseless khaki-colored casual slacks he had on were way too short and in no better shape than the shirt and his shoes were plain brown beat up looking lace-ups.

Keats tried to get a handle on the man's temperament. The guy looked real bothered. As a matter of fact the fingers of his right hand were so tightly clenched the hand was absolutely white-knuckled. Keats studied the guy's face. His eyes were mere slits and the muscles in his cheeks were twitching.

Keats let his eyes glide back to Elizabeth. She'd been watching him assess the guy and there was absolutely zero apprehension in her eyes. She wanted the perverted bastard dispatched and was convinced he could handle whatever this sorry bastard could dish out.

# CHAPTER THREE

In an instant Elizabeth was on her feet. Then she was dashing into the street, adjusting her skirt as she ran. Fortunately the traffic flow on Strand Street wasn't terribly congested yet so she managed to traverse the entire roadway quickly without being struck by a car or a truck or whatever. As she neared the curb Keats started ignoring her. That's because her pursuer had also stepped into the street and Keats had his eyes fixed on him.

The man paused momentarily, waiting for several vehicles to pass. Keats took another quick look at Elizabeth as she stepped onto the sidewalk in front of him. He watched her take two steps toward his table, stop and set her purse down.

She said, "His cell phone is in my purse. Don't let him take it away from you." Then she abruptly altered her course by ninety degrees and began scurrying up the sidewalk in a northerly direction.

Keats was oblivious to the second turn she took; that turn also ninety degrees; that turn onto the avenue at the end of the next block. Elizabeth's whereabouts were of absolutely no concern to him at that particular moment. Her pursuer was his only focus. Keats stood up and swept Elizabeth's purse off the table into the empty chair on his left. Then he pulled the chair around behind him.

Elizabeth's abrupt departure had taken the guy completely by surprise. When he did manage to get underway again the progress of his pursuit was severely hampered by the traffic flow, that, and his lack of coordination. The result, the clumsy bastard used up six or seven seconds just getting to the middle of the street. By that time Elizabeth was long gone.

The man stopped and stood in the middle of the street. He appeared to be staring at the surface of Keats table. He was obviously looking for Elizabeth's purse. When he didn't see it he looked back at Keats. The ferocity in the man's eyes would have made the blood of the average man on the street run cold, but he could tell Keats wasn't going to cower. It was probably Keats obvious lack of fear that made him hesitate a bit longer than he should have. And it was that extra moment of hesitation that did him in. The truck that hit the man was a Ford F-250 Super Duty Crew Cab pickup. Keats watched the vehicle slam into him. It wasn't a real messy thing, but the guy did look a lot like a ragdoll when he hit the concrete. Anybody could tell he was down for the count.

Keats sat back down. He stuck another chunk of ice in his mouth and crushed it between his teeth. Then he did a quick visual assessment of the unfortunate man's injuries, from a distance of course. The man had sustained some impressive abrasions and contusions. And he probably had compound fractures of his right ulna and maybe his radius. Greenstick fractures of a long bone or two were also distinct possibilities. Keats decided he probably hadn't sustained internal injuries of any significance and in his opinion, the guy would survive. Elizabeth would have plenty of time to notify the authorities. He could testify with regard to what he'd just witnessed, sign a written statement, and they'd be out of the loop. At least for rest the weekend, they would.

Keats watched as two male bystanders checked the injured guy out. One had a cell phone in his hand, obviously dialing 911. Keats looked back at the Ford truck. The driver of the truck was a female. She was just a kid and she remained in the driver's seat, simply going to pieces. And of course the occupants of passing vehicles were all rubber-necking, everybody exhibiting the standard amount of morbid curiosity.

Keats watched a sizable crowd begin to gather on the sidewalk, on both sides of the street. More than a few of the onlookers were grimacing, empathizing with the poor unfortunate bastard lying in the street. But Keats continued to watch from where he was sitting.

He wondered who the guy was. Wondered where Elizabeth had gone and how the hell she gotten her hands on his cell phone. He swallowed what was left of the ice in his mouth and snatched Elizabeth's purse from the chair. He put it on the table and raked most of its contents onto the table top.

She had an unbelievable amount of crap in her purse. He spread it all out. Her personal cell phone wasn't there, but he found another phone. He assumed that was the cell phone belonging to the injured guy. Surprisingly, there was also a midsize handgun lying among the refuse. Keats didn't think Elizabeth had a Concealed Handgun License, but there were a lot of things he didn't know about her. He simply shrugged, shoved the gun back into her purse and continued to sort.

Keats looked up as an ambulance from an outfit called Safe Harbor Emergency Medical Services arrived at the scene. He watched the paramedics jump out and start their scramble. It was something to see. They performed with perfected expediency, like someone had choreographed their every move. Within two or three minutes they had the injured guy on a gurney and prepped for transport.

# CHAPTER FOUR

Keats cell phone chirped one time. He removed it from his shirt pocket and took a look. It was a text message from Elizabeth. That came as no big surprise. She hardly ever used her cell phone to actually talk to anyone. Texting, she said, was more expedient, or something to that effect. In her case, Keats couldn't disagree. Most of the time she was a bit wordy, but this time she'd been extremely brief. Her text consisted of only three words.

*Is he dead?*

Keats responded with an easy to understand text message of his own.

*No. But he'll probably be in a body cast before long. He's totally out of commission. It's all over. There's no reason to be frightened. No more texting. We need to talk face to face. Come on back here.*

And that was that. Signed, sealed, and delivered. Keats folded his cell phone and put it back in his shirt pocket. But he didn't get it back in his pocket good before it chirped again. It was another text from Elizabeth. What part of *'no more texting'* did this woman not understand? He shook his head in disbelief and tried to ignore it, but he couldn't. He took a look.

*I'm not afraid! I can't return to the café. I have issues. This isn't about to be over.*

Keats waited for more from Elizabeth. But that was it. He was composing himself to type a scathing response when his cell phone chirped again. Elizabeth had added quite a bit. He read her addendum.

*Put EVERYTHING back in my purse. Get in your car and drive to the west end of Galveston Island. Cross the San Luis Pass Causeway. Stay on Highway 257 and go exactly three miles. You'll see two huge sago palms in concrete planters on the bay side of the road. Turn right between the two sagos. The property is gated, but the gates will be open. You'll be on a blue rock road. The road is several hundred yards long. There's an unusually large bay house and some other odd looking buildings at the end of the road. Meet me there.*

Keats was getting more than a little steamed. He reflected for a moment or so then he answered her with another text.

*Do you think I'm an idiot? Of course I'll put EVERYTHING back in your purse. The son-of-a-bitch has been neutralized. Come on back here and we'll talk about things. There's nothing to worry about.*

Elizabeth's response was almost immediate. He read it.

*You're very wrong. And whatever you do, don't contact the authorities. I'm caught in the middle of something extremely bad. I can't explain that right now. Just meet me where I asked you to. Please do as I ask, David.*

Keats thought about everything that had just happened. He reread Elizabeth's text message, entirely. None of this added up. He texted her a response.

*I'm leaving now.*

He waited a moment or two, got nothing else from Elizabeth. So he left.

# CHAPTER FIVE

## Cold Pass Pawn Shop

Keats cleared the San Luis Pass Causeway about thirty-five minutes later. He'd been re-thinking all the things that'd happened. He'd seen a lot of bad shit in his lifetime and some of it had been an out-n-out nightmare. Hopefully, Elizabeth was making this out to be more than it was. After all, she did have a vivid imagination. He decided to suspend judgment until he'd he had a chance to find out what she was actually talking about.

There were probably some loose ends he needed to take care of before he did anything else. For starters, he really needed somewhere to park the handgun he'd found in Elizabeth's purse. It probably wasn't hers. Maybe it belonged to the injured guy. But then again, maybe it didn't. Whatever the case, the very thought of her handling the weapon made him weak in the knees. God only knows how she'd gotten her hands on it. Why hadn't she used the damn thing to defend herself? One thing was for sure, she'd not touch it until he had some pat answers and maybe not even then.

There was a pawn shop at the first caution light past the San Luis Pass Causeway. He decided he'd leave the handgun there and maybe pick it up later in the evening or maybe the next day or maybe never. He pulled up in front of the shop. It was a *Mom and Pop* outfit, or so he'd been told. He sat in his car for a few seconds, studying the place. It was certainly rundown and raunchy-looking. There'd been multiple add-ons to the original building and each new addition looked like a bad after thought. But, he decided it'd do, got out of his car and went inside.

*Pop* was there. But *Mom* was nowhere around as far as he could tell. He studied the old man. The guy looked like skepticism personified. Keats decided if you looked up the word, *codger,* in a dictionary, you'd likely find a picture of this guy.

Keats approached the counter on the far side of the room then stopped and stood there. The old man looked up, but he didn't say anything. He just stood there, mouthing a soggy nasty-looking unfiltered cigarette stub. Keats noticed there was a *No Smoking* sign hanging on the wall behind the guy. He cut his eyes at the sign then back at the old man. When the old man saw him do it, he immediately took the stub out of his mouth and placed in an abalone shell which was sitting on the glass countertop in front of him. Then he looked back at Keats with suspicious eyes. Keats produced the handgun, pressed the magazine release lever and let a fully loaded clip dropped into his hand.

"Hey!" yelped the old man. "What's your problem, Marine? The sign on that damn door clearly states you can't bring no loaded weapon into this shop. You never learned to read, or what?"

Keats glanced at the smoldering cigarette stub sitting in the abalone shell. He asked, "Mind if I bum a cigarette?"

The old guy got the point. He grunted then extinguished the smoldering stub with his thumb.

"What the fuck do you need?" asked the old man.

"I need to leave this handgun here," said Keats. "A friend of mine gave it to me and I don't want it. I don't know where she got the gun. And until I get an explanation, she isn't getting it back."

Keats laid the weapon on the glass countertop. The old man cautiously scrutinized the weapon, but he didn't pick it up or even touch it. He just looked at it, first from one angle and then from another. Then he asked Keats a question.

"You know what you got here, son?" Keats didn't answer him. So the old man volunteered an explanation.

He said, "That's a military issue model M9A1 Berretta. It was built for the United States Marine Corps, but a lot of Navy Seals consider that handgun the weapon of choice." He looked at Keats a little crooked and asked, "And you don't want it?"

Keats said, "That's right. I've already got all the handguns I need."

The old guy looked at the Berretta again then back at Keats.

"Marine. Ain't nobody ever got all the handguns they need," said the old man.

"I've never been in the Marine Corps," said Keats.

The old guy got a crooked grin on his face. He said, "No shit?" It was easy to see the old guy was an accomplished smartass. Keats didn't respond.

After a few more seconds the old guy asked, "What do you expect me to give you for this piece?"

"I don't know," said Keats. "And I don't really care. Just give me whatever you want."

The old man didn't respond to what Keats had just said to him. He just initiated a sustained stare. Keats decided he was probably thinking he had a genuine moron on his hands. He decided he'd give the old guy as much time he needed to make up his mind.

Finally the old guy gave the glass countertop a double tap with his knuckles and said, "You don't look like no dumbass to me. Guess the reason you don't give a shit is because you already got more money than you need. Tell you what I'm gonna do. How bout I just hold the piece for you? You gimme some ID and I'll give you a receipt for a dollar. But I ain't gonna bother with no other paperwork, cuze you'll be back for it before this weekend is over. Trust me on that."

*Trust him*, thought Keats. *That'll be a cold day in hell.*

Then Keats got his wallet out, produced his Concealed Carry License and handed it to the old man. The old guy scrutinized Keats face then compared it with the photograph on the license. Then he grinned.

He looked back at the license and said, "So you're a doctor?" Keats nodded.

The old guys grinning puzzled Keats a little. But not enough for him to ask what he found so amusing. Finally the old fart started filling out a receipt. When he was done Keats took his copy and the one dollar bill the old man placed on the countertop, turned around, and left. Just before the front door slammed completely shut behind him, Keats heard the old guy say, "See you later, Doc." The inflection the old guy put on the word *Doc* sounded really strange.

# CHAPTER SIX

## The San Luis Bay House

Fifteen minutes later Keats reached the place where Elizabeth had told him to meet her. The property was in fact, gated. But the gates were wide open, just like Elizabeth had said they'd be. He turned between the two huge sago palms and stopped just inside the gates.

It was easy to see the landscaping on the property had been done by a professional. There were sea oats and a variety of exotic tropical grasses interspersed among patches of the local stuff; the stuff everybody along the Texas Gulf Coast is familiar with; needle grass, scrubby oaks, knotty-bark hackberry trees, etc. And like Elizabeth had said, he was on a blue rock road. The road meandered through the vegetation and between the sand dunes like some exotic azure serpent. It was totally unique for the neighborhood. Elizabeth had been adequately explicit. Hell, there was no way to mistake the place. This was it alright.

Keats drove to the end of the blue rock road and found all the buildings on the property were clustered closely together. He scanned all the buildings. They were definitely out of the box. For instance, the main house rested on massive twenty-five foot concrete pilings and there were absolutely no wind-resistant vertical surfaces anywhere, none what-so-ever. Matter of fact everything had obviously been constructed with storm surge and hurricane force winds in mind. The smaller out-buildings, and there several of those, were all of similar design. However, each building was distinctively different from the others. Keats could see no apparent reason for any of the differences. Actually, taken as a whole, the place simply dominated the surrounding area, with all the taller structures offering commanding views of West Galveston Bay to the north and the Gulf of Mexico to the south.

As he approached the main house, it was easy see there were no other vehicles there. As a matter of fact he couldn't really tell if anyone else was there at all. But he went ahead and parked his car on a concrete pad next to a boat-less galvanized trailer and waited.

Ten minutes he waited. Hell he was entirely too restless to just wait there in the car so he decided he'd get out and look around. He opened the driver side door and stepped out onto the concrete. Then he surveyed the underside of the interconnecting decks. There was a rather large open-air elevator on one end of the main building and stairs on the other end. He decided he'd have a better vantage point to watch for Elizabeth from the second-level and elected to use the stairs to get there. He took the steps two at a time.

When he reached the top step he could see that the entrance to the main house was via the deck on the east side of the second-level. But he didn't go there right off. That's because his attention was drawn to an elevated boat house which was connected to the main house on the west side by a ramp. Keats stood at the top of the stairs and studied the boat house. It was situated over a sizable turning basin and there was a canal connecting the basin to the bay. The canal was probably thirty feet wide and at least a hundred yards in length. There was a large yacht-like watercraft moored next to the boat house. If he was going to hazard a guess, he'd have said the protuberances on either side of the boats' bow probably housed a full complement of-the-best-that-money-can-buy marine technology. A number of other inexplicable modifications to the hull suggested the boat was probably one of a kind. But that was just a guess.

He looked at the other structures near the boat house. There were what looked like three medium size storage buildings at ground level and two aerated ponds surrounded by levees not far from the buildings. And adjacent to the largest pond was a helipad. As he turned his attention to the largest of the out-buildings, an unfamiliar voice interrupted his snooping.

"David?"

Keats turned and found himself face-to-face with a woman he'd never, ever before, laid eyes on. He was firm with that, because there was no way he could ever have gotten the image of this woman out of his head.

# CHAPTER SEVEN

Hard to say how long the woman had been standing behind him. There'd been absolutely nothing to telegraph her approach, no creaking boards, not a hint of a vibration, no indication of any kind. She was simply suddenly standing there, close enough to touch and maybe even smell if she'd been standing upwind from him. He looked at what she had on. She was draped in a white translucent ankle length cover-up. His best guess, she'd just taken a shower because her shoulder-length hair, which was as black and shiny as polished obsidian, appeared to be quite wet.

He studied the woman's features. She was put together like a fine piece of art; an alluring ethnic collage; part Asian or perhaps Pacific Islander; possibly of European extraction, because the way she spoke hinted at ancestral French in her genes. And there was also something else unusual about her, something he couldn't quite put his finger on. Took him the better part of a minute before he realized he was just standing there like a statue, staring at the woman like he was an idiot. Suddenly he remembered she'd said his name. It had sounded like a question. He gave her an answer.

He said, "That's right. I'm David. David Keats."

She smiled and offered him the package she was holding in her right hand.

She said, "Elizabeth asked me to give you this, David."

The way she'd said *David* had subtle tinges of inappropriate familiarity. Keats didn't think Elizabeth had disclosed the nature of their relationship with anyone, but he knew he could be wrong about that. He stared at the package the woman was pushing in his direction. He reached for it. She gave it to him, turned and walked off.

Keats stared after her. He looked at the package he was holding in his hands and thought about what she'd said. Elizabeth had been there. Obviously, she'd come and gone. He looked back in the Asian woman's direction and stood there until she disappeared into the main house.

He thought about Elizabeth again. *Where in the hell had she gone?* Keats hefted the package and realized it was unusually heavy for its size. He looked across the deck then back at the entrance to the main house where the woman had disappeared. She hadn't offered him any kind of explanation or told him what to do with the package or told him to follow her or anything else. She'd simply handed him the package, delivered Elizabeth's message then turned and walked off.

Keats studied the package. Maybe whatever was in it would answer some of his questions. He decided he'd better be careful when he opened it, thinking perhaps there could be something fragile inside. He looked around. But didn't see anything he could set it on while he opened it. So he walked back to the stairs, descended to the landing at the bottom, took a seat on the third step up, set the package in his lap, and began working on the bindings.

He stripped the paper away from what turned out to be a plain brown cardboard box. He folded back the flaps and found the box was filled with extruded polystyrene foam. He plunged his hands into the stuff. There were quite a few things in the box. As he worked his way toward the bottom of the box the more confused he became. And then he found it…another goddam gun.

# CHAPTER EIGHT

Keats cradled the box in the crook of his left arm and tapped lightly on the door facing. When the Asian woman opened the door he said, "I'd like an explanation." The woman smiled, but she didn't say anything.

"OK then," said Keats. "You know my name. What's yours?" Her smile broadened a bit, but again, she didn't respond verbally.

Keats stared into her face. It was flawless; beautiful bone structure; the contours of her checks, lips, nose, all of her; absolutely perfect. But none of that moved him, not now. This was getting old. He demanded she give him an answer. The abrupt way he did it put a look of disdain on her face. In retrospect, he wished he'd not been so harsh.

She ignored his demand that she tell him her name and instead said, "I was under the impression you already knew what the box contained. I know now I was wrong. If you'll relax I'll share what I know."

Keats mouth was not yet in sync with his brain and he blurted, "I am relaxed. Just get on with it." Again, his tone was harsh and abrupt.

The look of disdain disappeared and she began with a question for him. She asked, "Are you familiar with the type of handgun in the box? Have you ever used one of these weapons?"

This one was exactly like the gun he'd just left at the pawn shop. The gun he'd found in Elizabeth's purse. He recalled what the old man had told him about the other gun.

He said, "Am I familiar with it? Certainly. It's a model M9A1 Beretta, developed for use by the Marine Corps. Have I ever owned or fired one? No I haven't. But it's just another ordinary automatic hand gun. What the hell is there to know?"

The woman looked him directly in the eyes. There was something steely in the way she did it. He was convinced there was no real way to intimidate the woman.

Matter of fact, he was starting to think he'd better not press her to do or say anything else. So he contained himself.

Her eyes softened, she lackadaisically cleared her throat and started talking. She said, "I've used one of these weapons in the field and there's nothing ordinary about it. It's a state-of- the-art automatic. The tactical reloading characteristics of the weapon are absolutely superior to any handgun I've ever used. There's a tactical light and Viridian Laser installed on the accessory rail. They're the best that money can buy. If you're circumstances are what I've been led to believe, this weapon is perfectly suited for your needs. Agreed?"

The woman cleared her throat a second time and waited for his response. But he didn't respond. He wasn't ready to say anything quite yet. He was hung up on the *'your needs'* part of what she'd said.

She continued talking. "Since you've never used one of these handguns, I suggest you find a place to test fire the weapon soon, before you're actually forced to use it."

Still, Keats said nothing.

The woman cleared her throat again and added, "You asked me for my name. It's Angie. I think it's better for both of us if we keep things on a first name basis for now."

Keats stared into the woman's face for two or three more seconds then he nodded.

She stared into his face for another second or two then said, "I'm ready for your next question." Her brow was smoother now and a slight smile had started to bloom on her face again.

Keats realized he was holding his breath. He exhaled and asked, "Do you have any idea where Elizabeth is?"

He thought of something else he wanted to ask, but before he got to ask it she said, "Elizabeth told me she was going to your house. Perhaps she's there by now. Hopefully she'll have answers for all of your questions when you get there."

Keats didn't budge. He said, "Going to my house." He was having difficulty wrapping his mind around this entire scenario. None of this made any sense.

"And be very careful," said the woman. "Elizabeth told me you were in grave danger. She left me with the impression you already knew that. But I'm beginning to think I got the wrong impression."

Keats didn't comment. He decided he'd heard enough and did an abrupt about face. He returned to the stairwell and on the way down took the steps two at a time. When he reached the landing at the bottom, he stopped and did a quick three-sixty.

Everything downstairs was exactly as it had been when he'd first arrived. It still looked like absolutely nobody was home.

He thought about what Angie had said. Elizabeth had told her he was in *grave danger?* Evidently Elizabeth really believed that. Well was he? This entire scenario was more than just alarming. He decided he had a valid and compelling reason to exercise extreme caution.

He was totally uninformed. That was his most immediate problem. It put him at an extreme disadvantage. He decided he'd better settle down. Decided he needed to maintain adequate vigilance and try to gather some solid *intel.* He revisited the word. *Intel.* That was military jargon. Something he'd just resurrected from a past life. Keats had absolutely no desire to go back in time and relive that part of his life. He tried to refocus on the present and thought about his prevailing circumstances. Right now his personal safety seemed to be the issue. He decided he needed to get his shit together. Prioritize some things. And for starters, he needed to test fire this newly acquired weapon.

# CHAPTER NINE

## Follett's Beach

Keats stopped between the sago palm clusters at the entrance to the property. He looked east then west. He looked straight ahead. All he could see in front of him was a deserted stretch of beach and the open waters of the Gulf of Mexico. He couldn't see any cars or trucks coming from either direction. As far as he could tell he had nothing to worry about out here.

He made a left turn onto the blacktop road and began driving due east. He was replaying the events of the afternoon in his mind as he drove. About a quarter mile from the Bay House, his cell phone began chirping again. He picked it up and took a quick look. It was another text message from Elizabeth. It was about time. There was a sign indicating 'beach access' just ahead and to the right. He passed the sign, turned onto the sand road, drove between the dunes, and stopped when he reached the open beach. He killed the engine of his car and read the text message. It was a three word question, *Where are you?* He decided not to answer any more questions. Not until he got some answers.

He responded with the same three words, *WHERE ARE YOU???* He used all caps and redundant punctuation to telegraph his emotional intensity. He waited for Elizabeth's response. He got nothing from her.

He typed another text message and pressed send. *I'm going to the authorities, Elizabeth.*

Her return text came almost immediately. *You're going to get us both killed if you do.*

He typed a response and pressed send. *OK. I won't do that yet. But you have to tell me where you are. And I want to know what this is all about.*

Again, her response was evasive. *Where am I? Tell me where you are first.*

He didn't respond. He had a condo on the mainland in the Village at Tiki Island. That was his home. That's where Angie had said she'd be going. That seemed reasonable enough to him. After all, she did have a key to the place and some clothing there. Most of it was stuff she slept in, but not all of it. The last time he'd seen her she was a mess. If she wanted to shower and change her clothes she could do that there. He continued to wait. After a minute or so he got another text.

It read, *OK. I'm on my way to Tiki Island. I'm assuming you were told to go there. Are you there yet?*

She was en route. That's all she'd said. That was not a definitive answer. Obviously she didn't intend to give him anything of real substance. He thought about that. He wouldn't give her anything substantial either. If she'd involved him in some sort of cloak and dagger crap, she'd have to be totally open and honest with him before he'd cooperate. He typed another text message and sent it.

It read, *I've been told I'm in grave danger. What's that supposed to mean? And where exactly are you? You call me. I have to know this is you sending these text messages and not someone else.*

He waited for a response; one minute, then two, then three minutes. He got nothing, not even another text message.

*"Good enough"*, he thought. He decided he wouldn't go home, or to the office, or anywhere else someone, or anyone for that matter, might think he'd turn up. Not until he had some concrete answers.

# CHAPTER TEN

Keats needed to take a leak so he laid his cell phone on the dash, pushed the car door open and stepped out onto the beach. He did another three-sixty to make sure he was still totally alone. There were no other cars or trucks, no children or dogs, absolutely nothing anywhere.

He decided he'd do more than just take a leak. He decided he needed to make sure the Berretta Angie had given him would function properly. He leaned back into the car, reached across the driver's seat, and removed the cardboard box from the passenger side. He set the box on the hood of his car, removed the Berretta, and shook it a little to get rid of a few pieces of clinging Styrofoam. Then he depressed the magazine release lever and let the clip drop into his hand. He checked the clip and found it was fully loaded with 9mm hollow-point rounds. He re-inserted it back into the grip and chambered a round. He set the safety then shoved the weapon inside the waistband of his jeans at the small of his back. He walked across the beach halfway to the water's edge and stopped. He did another three-sixty and decided that spot was as good as any.

There was a slight breeze coming from the north blowing directly into the open waters of the Gulf of Mexico. He was facing downwind so he unzipped his fly and relieved himself. Then he tucked his business away. Done with that, he removed the Berretta from the small of his back.

He stared at a tiny Sanderling scurrying about on the beach not far from the fringes of the breakwater. There were several of the little birds chasing the surf seaward as the water retreated from the beach. When they reached low ebb they'd scamper around on the wet sand, pecking at anything that wiggled. As each subsequent breaker rolled in the birds would scurry toward the dunes again. Then as the wave collapsed on the beach, they would immediately reverse themselves and chase the retreating seawater southward. They repeated this over and over again.

Keats decided he'd test the Viridian laser first. He pointed the Berretta at the damp sand between his feet and depressed the laser's switch. A tiny green dot appeared there instantly. He looked around. One of the tiny birds was standing perfectly still, not twenty yards away. He placed the laser's green dot on the wet sand about five inches from where the bird stood, released the gun's safety, and pulled the trigger. Miniscule particles of debris, pieces of broken shell and granulated quartz peppered at least half a dozen birds. The targeted Sanderling, as well as three or four by-stander birds, went down. They looked like they'd been hit by shrapnel. But they all managed to get up and either run off or fly away; all except the targeted bird; that bird was afflicted; matter of fact, it was really struggling.

Keats watched the wounded Sanderling finally right itself. Then he watched it hobble a few feet, stop, and shake the grit and debris from its body. After a few more seconds it spread its wings. The north wind created just enough draft for the bird to finally lift off. Keats returned the Berretta to the waistband of his jeans, pursed his lips and started staring trance-like at the two drilling rigs a mile or so off shore in the Gulf of Mexico.

# CHAPTER ELEVEN

The sound of a decelerating pickup truck brought Keats out of his trance. He couldn't see the vehicle because it was still on the blacktop road and a stretch of sand dunes, maybe fifty yards across, separated the beach from the blacktop. But he could tell it was a big truck and he could also tell it was decelerating real fast. Its exhaust pipes were popping erratically and the rumbling sound of knobby oversized sand tires on the asphalt was changing pitch. As a matter of fact the pitch was dropping rather rapidly. The intent of whoever was behind the wheel was obvious. The driver was attempting to negotiate a turn onto the beach using the access road about a hundred yards west of the one he'd used.

As soon as the rumbling stopped Keats knew the truck was on the access road and would be on the beach soon, probably within ten or twelve seconds. He also knew the vehicle had definite problematic potential. He needed to get the hell out of harms' way and he needed to do it posthaste.

Within two or three seconds Keats was back in the driver's seat of his car and getting it started. He slammed the vehicle into reverse and retreated from the beach via the access road where he'd entered. His retreat took no longer than five or six seconds and once clear of the beach his car was sandwiched between the sand dunes and adequately concealed. He shifted to park, got out of the car, and left it running with the driver's side door ajar. Another three or four seconds and he was crouching in the dunes. He had the Berretta he'd gotten from Angie in his right hand. He'd left his personal cell phone in his car, but he did have the injured guy's cell in his shirt pocket. He'd left the cell phone on, but he'd silenced the ring tone. He decided if whoever was in this truck was a going to be a problem, he was about ready as he'd ever be.

In two or three seconds the big truck rolled onto the beach. Once on the beach it took a sharp right. It traveled away from him about seventy-five yards, turned facing the Gulf of Mexico, and stopped.

The truck was a big black jacked-up 4X4 Dodge Ram crew cab. It sported a pipe grill and wench, had a roll bar behind the cab and all the glass had been heavily tinted. It just sat there, belching exhaust gases for maybe three or four seconds before the occupants of the vehicle killed the engine and decided to bail out onto the beach. Two men got out of the front seat and walked around in front of the truck, their heads swiveling in concert as they walked. Then they stopped and just stood there, both men staring at a tangle of seaweed and debris lying in front of them on the beach. Keats decided this might be an opportune time to gather a little 'intel'.

He took the injured guy's cell phone out of his shirt pocket and unlocked it. He looked at the last number that had been called and touched *redial*. He let it ring twice then terminated the call. Within three or four seconds the cell phone in his hand began to vibrate. He didn't answer it and whoever was on the other end didn't leave any voicemail. He waited. After a few more seconds the caller gave it another shot. Again, Keats didn't respond. Again, the caller left no voicemail.

# CHAPTER TWELVE

About half a minute passed. Then the two men on the beach looked back at the truck. They followed that with a double-take, then turned and walked back toward the truck. They walked around to the side opposite Keats and stopped near the rear door. Then they just stood there, doing nothing, saying nothing. A little more time passed then the right-side rear passenger door swung open. But no one got out. A conversation appeared to ensue. A person, or persons, sitting in the back seat of the truck and the man who'd been driving looked like they were engaging in a heated verbal exchange.

When the talking stopped several items changed hands. The individual, or individuals, inside the truck appeared to be calling all the shots. The two standing men had obviously been given some orders, because they both knelt. Keats couldn't actually see what they were doing, but when they stood up again he could see they'd made adjustments to their clothing. Both had arrived with their shirt tails tucked in. Now their shirt tails were being worn outside their pants. They looked one another over, top to bottom then the driver pointed at the other man's right ankle. The man looked down then did a little *shake your leg* routine. Keats had seen that routine before, a multitude of times. He was convinced the two men standing next to the truck were now both armed. They were probably carrying multiple concealed handguns, at a minimum, two each. Keats opinion, they both had one under their shirt tails, probably inserted inside their pants in the back at the waist and probably another one tucked into an ankle holster and concealed beneath a pant leg at the cuff.

Keats thought about what he'd just seen. The rear door of the truck was still ajar and the two men standing outside the truck began looking up and down the beach. Keats unlocked the injured guy's cell phone again and touched redial. He placed the phone next to his ear and listened. The instant he heard the ringtone the heads of both men standing on the beach rotated ninety degrees.

Keats terminated the call the instant he heard the ringing stop and someone answer. There appeared to be a brief verbal exchange between the driver and whoever was sitting inside the truck. Then the rear door slammed shut and the two standing men were instantly on the move, scrambling to get into the front seat. There was no doubt in Keats mind. The individuals in the truck and the guy who was hit by the truck in downtown Galveston were in some way connected.

Keats continued watching. The man behind the steering wheel had the big Dodge cranked up and underway almost immediately. The oversized sand tires broadcast a huge rooster tail of grit and debris in a perfect arc as the truck began to come about and make for the dunes. Keats was on the move before the driver of the truck managed to complete his initial maneuver and reenter the access road.

Keats had left his engine idling and the car door ajar so he could get behind the wheel in the shortest time possible. That helped him a lot. He was behind the wheel and edging toward the beach within three or four seconds. He hesitated just short of the beach and waited until he could hear the rumble of the knobby sand tires on the blacktop. Then he pulled onto the beach and headed for the access road the truck had just vacated. He intended to turn onto that access road, stop halfway to the blacktop, get out and climb into the dunes again. That way he could keep an eye on the truck. Hopefully they'd not check the spot he'd just left, see his tracks, and come after him. Keats got lucky and the truck continued to accelerate. He watched it travel east on the blacktop until it finally disappeared from view.

He turned and looked back at the beach. About ten yards from where the Dodge pickup had stopped there was a sizable pile of seaweed and all kinds of debris. There was something lying there in that mess that had attracted and held the attention of the two men who'd gotten out of the truck. Keats decided he'd take a look.

# CHAPTER THIRTEEN

When Keats reached the spot where the two men had stopped and stood, he discovered a woman lying in the pile of seaweed. He took a quick look at her. Then he looked up and down the beach. There was no one else anywhere, not as far as he could see.

He knelt and took a good look at her. She'd been shot in the chest, not just once, but several times. She was still alive, but bleeding profusely. His best guess, none of the bullets had done significant damage to her heart. However, the damage to her lungs had to be massive. The woman was literally drowning in her own blood. She be dead soon. Keats knew that and he could tell that she knew it.

He looked at what she was doing with her hands. She had her left arm bent at the elbow, her forearm resting on her abdomen. She'd curled her wrist inward and had twisted a wad of her blouse in her left hand. She was repeatedly jerking down on the blood soaked material. The jerking looked mindless and irregular. What this woman was doing with her left hand was extremely telling. It spoke of shock and desperation.

The woman's right arm and hand were telling the same story, but in a different way. Her right arm was perpendicular to her torso, fully extended and resting in the seaweed. She'd rolled the right hand over, palm down, and had her fingers splayed wide. That hand had a very definite purpose. With that hand she was reaching for a small caliber automatic handgun. The weapon was lying only a few inches from her fingertips, but anybody could see that was an exercise in futility.

Keats studied the handgun. It had a few small pieces of debris stuck to it, but there was little to no sand clinging to the weapon. No blood on the gun at all. He reached for it and got it, examined it, shook off the debris then pulled the slide back a tiny bit. There was a live round in the chamber and judging from the weight of the weapon there were still other rounds in the magazine. The safety was off.

He looked back at the woman, studied her face. The look in her eyes was unmistakable. She knew she was finished and just wanted her ordeal to be over. Keats believed almost anyone in her situation would've felt the same way.

The woman lifted her right arm and pointed a trembling finger at the gun. He could see she'd fired the weapon recently because there was a small bit of gray powdery residue on the back of her hand, on the fleshy part between her thumb and forefinger. He shifted his focus back to the woman's face. She was looking directly into his eyes now, trying to connect with him. He didn't have to be a mind-reader to know what this woman wanted. She wanted him to help her get it over with. Finish her. He considered the possibility, but then dismissed the thought. He could tell she knew it.

The woman turned her blouse loose, reached up with her left hand and grasped the barrel of the gun he was holding. Somehow she managed to muster the strength to get her right hand on top of the weapon. She tried desperately to slip her right thumb inside the trigger guard, but Keats prevented her from doing that. She tightened her grip. Then she began to struggle with him. The woman's strength had ebbed to damn near nothing so that was no real contest. But the weapon did finally fire a round. But the bullet missed her head by more than a foot. Evidently that was all it took, because both her hands instantly relaxed. Keats looked into the woman's eyes. She was dead. The report of the gun had punctuated her passing.

# CHAPTER FOURTEEN

Keats leaned back, sat on his heels and stared blankly into the dunes. He studied the gun he was holding in his right hand. Both the weapon and his hands were covered with blood. He needed to do something with the gun. He searched for a spot to lay it. But the search didn't last very long. That's because he caught a glimpse of someone coming down the beach. Whoever it was was headed in his direction. They were still quite some distance west of where he was kneeling, but coming on fast.

Keats rose slowly until he was standing. He lowered his hand to his side and released the weapon. Then he did a slow one-eighty, rotating to the right, turning slowly from north to south. As he turned he visually swept the terrain to the east. Things still looked totally deserted in that direction. He paused momentarily, staring pensively into the open waters of the Gulf of Mexico. He thought about the dead woman lying behind him in the pile of debris. He ran the fingers of his left hand through his hair then began massaging the back of his neck. While he did that he twisted his head slowly to the west until he had the individual headed in his direction in his peripheral field of view. And that was sufficient for him to garner enough to tell him what he needed to know.

There was another woman on the beach. This one was also a stranger. It didn't look like she had anything in either of her hands, but she was moving at a rapid clip, closing on him real fast. As a matter of fact, only about fifty yards now separated Keats and this new woman.

Keats made his move. He turned abruptly and faced her. She was really close now and he could see she had a strange look of determination on her face. The woman was probably no more than twenty yards from him when she stumbled, staggered a step and fell face-forward into the sand. Keats did a double-take as she went down. What he'd just witnessed was surreal. Someone had just put a bullet in woman number two.

There wasn't a moment of hesitation on his part. He immediately broke for the sand dunes, running like a wild man. He left his personal concealed carry handgun, a Walther PK 380, stuffed inside the waist band of his jeans at the small of his back. There was a fully loaded clip in the weapon and a live round in the chamber, but he didn't waste any time trying to go for the gun. He had no idea where the bullet had come from.

Within three or four seconds Keats was clear of the beach and hurling himself into the needle grass between the dunes. He quickly rolled over, sat up, and looked back at woman number two. He could see she was still alive and trying to crawl in his direction. He knew he needed to think fast. He needed to act fast. He was the only chance this new woman had.

He watched her for a few more seconds. She was at least fifteen yards from the dunes, totally exposed, and getting nowhere fast. The look in her eyes was unmistakable. She was pleading with him to do something to help her. But where in the hell was the *shooter*? There was no way he could just go out there and get her and drag her into the dunes. He'd more-than-likely get his ass nailed too. He reflected for a moment. Maybe there was another way.

He thrust his left arm forward; hand up, palm open and facing her, the standard gesture for 'stop'. He produced his Walther and held it in his right hand. He showed her the weapon. As soon as she saw his handgun she stopped trying to crawl, but she didn't stop looking at him.

He silently mouthed some orders, *"Die and stay dead."* Then he pointed at her and demonstrated what he wanted her to do. He wasn't overly dramatic, but the woman got the message and immediately followed orders. What she did was quite convincing.

Keats watched her for just a moment more, then weighed the possibilities. First possibility, the *shooter* would believe the woman was actually dead now and would leave soon. Second possibility, the *shooter* was still watching and in a few minutes he'd shoot her again just for good measure. Third, and probably the most likely possibility, the *shooter* would just wait him out.

He decided he'd better try what he was thinking. It was risky. Probably downright stupid on his part. But he decided he'd give it a shot anyway. Maybe it would save the woman's life. He looked back at her. She still *looked* quite dead.

In a muffled tone he said, "Don't move and don't say anything. Just listen to me." He got no visible reaction from her. He began to explain her situation.

He said, "The person who shot you may decide to shoot you again, soon, very soon. We can't let that happen, can we?" Again he got no response from her. She'd obviously understood the question was meant to be rhetorical. He went on, "For me to come out there and try to drag you back here would be suicide for both of us. So I'm not going to do that. I'm going to try something else instead. I'm coming out there and just look you over. I may even kick you a time or two. It'll all happen real fast and I'm hoping it convinces the shooter you're actually dead." Keats hesitated. Still he got no reaction from the woman. He added, "Your job will be to stay dead. I hope you can handle this." After a brief pause he added, "Tell me if you can't. But be quiet about it and don't move anything, not even your lips."

The woman cooperated, didn't move a muscle and remained totally silent. Keats decided to get on with it. He took a deep breath, exhaled, and made his move.

# CHAPTER FIFTEEN

He stepped out into the open, hesitated for a fraction of a second then took a second step in the woman's direction. She was doing her part, didn't look like she was even breathing. Finally Keats reached her, stopped and stood next to her. Then he looked up and down the beach, just a quick glance in each direction. He looked at her again, shook his head empathetically and nudged her arm with his foot. He did it a second time. Then he quickly spun around and returned to the safety of the dunes. He'd exposed himself for maybe four seconds and he was still alive. Maybe the *shooter* wasn't interested in him. Maybe he was gone.

Keats looked back at the woman. Had he convinced the *shooter* the woman was dead? If he had, would the *shooter* leave now? Keats had only one feasible option. That was to give it some time. Three minutes ticked by without another shot being fired. That was a good sign. However, now Keats realized the woman who was supposed to be *dead and done for* was actually trying to get his attention. She wasn't moving or anything, but she was speaking, softly, trying to tell him something. Keats listened and tried to understand the woman, but he couldn't. What she was doing was so stupid.

Keats kept his volume as low as he could and spoke to her. He said, "Listen to me. The *shooter* could still be watching you and looking for any sign of life. So don't be talking." The woman didn't stir, didn't answer him either. Keats reflected for a moment.

He added, "I'm going to move around a bit and see what I can find out. You be quiet and remain perfectly still." He'd said that softly, but emphatically. He hoped she'd heard him and hoped she'd cooperate.

He watched her for a few more seconds. She appeared to *stay dead*. But she did speak again, this time a little bit louder than before. She said, "Do what you have to. You're lucky the bitch didn't kill you."

Keats thought about what the woman had just said. It sounded like she knew who'd shot her. He wanted to ask her for clarification, but knew it was unwise to ask her anything at this point.

He simply said, "I understand. Now please keep your mouth shut." But the woman wasn't done talking yet.

She said, "Be careful, David. Elizabeth may be around here somewhere."

That blew Keats mind. The woman had just called him by his first name. As far as he knew, this woman had never seen him before today. And he was absolutely positive he'd never ever seen her before.

Before he could stop himself he blurted, "How the hell do you know who I am?" Then he grimaced because he realized he'd said that entirely too loud. It was too late to worry about that now. He just listened for her response. If she said anything, it wasn't audible. He was about to press her for an explanation when he remembered she'd also mentioned Elizabeth.

"How do you know Elizabeth?" he asked. "How did you get involved in this?"

"Elizabeth and I are coworkers," said the woman.

Well, that didn't explain anything. But Keats let it slide. He knew he couldn't afford to waste any more time trying to get answers. They had much more pressing needs. He had to come up with a strategy that could save both their lives.

"That's enough for now," he said. "You have got to be quiet. Give me some time to think." His come-back had been quick and simple, and fortunately, it effectively eliminated any additional chit-chat.

It took Keats several minutes to concoct a plan and the woman remained silent the entire time. She was so quiet and still he was beginning to think maybe she'd lost consciousness, but that didn't matter. He assumed she could still hear him and he told her what he thought she needed to know. He was careful to be very quiet about it this time.

"Listen to me," he said. "I don't want you to say another word. And whatever you do, don't move." The woman appeared to cooperate.

He said, "Maybe you're seriously wounded, maybe you're not. But you definitely need to be examined, and soon. So here's the deal. The person who shot you may think you're actually dead. Or maybe the person's gone. Right now, I have no way of knowing that. But I do need to find out." He paused to catch his breath then went on.

"I'm going to move around a little and expose myself again. If the shooter is still out there he may take a shot at me. If he does, I'm going to return fire. If he does nothing, I may fire a few random shots where I think he might be hiding." Keats hesitated. Again, the woman didn't attempt to do or say anything. He continued talking. "Here's what you're going to do. You're going listen and that's all. The person who shot you used a high powered rifle. You heard the sound of the rifle when it was fired. My handgun doesn't sound anything like that when it's fired so if you'll simply listen you'll be able to tell the difference. You'll know exactly who's getting shot at and who's doing the shooting. There'll be no warning prior to shots being fired and you mustn't allow yourself to be startled and move when-and-if there is gunfire. Even if you get shot at again, do nothing overt. I repeat. You must not react overtly to anything that happens." Keats paused to see if he'd get any feedback. Again, he got nothing. He added, "I sure as hell hope you're good with all this." As soon as he said that, he got an instant verbal *'I am'* from the woman.

# CHAPTER SIXTEEN

Keats decided it was time to get on with it. He took one more look at the wounded woman then stood up and made his first move. He moved one sand dune closer to the road and took cover behind the neighboring dune. He was out in the open for a good two seconds and no shots were fired. He turned and looked back at the wounded woman again. She still looked quite dead.

He moved again, same direction, one more dune, took him about two seconds again. He immediately moved again, diagonally, one more dune, toward the blacktop road again, but this time to the northeast and hopefully away from the *shooter*. This move took him no more than two seconds.

Keats double checked his surroundings. The blacktop was only two dunes away now. He intended to move east and north again, but this time with a twist. He'd dart out then back. And he'd be quick about it. He sucked in a deep breath and made his move. Instantly out, instantly back. The *shooter's* bullet punched through the near edge of the neighboring sand dune about midway up then smashed into the base of the dune behind it. Had Keats repeated the pattern he'd established, he'd be dead or dying. But his strategy had worked and he was still unscathed. And better yet, he had some solid *intel* to work with. Now he knew the *shooter* was still out there and intended to kill him if given half a chance. This was a game changer.

Keats went right to work analyzing everything he'd observed. He used the trajectory of the last bullet fired to draw an imaginary line in his *mind's eye* from initial point of contact with dune 'A' to the point of final impact near the base of dune 'B'. That gave him a tentative directional fix and approximate elevation on the *shooter*. Furthermore, all he had to do was get back to the dune where he'd started and he could use the exact spot on the beach where the wounded woman had been initially hit, do a little triangulation, and he'd damn near have the *shooters'* exact position pinpointed. Then he'd be on the hunt. Hell, any sniper with even an ounce of special ops savvy would be hauling ass.

While Keats was thinking about all that the wounded woman had also been drawing some conclusions of her own. She'd heard the *shooter* fire his weapon at Keats, decided she was no longer being watched and started crawling again. Keats thought she might do that so he was instantly on the move himself.

This time he skirted the dunes beachside where he had decent cover. He managed to reach his initial position a little before the woman did and he watched her crawl the last two or three feet. She was moving quite well now. He decided perhaps she hadn't been as badly wounded as he'd first thought. He hurriedly examined her and decided her wound was probably superficial.

He asked her if she'd seen Elizabeth today and if so, where. He asked her if she was OK. The woman said she'd left Elizabeth at a beach house that was under construction about a half mile away an hour earlier and she was fine then. She added she didn't know where Elizabeth might be at that exact moment or what her current circumstances might be. Keats considered using the *injured guy's* cell phone to text Elizabeth, but decided against it.

He asked the wounded woman if she knew who'd shot her. She said she had no idea. He asked her if she thought perhaps the same person who'd shot her had also shot the woman he'd found on the beach a little earlier.

She answered that question quickly with an *uh, uh*. She pondered momentarily. Then added *a different person* shot that woman.

That puzzled Keats. "How can you be so sure?" he asked.

She wouldn't tell him. She simply said, "You'll just have to take my word for that."

Keats dropped the subject. He needed time to think, needed time to develop a fresh new strategy.

The woman considered his silence an invitation to ask him a few questions. She started with what he thought *they* should do next. He didn't share his first thought with the woman. It was something like, *"You need to shut up and give me time to think, you idiot."* But, he simply gave the thought a moment to pass then asked her for her name.

The name she gave him was Tricia Compton. He asked her how she fit into the scheme of things. The explanation she attempted to give him was totally confusing, morphed into a Q & A session, and would've gone on for God knows how long if it hadn't been cut short by new rash of gunfire.

# CHAPTER SEVENTEEN

This new gunfire was some distance away. The sound of the weapons involved was very distinctive. There were short bursts from some sort of small caliber fully automatic weapons. There were rounds fired in multiples of two or three from more than one semi-automatic handgun. That had all been preceded by a single shot fired from a high caliber rifle. From what Keats had heard, he determined there were at least three individuals doing the shooting and probably considerably more than that.

The exchange of gunfire had taken no longer than five or six seconds. When it ended he was convinced the first shot fired had come from the same weapon that had been used to wound Compton and take a shot at him about ten minutes earlier. Compton concurred with his opinion. She told him she thought the shots they'd just heard sounded as though they'd been fired in the general vicinity of the beach house where she'd last seen Elizabeth. She said the beach house wasn't a hell of a long way from where they were. Said, in her opinion, they were probably no longer being targeted. Keats agreed with that and asked her whether or not she was up to taking him to the beach house and if so, how fast she thought she could move. She told him she was fine and she could handle whatever he could. He knew that was total bullshit, but he decided he wouldn't tell her that. He simply asked her if she knew what this was all about. She told him she didn't have a clue. Anybody could tell the woman was lying, but he dropped the issue.

Compton produced a small semi-automatic handgun from a pocket in her jeans. Keats had quickly examined her wound, but he'd not bothered to check her pockets for weapons. He wasn't usually that careless, but he shrugged it off and simply asked her if she had any extra clips. She said she didn't. All she had was seven rounds, total. Keats had two spare fully-loaded clips with him, but the Berretta was a nine millimeter weapon and his Walther a 380. Her weapon was much smaller. Hers was a thirty-two caliber. He told her if they got into a fire fight she'd have to remember to conserve her ammunition. What he did not tell her was that he intended to relieve her of her weapon and probably disable her long before they came anywhere near the beach house.

# CHAPTER EIGHTEEN

The woman told Keats they needed to get back on the beach and go west for about a half mile. She said there was nothing but open beach and more sand dunes between where they were sitting at that moment and where the beach house was being built. He told her they needed to get there as soon as they could. She agreed and said she was ready to go.

Keats helped the woman get to her feet and watched her try her legs. She was a little shaky at first, but good enough to give it a go. They exchanged nods. Then Keats did an about-face and broke for the beach. The wounded woman followed him. It was slow-going for the first ten or fifteen yards, because the sand was so loose and deep and dry. But they were able to pick up the pace once they reached the damper sand. That sand was much more firm, almost like running on pavement.

Suddenly the woman yelled, "Stop, David."

Keats immediately stopped running and turned to look back at her. As he turned he felt a weird sensation low on his chest. The sensation was accompanied by a hissing sound. The hissing was followed by the distant crack of a rifle.

A bullet that had been meant for him had missed its mark and struck the woman in the uppermost part of her right thigh. He watched the bullet knock her completely off her feet. He ran back to her, grabbed a wad of her jeans, hefted her out of the sand, and started running toward the dunes. She didn't weigh all that much so he managed to get her off the beach before the *shooter* got off a second round.

He took a look at her leg. The bullet had gone completely through her right thigh. It looked like it hadn't hit any bone and it'd more-than-likely missed her femoral artery. She'd obviously dropped her weapon back on the beach because she was using both her hands to apply direct pressure to the entry wound in the front of her leg. He used his left hand to put pressure on the exit wound in the back of her leg.

He kept his Walther in his other hand while he did it. He looked at her face. She was becoming very pale.

He asked, "Is it painful?"

She said, "No." The way she'd said it sounded snippy.

He said, "Good."

She was avoiding eye contact with him. He said, "Look at me." She did. "How'd you know that was about to happen? Did you see something move in the dunes?"

"I didn't see anything or anybody," she said. "I have no idea how I knew that was going to happen. I just did." She removed one of her hands from the front of her thigh and Keats insisted she put it back.

He told her, "You can't afford to lose any more blood, Compton. You'll go into shock." She sneered at him. He added, "You're probably going to do that anyway."

She snapped, "No I won't."

Keats wanted to say *bullshit* to that too, but he didn't.

# CHAPTER NINETEEN

They were both quiet for several minutes, both thinking, both listening. It was fundamentally impossible to separate the sound of the pounding surf and the chatter of the noisy shore birds from any potentially critical sounds so Keats finally stopped listening and started asking Compton more questions.

He opened with, "Tell me this. How much time do you think separated the impact of the second bullet that hit you and the sound of the rifle being fired?"

The woman thought about it then said, "A second, maybe two. I don't really know."

Keats noticed everything she was asked seemed to irritate her. He ignored her irritation and gave her his opinion.

He said, "It had to be at least a full second, maybe even longer. I know you were definitely on the ground before I even heard it. I'm convinced the bullet had to come from somewhere way off." He paused, thought a second or two then added, "The *shooter* intended for that bullet to hit me in the chest." He touched a spot just below his left pectoral muscle as he said it. Then he added, "That would've been lights out for me." He looked away and stared pensively at the dunes to the west. He said, "The angle and elevation of the bullet precludes any possibility the shot was taken from a sand dune anywhere near here. Whoever fired that shot did it from a roof top or something else pretty tall."

Keats reflected for another moment then asked, "What was the elevation of the beach house where you last saw Elizabeth?"

"It was built on eighteen or maybe even twenty foot pilings. There were two levels above that. No wait. There were three levels. The third one was just a small room, one of those *crow's nest* things."

"Were there any other unusually tall buildings in that vicinity?" asked Keats.

She said, "No. There weren't any other beach houses anywhere around there."

"Could you see any other tall structures in the vicinity?"

She gave his question a little thought before she answered. Then she said, "The closest thing I noticed was a water tower near the bridge at San Luis Pass. But that's at least a mile away, maybe even more. There were a lot of telephone poles. And there was a cell phone tower, but I'm not really sure how far away that was. It was definitely a long way off." She paused then asked, "What are we going to do now? Have you got any idea?"

"Do now?" asked Keats. "Not a damn thing. We're going to wait right here until after it gets dark. It should be totally dark within half an hour. In the mean time, let me take another quick look at your wounds."

Keats had the muzzle of his Walther pointed in her direction. She pushed the gun aside and said, "You don't have to examine me. I'm fine."

He said, "You let me be the judge of that. Roll over on your side and pull down your jeans. I need to take a better look at the back of your leg, make sure the bleeding has subsided."

She didn't offer any more resistance and did exactly what he told her to do. He poked around quite a bit and took his time about it.

Finally he said, "Things look ok in the back. You're mighty lucky. The bullet went through-and-through and it looks like it missed the larger arteries. There is considerable tissue damage, but the bleeding has stopped almost completely. You better hope the clot holds. Now let me see your front side."

She rolled onto her back and showed him the entry wound. He looked at the hole in her leg, first from one angle then from another. Again, he poked around quite a bit. During the process she squirmed a little, but she didn't make a fuss.

Finally satisfied, Keats sat back and said, "Everything looks ok in front too. I hope I didn't hurt you."

"You didn't," she said. She had a sarcastic tone in her voice when she said it.

He was getting tired of her attitude. He said, "You listen to me." She looked away. He said, "Look at me." She did.

He added, "You've been shot twice with a high powered rifle. You're lucky you're not dead. So cut the sarcastic bullshit. I'm in no mood for that kind of crap."

He was quick to find out the woman was not about to take a scolding from him lying down. She abruptly sat up and said, "You're an abusive son-of-a-bitch."

That took Keats completely by surprise. He reflected for a moment then said,

"Ok. Settle down." Then he explained his perspective. "There's a dead woman lying out there on the beach. We just heard more than a dozen shots fired. Things have been very quiet since then." He hesitated a few seconds then added, "We just might have more than one dead woman on our hands by now. I'm extremely worried about Elizabeth." He stared pensively out into the Gulf of Mexico for a moment and thought about what he'd just said. He added, "Compton. I honestly don't know what to do next."

She thought about that then she asked him a question. "You do have a cell phone with you, don't you?"

He nodded 'yes' and tapped the cell phone he had in his shirt pocket with the business end of his Walther.

"I've got an idea," she said. "Let me have the phone."

He asked, "Why?"

She didn't give him an answer and before he could do anything about it, she'd snatched the cell phone from his shirt pocket. In a split second she entered a single digit and pressed 'send'. Keats tried to take the phone away from her, but she turned away from him, clutched the phone in both hands and pressed it tightly against her chest.

"You shouldn't be using that phone," blurted Keats. "It doesn't belong to me." She looked at him like he was an idiot.

Something suddenly dawned on him. She'd only entered a single digit. He insisted she give up the phone.

"Be still," she said. "And be quiet."

She said that because someone on the other end had answered her call. He shut up and tried to listen in. She began conversing with who ever had answered the phone. He couldn't actually hear both sides of the conversation, but he could tell the other person was a male. She gave the individual their approximate location and told the person she'd been wounded. She quickly terminated the call and set the cell phone on Keats thigh. The entire conversation lasted slightly less than thirty seconds. He expected an explanation, but she didn't volunteer one.

He insisted. "You tell me who in the hell you were talking to just then."

She said, "A friend of mine, someone who'll come for us." She looked at him like he was a fool and added, "Relax. Everything's going to be just fine."

He said, "You pressed a single digit. Explain that." She ignored him.

He insisted, "You better start explaining yourself right now."

She ignored his demand and instead said, "Use the light from the phone to check my wound. I think I've started bleeding again, in the back. Be sure and keep your hand over the screen so the light from the cell phone can't be seen." He didn't comment. He just let her go on talking. She said, "I have a knife with me. If you want to cut away part of my jeans, you can do it with that." She produced the knife and offered it to him.

Again, he said nothing. He simply laid his Walther in the needle grass, took the knife from her, and started doing what she'd suggested.

# CHAPTER TWENTY

Keats had all of her wounds exposed in ten or twelve seconds. He took a thorough look at her, front and back. His findings were a mixed bag. She wasn't bleeding at all in front, but when he rolled her onto her belly he found her backside was a totally different issue. The woman had been correct. The blood clot in the back of her leg had dislodged and she was bleeding again, profusely. He needed to do what he could to stem the blood flow and he needed to do it fast. He used her knife on the back of her britches, completely exposed her thigh then began preparing a dressing. All he had to work with was their clothing so he cut pieces of cloth from the back of her blouse and used the material to pack the wound. Then he tore several long strips of cloth from the front of his own shirt, tied the strips together, and used them to hold the packing in place. He applied direct pressure to the wound using his left hand. Compton lost consciousness while he was getting all that done.

He picked up his Walther and kept it in his right hand. He stared into the darkness and thought about Elizabeth. *Where in the hell was she? Was she even still alive?* He knew if he left now to search for Elizabeth, Compton would most probably die. He thought about her phone conversation. Who'd she talked to? Who'd be coming? He hoped the crew in the Dodge truck wasn't headed in their direction. He'd definitely have his hands full if they were.

# CHAPTER TWENTY-ONE

An hour had gone by and no one had come for them. It was totally dark now, the sky was cloudless and the moon was full. The full moon made every object on the beach look like a silhouette. Keats stared at several of the shore birds standing on the beach not far from the waterline. They were standing very still. To him they looked like comatose yard ornaments. He looked out into the Gulf of Mexico. The surf was completely flat and the seawater had become placid as far as the eye could see. There was no hint of a breeze. Keats felt like he was waiting in a tomb.

He took a look at Compton again. He couldn't see the rise and fall of her chest anymore. He thought, *"Is she even breathing?"* He checked her pulse. She had almost no pulse at all. He placed his fingers against her carotid artery. Then he waited. In less than two minutes the woman's heart played out completely. He tried to resuscitate her, but there was no way to bring her back. She'd lost too much blood.

Her death was definitely a game-changer for Keats. He double checked his weapon for grit and found it was clean enough. There was the other gun and more ammunition in his car. But even with what he had at his disposal, he felt like he was still inadequately armed. He thought about the Cold Pass Pawn Shop. He knew he could probably get exactly what he needed from the old man. All he had to do was get back to his car and drive there. He knew his vehicle could be the bait for a trap. He thought about it then decided if that's the way it was, he'd just have to handle it. He took one last look at the Compton's corpse then stood, turned, and started working his way through the dunes.

Keats' movement was due north this time and when he reached the blacktop road he crossed it, went through a shallow ditch, came to a barbed wire fence, slipped through it then looked around to see what he could find that might be useful. He was going to need a few odds and ends if he was going to do what he had in mind so he looked around. He found a few desiccated chunks of cow manure. He picked up three round flat pieces. Found a little driftwood and some other trash, selected what he thought he might be able to use, returned to the ditch, laid down in it and waited there. He needed to make certain there were no vehicles coming down the road before he tried crossing the road. And he was glad he waited, because within three or four seconds he heard a distant rumbling sound. It was the sound of knobby sand tires on the asphalt and the pitch was dropping rapidly. He knew exactly what was coming down the road, the Dodge Hemi. It went right by him, slowed then turned left onto one of the sand access roads. Not the one where his car was parked, but the one just before it.

Once it made the turn Keats got up and re-crossed the blacktop. He made his way through the dunes then stopped when he reached the beach. He knelt on the sand behind a large piece of driftwood and kept an eye on the truck. He watched it move slowly down the beach in a westerly direction. The red glow of its tail lights intensified as it came to a halt. There was some movement around the truck and the tailgate went down. The cargo light came on. Light flooded the bed of the truck and a small patch of the beach behind it. Keats watched two featureless men drag the body of the woman he'd found lying in the seaweed around to the rear of the truck and toss her body into the truck's bed like a sack of potatoes. Two more men were approaching the truck from the rear. Those two were dragging Compton's body. They laid her on the tailgate and one of the men started tearing at her clothing, searching her. The man was a savage. Keats could almost swear the search included the woman's body cavities, but it was hard for him to tell because the other three men were standing in the way. They were all leaning in real close, obviously enjoying the intrusive spectacle.

The search was over in three or four minutes and it didn't look like the guy who'd conducted it had found what he was looking for. Even from that distance you could tell the man was pissed because he jerked Compton's body off of the tailgate and let it flop onto the beach. Then the four men stood there, staring down at her, and talking things over.

Keats got an idea. He removed the *injured guy's* cell phone from his shirt pocket and switched it on. He was careful to keep the light from the phone completely shielded. He found the single digit Compton had used to call for assistance. He touched *call*. After a few seconds the man who'd conducted the search reached into his shirt pocket and pulled out a cell phone. Keats immediately terminated the call. The man on the beach peered at the face of his phone then appeared to be typing a text message. As soon as he was done, the cell phone in Keats hand began to vibrate. It was a text message from the guy. He read it. *'You're a dead man'.*

Keats typed a response. His response read, *'Really? Think about this. You didn't find what you were looking for. So where is it? And what makes you think I'm a man? You don't know who I am. You don't know where I am. Do the smart thing. Get out of the light and leave before it's too late.* Keats reread what he'd typed then pressed send.

The man looked at his cell phone again. He read Keats text message. He must've read it aloud, because when he was done reading it was instantly balls-to-the-walls. On the beach all four men were scrambling to get out of the light and get into the cab of the truck. As the last door slammed shut, the man behind the wheel killed all the lights, started the truck and hauled ass down the beach. They must have driven a quarter mile before Keats saw the tail lights come on again. But they didn't stay on long. He was trying to negotiate a turn onto a beach access road and had more-than-likely touched the brake pedal by accident. Keats watched the truck disappear then listened for the sound of the knobby tires on the asphalt. He was satisfied with what he finally heard. The Dodge Ram sounded like it was headed west and away from him. He'd probably have to deal with the crew in the Dodge truck sooner or later. But for now, they were gone.

He looked back at Compton's corpse. Now he knew what the woman had done. She'd called the man in the Dodge truck. Compton was in league with these people. He stopped looking in Compton's direction, stood up and checked his immediate surroundings. Looked like he was totally alone. He gathered up the stuff he'd collected and left.

# CHAPTER TWENTY-TWO

Keats crossed the blacktop again then wormed his way north through clusters of scraggly brush and scattered patches of prickly pear cactus. After he'd covered about two hundred and fifty yards he altered his direction of travel and started moving due east. He gradually angled back toward the blacktop then stopped when he reached the roadside ditch. He rechecked his surroundings, decided he'd gone far enough and selected a spot that was suitable for what he had in mind. He picked up two large sticks and two flat disc-shaped pieces of cow manure and placed the manure and one of the sticks under his arm. The other stick he hurled in the direction of his car. As soon as the stick struck the brush he hurried across the road. He stopped and dropped everything on the ground. He took the largest piece of manure and tossed it across the road. It struck the ground with a thud. He detected movement in the dunes. A head had turned about twenty yards from where he was crouching.

Keats didn't make the slightest sound getting to the person waiting to ambush him. But somehow the son-of-a-bitch sensed his advance. A fraction of a second before Keats reached him, the head of the *shooter* rotated slightly in his direction. But that made no difference. Keats throat strike instantly crushed the man's larynx. For all practical purposes, the *shooter* was as good as dead. But, in these types of situations, there's no such thing as overkill. Keats pinned the dying man to the ground and held him down until his vital signs told Keats every organ system in his body was shutting down. Finally his body went limp. Keats rolled off the guy and relieved him of his handgun. He also took the sniper rifle and a SAT phone he had with him. He laid everything aside and searched the *shooter's* body thoroughly in hopes of finding something else. But that's all he had on him. Keats rolled him over. Something about the dead guy didn't feel right. He removed the cell phone from his shirt pocket and used the light to look at the dead man's face. Keats discovered he'd been laboring under a false assumption. He wasn't looking into the face of a man. The person he'd killed was a woman. She was wide-eyed and all the color had drained from her face. He stared into her soon to be stone-cold-dead face. The face was smudged and dirty and extremely contorted, but that didn't hinder recognition. The face belonged to Linda Cunningham. The pieces of the puzzle were beginning to fall into place now. Cunningham had been planted in his class. All of these people were connected. He and Elizabeth were obviously caught up in some sort of bizarre conspiracy.

Keats continued to stare into Cunningham's face. Her eyes were wet, literally flooded with tears. She convulsed one final time, but that was the end of it. He gently closed her eyes. Then he picked up her rifle and examined it. It was a high tech sniper rifle equipped with a night vision scope and a flash suppressor. He drew the bolt back a hair and checked to make sure there was a bullet in the breach. There was. And there were several other rounds in the magazine. Keats pushed the bolt forward and closed the breach. Then he sighted through the scope. He located a large clump of prickly pear cactus on the other side of the blacktop. He could see every tiny detail of the plant as clearly as one might mid day. He panned the terrain around him. It didn't look like anyone else was there. He sat back on his heels anyway and waited a while. He heard nothing. Nothing else happened. No one else came. Finally he convinced himself he was all alone and began silently and cautiously working his way through the dunes. The trek back to his car proved to be totally uneventful. He retrieved his personal cell phone from the glove box and checked it for missed calls or additional texts. He found nothing. He thought about Elizabeth. He knew he'd better not attempt to call her or send her a text message. There were entirely too many unknowns. If anything was going to pass between the two of them, Elizabeth would have to be the one to initiate it. Keats knew he couldn't contact the authorities either. There were dead people all over the place and he'd be considered suspect number one. They'd arrest him on the spot. He knew there were a multitude of other issues he hadn't even thought of. He recalled the other shots he'd heard fired in the distance. There was no way to get anything even approaching an accurate body count.

Elizabeth's friend, Angie, was probably his only ally. What Elizabeth had told Angie was true. His life was in danger. Matter of fact, he was convinced they were all three in danger. Keats decided his most pressing need was to get himself adequately armed. He knew exactly where he could go and accomplish that.

# CHAPTER TWENTY-THREE

### Cold Pass Pawn Shop

Keats pulled his car around the west end of the pawn shop and stopped next to a badly rusted dumpster. He put his car in park, killed the engine, picked up the Berretta Angie had given him and chambered a round. He pressed the magazine release lever and let the clip drop onto the seat. He fished a single bullet out of the cardboard box and reloaded the clip to maximum capacity. Then he reinserted the clip into the magazine and made sure the safety was off.

He pushed the driver-side door open and got out. He kept the Berretta in his right hand and ready while he checked to make sure his car couldn't be seen from the road. Then he walked back to the car, shoved the Berretta inside the waistband of his jeans at the small of his back, reached inside the car and retrieved the cardboard box. He set it on the hood and removed three more fully loaded clips. He inserted two clips in the left rear pocket of his jeans and the third he shoved inside his waistband, in front, just left of center. Then he placed the cardboard box back on the floor and shoved it under the steering column as far as he could. He quietly pushed the car door shut, walked to the corner of the building and took a quick look out front. It looked like there was no one else anywhere around. He checked the road for traffic. Nothing was coming from either direction, not from the east or the west.

He rounded the corner of the building. The lights inside the shop were still on and the sign in the window indicated the pawn shop was open for business. He entered and found no one up front. He approached the counter near the cash register and rapped lightly on the glass counter top with his knuckles. No response. He shuffled a little to his left and tried to look through the partially open door and into the next room.

He said, "Hello."

Again, he got no response. He placed his left hand on the glass counter top and leaned in as far as he could. He couldn't see a soul in the other room. But he did hear the voice.

"Don't turn around and don't move a muscle. If you do, you're a dead man."

It was the old guy. Keats remained frozen in place, started to say something.

The old guy issued another edict. He said, "Don't you even think about opening your mouth. You just listen. This shop's all locked up now. If someone rattles the doorknob, you ignore it."

The old man stopped talking. Keats remained quiet.

After about ten or fifteen seconds the old guy started talking again. He said, "I appreciate where you parked your car. I got to watch you get out of your car. Got to watch everything you did. You know what? You're one dumb son-of-a-bitch. The security camera captured everything you did on tape. It's so easy to see you're packing again. And the weapon in your pants is loaded. There isn't a law enforcement officer anywhere in the State of Texas who'd give me any shit at all for killing you right now, right where you stand. And have no doubt about it. I'll do that in a heartbeat." The old man hesitated.

Keats felt a need to explain himself. He decided he was going give it a try. But before he could even get one word out the old man stopped him with an 'uh-uh'.

He said, "Don't talk until you're told you can. Just nod your head up and down if you comprehend everything you've been told so far." Keats nodded.

The old man continued to talk. He said, "I'm going to relieve you of the weapon in the back of your britches and the two clips you've got in your back pocket. While I'm doing that, the barrel of my weapon is going feel mighty cold against the base of your skull, but don't you even think about flinching. This isn't my first fucking rodeo."

It took the old man a while to get done what he'd said he was going to do. When he did finish he said, "Good boy. Next, when I tell you to, you're going to grab the bottom edge of your shirt on either side and slowly lift it up until its nipple high. Then you're going rotate counter-clockwise. You're going to do that real slow. You're going to keep doing that until I tell you to stop." The old man hesitated then added, "Nod if you think you can do all that." Keats nodded. The old man said, "OK. You can begin now."

The old guy scrutinized Keats as he lifted his shirt and turned. As soon as they were face to face he told Keats to stop. Then he said, "You can leave that other clip in the front of your britches. Now let go of your shirt and get your hands over your head. And keep them there."

Keats was getting tired. He was also getting frustrated. He decided he was going to try and explain himself again. As soon his lips parted the old man said, "Shut up. I didn't give you permission to say anything." A brief period of silence followed that.

Keats couldn't tell what the old guy had done with the two clips. But he had the gun he'd taken from him in his left hand and he was examining it. It was identical to the one the old man was holding in his other hand, the same make and model, the same kind of light and laser.

"You get this gun and the one you left here earlier from the same woman?"
Keats shook his head from side to side.

"You didn't? Then who gave you this other piece? Speak up."

"A woman I'd not met before today," said Keats. "She called herself Angie."

"And the first woman, what was her name?"

"Elizabeth."

The old man got a disgusted look on his face. He squinted. He slowly shook his head from side to side and said, "Women don't ever tell you their last name?"

"Not always," said Keats.

"Elizabeth's last name is Davenport," said the old man. "Would I be right about that?" Keats was shocked and nodded his head 'yes'.

"You're a Doctor," said the old man. "You and Elizabeth work together, don't you?"

"No," said Keats. "We're just friends. And I'm not an MD, if that's what you're thinking. I have a PhD. I'm a Professor at UTMB."

The old man reflected for a second or two then asked, "Why'd Elizabeth give you the other gun?"

"She left her purse with me and the gun was in it. I was surprised to find her in possession of the weapon. She told me guns have always frightened her."

The old man drew a deep breath through his nostrils then expelled it slowly through clenched teeth. Keats could see skepticism written all over his face.

Finally the old guy asked, "Did Elizabeth send you out here to get this other weapon from Angie?"

"No," said Keats. "I was simply supposed to meet Elizabeth somewhere out here."

"And there was no Elizabeth waiting for you when you got to the place you refer to as *somewhere out here?*"

Keats was getting more and more irritated. He said, "That's right. And I don't know who Angie is. Like I said, I've never seen her before today." The irritation in Keats voice was becoming very obvious.

The old man gave what Keats had just said a little thought. Then he said, "I think that's all a bunch of bullshit. You're a liar, Amigo."

Keats had his fill of the old guy. He said, "Everything I've told you is the absolute truth. And I don't give a shit what you think." Keats began relaxing his arms. Began to lower his hands.

The old guy squinted and said, "You better keep your fucking hands up." He paused then added, "This chit chat is over."

The malignant look on the old man's face told Keats a lot more than he wanted to know.

# CHAPTER TWENTY-FOUR

The old man took three steps backward. There was a free-standing metal rack on his left and he laid the gun he'd taken from Keats on a partially cleared shelf. Then he transferred his own weapon to his left hand and removed a cell phone from his right front shirt pocket. He looked down. Began touching the face of his cell phone with his thumb. Keats let his eyes wander while he was doing that, trying to take visual inventory of everything in the room.

As the old guy raised the phone to his ear they re-established solid eye contact. Then both men waited. After the eighth ring someone answered. Neither of them had blinked even once during the interlude.

"There's a man in my shop," said the old man. "He presents himself as Dr. David Keats. This is the second time he's been in here today. This time he came in with blood on his clothes. He also entered the shop loaded for bear. I've relieved him of his weapon and right now I'm holding him at gunpoint. We've had a little talk and he dropped two names. One was Elizabeth's and the other one was yours."

Keats knew Angie was on the other end of the call. The conversation that ensued lasted maybe five minutes. It was fundamentally one sided with the old man simply listening. When it was over, the old guy terminated the call without saying *goodbye* or anything else. Then he just stood there, grinding his teeth. Now Keats was really worried.

After maybe fifteen seconds the old man put his cell phone back in his shirt pocket, shifted the weapon he was holding to his right hand and retrieved the other handgun from the shelf. Then he approached Keats and stopped about four or five feet away. He reversed the gun he was holding in his left hand, and gripping it by the muzzle, offered it to Keats.

Keats was dumbfounded. He asked, "I'm supposed to take the gun?"

The old man said, "Yep. Take it and put it back in your britches. You need my help. I'm willing to give you an assist if you're willing to accept it."

Keats took the gun from the old man and did exactly what he'd been told to do. The old man lowered the muzzle of the gun he was holding in his right hand, turned, retrieved the two loaded clips he'd taken from Keats and gave them back to him.

He said, "Put these where you can get to them. You still got the cell phone belonged to that son-of-a-bitch who got run over downtown?" Keats shook his head, '*yes*'.

The old man said, "Give it to me." Keats handed him the phone. The old man studied it for a few seconds then put it in one of the pockets in his pants. "We're leaving," he said. He looked past Keats into the back room and said, "Cover up ladies. We're coming through."

Keats thought about that. He'd said '*ladies*'. That was plural. Evidently there was more than just the old man's wife out back.

The old man walked past him and said, "Come with me." Keats followed him around the end of the counter and into the next room. They passed through two more doors then entered a fourth room. There were four individuals in room number four and not one of them was a woman. They were all young men, the oldest of the four being probably forty-something, and the youngest being maybe twenty-two or twenty-three. They were all sitting at a computer station. They'd obviously stopped doing whatever it was they'd been doing and draped a piece of black fabric over their monitors. The old man and Keats passed straight through the room and out the back door without a word being said.

Once outside they continued walking until they reached a dilapidated shack about a hundred yards from the shop. There was a rusty old Chevrolet pickup truck parked on the far side of the shack. The truck turned out to be their ride.

# CHAPTER TWENTY-FIVE

## Sand Luis Island Bay House

When they reached the entrance to the Bay House the old man drove straight through the gates, up the blue rock road, and parked on the concrete slab next to the boat trailer. As soon as he killed the engine he was out of the truck and up the stairs. He walked into the place like he owned it. Keats stayed with him every step of the way.

The first room they entered was huge. It was long and wide and had a very tall ceiling with a lot of heavy exposed timber overhead. The furnishings were ordinary. They were simple, practical and comfortable looking. And Angie was there, standing on the far side of the room, staring intently at something displayed on a huge wall-mounted monitor. As they approached her, she was slow to turn. That afforded Keats the opportunity to get a good look at her before they were face-to-face again.

She had on brown boots and non-descript street clothes. Everything she had on was drab and anything but new. But they were definitely her clothes. The fit was perfect and they were worn in all the right places. Keats studied her profile. She'd obviously flattened her breasts with some sort of sports bra, but the reduction had been only moderately successful. She had her hair pulled back and cinched up with something or other, it too was non-descript. She'd not been very deliberate with her hair. There were quite a few loose strands dangling here and there. The last thing he looked at was her face. She had on zero makeup.

Everything about her was ordinary. Looking like she did, she'd easily blend into a crowd on a busy street. Attract very little attention. Keats considered that her intent. He was careful not to overstay his stare. He could tell she knew what he was doing.

He tried to catch a glimpse of what was displayed on the monitor in front of her. But the angle of their approach was all wrong for that. That, and she blanked the screen before they got even halfway across the room. When they did reach her, she turned and exchanged hugs with the old man. Then she offered Keats her hand. He took it. But they didn't shake. She simply held his hand for two or three seconds. Keats felt some sort of strange camaraderie in the way she'd done it. As soon as she released his hand, she turned and walked off. The old man followed her. Keats followed him.

Next they entered what looked like a conference room. It was quite a bit smaller than the other room. Keats looked around. There was a wall-to-wall plate glass window on one side of the room. Two of the other walls were covered with a lot of maps and charts and photographs of people. It was the photographs that captured Keats attention. He took a comprehensive look, but he didn't recognize anybody. He looked at the last wall. There were three wall-mounted monitors mounted on wall number four. The table situated in the center of the room was surrounded by a lot of chairs. Angie and the old man grabbed a couple of the chairs and sat down. Keats followed suit.

# CHAPTER TWENTY-SIX

Angie immediately went to work. She removed something that looked a lot like a tablet-size laptop from somewhere under the table and set it in front of her. She tapped the cover of the device twice and it opened automatically. Then it folded itself in half, rotated 270 degrees to form a stand and adjusted itself for proper angle. Angie made one adjustment then brushed the grey surface of the device with her fingertips. All three monitors took on a pale green glow. Keats waited, expecting something else to happen. But nothing did. They simply sat there in silence.

Finally, the old man broke the silence and said, "You and I share some common knowledge, Keats. This made Keats curious. But he didn't ask for an explanation. He knew he'd get one when the old man was ready to give it.

"Keats, I know what happened in Paris twelve years ago," said the old man. "I also understand the significance of the *Venus de Milo Protocol*."

The *Venus de Milo Protocol* was a black ops identification/extraction protocol Keats had had to use to get out of Paris at the conclusion of a black ops mission. He was thinking this couldn't possibly be what it sounded like, but then again, maybe it was. He waited for more.

"I know the Sergeant Major," said the old man. "He and I are good friends. We served together. Do you need to know more?"

"No," said Keats. "You know about my *dark past*. You've convinced me we're not adversaries." He gestured at Angie and asked, "Does she know what you're talking about?"

The old man didn't respond to Keats question. He simply rotated in his chair, shifted his attention to the nearest monitor and said, "Show us what you've got, Angelique."

# CHAPTER TWENTY-SEVEN

Angie's fingertips literally danced across the surface of the device resting on the table in front of her and the three monitors mounted on the walls came instantly alive. Then Keats watched serial stop-and-go action unfold on the screens. First on one monitor and then on another and then another. What he was looking at was recently edited satellite surveillance footage.

Over the next half hour he watched the Dodge Hemi come and go. Watched himself find the wounded woman lying in the seaweed on the beach. Watched the woman die. Watched Compton shot twice, and watched her die. Saw the first woman's corpse recovered and Compton's dead body searched and abandoned. Watched himself terminate Linda Cunningham, drive to the pawn shop, get out of his car and go inside. At the end of it all, the three monitors went blank again and glowed green.

Keats found all of this hard to fathom. He wanted to know how the hell they'd managed to capture all that on satellite surveillance tape. He turned to the old man, not even knowing where to start. But the old man just sat there staring at him. The staring went on for maybe thirty seconds before the old guy said what he was thinking.

He said, "You're one hell of a survivor, Keats. You had absolutely no trouble saving yourself from becoming collateral damage. You killed the individual waiting to assassinate you like the professional I've been told you are. Then you did exactly what I'd have done. You returned to the pawn shop."

The old man paused. Looked like he was gathering his thoughts. Then he added, "Here's the situation. You've survived. You're here with us. Among friends. But Elizabeth is still out there and I'm not so sure she knows how to handle herself in the field. Right now we don't know where in the hell she is, who these people are, or why all this shit is happening. I'd say we need to do something about that pretty damn quick. Wouldn't you agree?"

Keats nodded and said, "Absolutely."

The old guy went on talking. He said, "If you have anything you want to say about what you just watched on these three monitors you get it said now. Get that part over with."

Keats said, "What happened, happened. But I do have a question for Angie."

"Get it asked," said the old man.

"While I was waiting in the dunes, Trish Compton called someone and requested assistance. I heard a man's voice on the other end. I'm convinced she'd called the man who searched her. Do you have any idea who the man is?"

Angie shook her head 'no' then said, "Not yet. And you need to know this. The woman the man searched was lying to you. She wasn't Trish Compton. I met Compton at the John Sealy Hospital about four months ago. I'd recognize her anywhere. Compton was the woman you found lying in the debris on the beach. She was the woman who died a few moments after you found her. I don't know who the other woman was and I have no idea who she called."

Keats thought about that then asked, "Did Trish Compton and Elizabeth work together?"

"That's what I was led to believe," said Angie.

Then she threw a quick glance in the old man's direction. Keats leaned forward, expecting to hear more from her. But evidently the old man decided whatever else Angie had to say could wait, because he intervened.

He said, "That's enough for now. You got anything else we need to know, Angelique?"

"Elizabeth sent me several text messages," said Angie. "They were all very vague."

The old man looked at Keats. He asked, "You got anything else, Keats?"

"I have some text messages from Elizabeth," said Keats. "And there's something else. I knew the woman I killed, the one who was waiting to ambush me if I returned to my car."

The old man pushed back in his chair and turned to face Keats. Obviously he found what Keats had just said very interesting, but he didn't ask him to elaborate.

Instead, he said, "How'd you know her? Who was she?"

Keats said, "She was enrolled in one of my graduate classes. She'd enrolled this fall as an Intern. She'd enrolled as Linda Cunningham. This afternoon at the end of the class period she started acting very strange. Then she insisted on walking with me to the faculty parking lot. I managed to get away from her and go to my office. I looked at her records. They'd been falsified. I have no idea who she really was. She'd been planted in my class and had orders to kill me."

Angie stood up.

The old man threw a glance in her direction. "Where do you think you're going?" he asked.

She said, "I thought I'd get us some coffee."

"Coffee's a good idea," said the old man. "But not right now. Take a seat."

It was easy to see Angie didn't want to do that, but the way the old man had said it left her no other option. She reluctantly sat down. Both men picked up on her reluctance.

The old man asked her a question. He asked, "You got your cell phone with you, Angie?"

Keats was thinking the same thing the old man was. Angie had something to hide.

She was slow with her answer. And when she did respond, she simply said, "No."

Her right hand was resting on the surface of the table. But her left hand was in her lap. She immediately moved the left hand to the surface of the table. Both of her hands were empty.

"Where's your cell phone?" asked the old man.

"I have no idea," said Angie. "It disappeared right after our last conversation."

The old man had both his hands resting in his lap. He moved both to the surface of the table. He had his Berretta in his right hand and the cell phone he'd gotten from Keats in his left. That was the phone belonging to the guy who'd been hit by the truck on Strand Street.

The old man placed his Berretta on surface of the table and studied the cell phone. After a few moments he began stroking the face of the phone with his right thumb. When he'd finished, he didn't press send. He silently reread whatever he'd typed.

"Keats," he said. "How many times you use this phone?"

Keats thought a moment then said, "Twice."

"You're sure about that? You used it only two times?"

Keats said, "I'm absolutely certain."

The old man handed him the cell phone. Keats took a look at what was displayed on face of the phone. The old man had written him a rather lengthy text message. He read it. Then he deleted the entire message and handed the phone back to the old man.

The old man looked back at Angie and asked her another question. "You're armed, are you not?"

Angie shook her head *'yes'*. She said, "I have a knife." The old man knew she was carrying more than that and nodded, urging her on.

"I'm also wearing an ankle holster," she said. "There's a Smith & Wesson Bodyguard 380 in the holster." The old man continued staring at her. She added, "That's everything." A deadpan look remained on the old man's face. She repeated herself. Said, "That *is* everything."

He nodded and said, "Keep everything where it is for now. I'm going to the kitchen and get us some coffee." He looked at Keats and said, "You might want to put your piece on the table, Keats."

Keats removed the Berretta from the small of his back, double checked the chamber for a live round then laid the weapon on the table right in front of him. The old man pushed his chair back and stood. When he left the room he was carrying his Berretta in his right hand.

As he walked through the doorway he said, "Make the call while I'm gone, Keats."

The old man had placed the injured guy's cell phone on the table right in front of Keats as he stood to leave. Keats thought about the text message he'd read on the face of the phone, the one from the old man, the one he'd deleted after reading it. There'd been a phone number in the text and he'd been instructed to commit it to memory. He'd also been instructed to call the number when told to do so. Keats waited about ten seconds then he picked up the phone and made the call.

A strange reverberating sound began to emanate from somewhere under the conference table. Keats could not only hear it, he could feel it. It was a vibrating cell phone. It was Angie's phone. Obviously its ring-tone had been silenced. And evidently, the cell phone had been placed in a cavity somewhere inside the table top. The net effect of the vibrating cell was an extremely amplified level of reverberation. Keats allowed the sound to go on for quite a while. There was never a voice mail prompt. He could tell Angie was getting a little rattled by the mere amplitude of the reverberation. When he finally decided to terminate the call he could tell Angie was relieved. She sighed several times. Anyone one could see she was angry.

Finally she said, "I had no idea where my cell phone was. But I know who put it there."

Keats wanted to hear more, but that's all she said pertaining to the phone. Instead she said, "I know all about your past. I know you haven't always been a College

Professor. Like you, I was also forced to use the *Venus de Milo Protocol*. Two years after you used it, but my circumstances were not much different from yours."

Now Keats knew. He stared into Angie's face for a few more seconds. He had a multitude of questions he wanted to ask her, but decided that exact moment was not the appropriate time to do it. He simply said, "Thank you." And he left it at that.

He shifted his gaze. Looked past Angie toward the open doorway behind her. Someone was about to enter the room through the door. Angie didn't bother to turn and look. She already knew who it would be. Elizabeth. And she knew the old man would be trailing a few steps behind her and that he'd be holding her at gunpoint.

They entered the room and approached the table. The old man said, "Go to the far end of the table, Elizabeth. Then stop and stand there and don't turn around." Then he looked in Keats direction and said, "When she gets where she's supposed to go, you pick up the cell phone, pick up your piece, and come over here to this side of the table. Then stand right here. Angie, I don't want you to lift a finger while Keats is doing any of that. If Elizabeth decides to do anything stupid, you let me handle it." The old man hesitated for a moment then added, "Do you understand the gravity of your situation, Elizabeth?" Elizabeth nodded, indicating that she did.

The old man said, "Time to make your move, Keats." Keats reached the spot where he'd been told to stand and stopped.

The old man told Elizabeth to raise her hands as high as she could and keep them there. Then he told her to kneel, lay face down and spread-eagle on the floor, and stay that way. The old man approached her after she was lying flat on the floor. He stopped a few feet away from her and looked her over. Elizabeth had a handgun under her blouse. She'd tucked it into the back of her jeans. The old man exchanged looks with both Keats and Angie. They nodded, each indicating they'd seen the gun too. The old man bent over and removed the weapon. He laid it on the table and slid it in Angie's direction. Then he told Elizabeth to roll over onto her back, keep her hands over her head and get up. Getting up without the use of her arms was a little difficult for her, but she managed. Once on her feet, he told her to walk slowly to the nearest chair, place both her hands flat on top of the table and keep them there. Then he told her to sit down. She did everything per his instructions. He looked satisfied. He left where he was standing and repositioned himself directly behind her. Elizabeth was pale and her bottom lip was beginning to quiver.

The old man looked up. Looked at Angie. She had her eyes locked on Elizabeth's face and she'd taken on an emotionally detached look. The old man shifted his gaze to Keats and kept it there. Then he removed a SAT phone from his hip pocket and punched in a single number. Someone on the other end picked up almost immediately.

"This is Tony Buchanan," said the old man. Let me speak to Nate Davenport." He listened for a moment then added, "That's correct. *Tony* is short for *Anthony*."

*Davenport.* That was Elizabeth's last name. Keats thought about that. *Surely Elizabeth wasn't married. Maybe she'd been married and was now divorced.* Keats mind began to wander. The old man could see that and interrupted his thoughts.

He said, "Keats. The individual that answered the phone told me to *'wait one'*. They say that every time you call. But they always make you wait considerably longer than a minute."

Then he switched the SAT phone to speaker mode and set it in the middle of the table. He obviously wanted everyone in the room to be able to hear both sides of the conversation he was about to have. Elizabeth appeared to be unbelievably shaken. Angie looked unmoved. As a matter of fact she looked absolutely aloof. Keats was engrossed in thought again. One of the things he was asking himself was whether or not Anthony Buchanan was the old man's real name. Neither Angie nor Elizabeth had looked at all surprised when he'd called himself that. Keats decided Anthony Buchanan was probably his name.

# CHAPTER TWENTY-EIGHT

Whoever Buchanan had called finally answered.

"Tony?" said the person on the other end. "You used an Agency SAT phone to call me. What the hell is wrong?"

Buchanan said, "You need to know I'm not alone, Nate. You also need to know this SAT phone is in speaker mode."

There was a moment of silence on the other end. Then the reply came. "Roger that." But that's all that was said.

Buchanan continued to talk. He said, "Elizabeth has gotten herself involved in some sort of cloak-and-dagger crap. Things have become lethal. The current body count stands at five and there may be even more dead bodies than that by now."

Keats thought about that. Buchanan had said *five*. There were two Keats didn't know about.

"Is Elizabeth alright?" asked the man on the other end of the call. There was obvious alarm in his voice.

"She's fine right now," said Buchanan. "But that could change at any minute. We're at the San Luis Bay House in the main conference room. Elizabeth is sitting at the table and I'm standing. Listen to me carefully, Nate. I'm holding her at gunpoint and I'm about to separate the sheep from the goats."

Davenport said nothing to that. There was simply a heavy-duty silence on his end. Buchanan stopped talking at that point.

Davenport finally said, "I'm still here, Tony. I don't know what I'm supposed to say." There didn't seem to be any alarm in his voice at that exact moment. The man's voice had simply taken on a rather resolute quality.

Buchanan said, "Three women and at least two men have been killed this evening out on Follett's Beach. Elizabeth may be the reason these three individuals are dead.

Two were shot to death by *'we don't know who'*, and a third woman was killed in self-defense by Dr. David Keats. Keats is a personal friend of Elizabeth's. Have you ever heard of him?" Buchanan paused to give Davenport an opportunity to comment on that, but he didn't. So Buchanan continued talking.

"Keats is a Psychologist, a College Professor. An ex-Navy Seal. He served with the ISAF as a member of a deeply embedded Delta Force Team Member for a short time. Then after leaving the Navy, Keats continued serving his Country in a slightly different capacity. I'm not at liberty to tell you which Governmental Agency he worked for or the nature of his assignment while he served."

Keats was flabbergasted. He was wondering how the hell Buchanan had found out that much about his past. He certainly hadn't told Elizabeth a damn thing about that part of his life. Keats continued listening with an interesting mixture of fascination and apprehension. But that was the extent of what Buchanan had to say about him. He turned his attention to Angie.

He said, "Angelique is here too. You already know all you need to know about her. I believe Angelique has told me everything she knows about what's happened out here on the Island tonight. But that doesn't amount to very much." Buchanan paused, took a long slow breath then said, "But Elizabeth knows a hell-of-a-lot. But she hasn't yet shared what she knows with us. However I'm ready for a little enlightenment." There was another short pause then Buchanan added, "The Agency SAT phone is sitting in the middle of the table. Sitting right in front of Elizabeth. That way, we can all hear what she has to say."

Buchanan adjusted the phone slightly, making sure it was properly pointed at Elizabeth. Then he said, "Now it's your turn, Elizabeth. Be thorough. That means you better not leave a one damn thing unsaid."

Elizabeth was getting more than a little red-in-the-face. Keats knew Elizabeth all too well. It wasn't embarrassment turning her face red, it was defiance.

Buchanan waited patiently for twenty or maybe even thirty seconds then he looked at Keats and said, "Make the call." He gestured at the cell phone Keats was holding in his hand. The one Keats had used to call Angie's cell phone earlier.

Buchanan repeated the order, "Make the call, Keats."

Keats did what Buchanan told him to. The strange reverberation began again. It went on for a quite a while. But it finally ended. It ended when Buchanan terminated the call by blowing a hole through the table with his Berretta. The bullet from his handgun literally obliterated Angie's cell phone. Wood splinters and fragments of plastic and metal from the phone slammed into the floor and skittered across the surface of the table. The spent shell casing ejected from the weapon and smacked into one of the plate glass windows behind Buchanan then tumbled end-over-end across the tile floor. To Keats it sounded a little like the clattering hooves of a horse on a cobblestone road. The only one really startled by any of it was Elizabeth.

Buchanan said, "Get on with it, Elizabeth. Tell us everything."

Elizabeth still didn't say anything.

Buchanan waited maybe ten more seconds then said, "Stand up. Take a moment to reconsider your decision. Then let me know what you decide. Think real hard. I intend to get answers one way or the other. I'd hate for you to lose the use of a limb or two in the process."

Davenport said, "Elizabeth is my granddaughter, Tony." The tone of the man's voice reflected genuine alarm.

Buchanan said, "I know that. And you've known me long enough to understand I'm not bluffing." Buchanan had said that without a hint of emotion.

At that point Elizabeth made a fist and pounded on the table. Then she addressed her grandfather, saying, "What am I supposed to do?"

A short period of silence followed. Angie and Keats exchanged quick glances. Then the legs of the chair Elizabeth was sitting in scraped across the floor and she stood.

"I'm not at liberty to tell you anything," said Elizabeth. The blood appeared to be draining from her face.

Davenport broke in. He said, "You have to tell him, Elizabeth. You've got no other option. He'll do it and we both know that."

# CHAPTER TWENTY-NINE

Elizabeth opened her mouth. Started to speak. But Buchanan didn't let it happen. He told her to shut up and sit down. Then he cast a glance in Angie's direction and said, "Go get us some coffee, Angelique. No need to get in a big hurry. Whatever Elizabeth has to say can wait until you get back here."

Angie got up and left right on cue. Elizabeth eased back into her chair. She knew she'd better not open her mouth. Not until she was told she could.

Two words popped into Keats mind simultaneously. The first was *command*. The second, *control*.

Keats hadn't said a word out loud, but that didn't seem to matter. Buchanan cut his eyes at him instantly. It was like the man had just read his mind. Keats tried to stop thinking, but the next two words popped into his head anyway. Those two words were *Jesus* and *Christ*.

This time the old man turned toward him, squared himself in his chair, and initiated a sustained stare. Keats decided he'd better stop thinking. Decided he'd better ask Buchanan a direct question.

He asked, "Is Anthony Buchanan actually your name?"

Buchanan cast a glance at the SAT phone sitting in the center of the table and said, "You want to answer the man's question, Nate?"

Davenport said, "That's what his name is right now. But I'm not so sure how long it's going to stay that way."

Davenport's statement put a grin on Buchanan's face. Keats decided not to ask any more questions. He just sat there replaying all the events of the afternoon and evening in his mind. Elizabeth had started looking down at her hands, fooling with her fingernails. Silence settled over the room like a blanket.

# PART TWO

# THE CONFESSION

"But I tell you that every careless word that people speak,
They shall give an accounting for it in the day of judgement.
For by your words you will be justified, and by your words you will be condemned."

The Book of Matthew—Chapter 12: Verses 36-37

# CHAPTER THIRTY

After about five minutes Angie returned with the coffee, set a steaming cup in front of everyone then took her seat back at the table. The coffee was extremely hot. Angie was the only one to lift a cup to her lips, but she didn't take a sip. She simply blew on it. Keats watched her do that for a second or two then looked at Elizabeth. She was staring at the steam rising from her cup. Then he looked at Buchanan. He had his eyes locked on Elizabeth. He told her to stop fidgeting. Told her she could start talking anytime she was ready.

She asked, "Where would you like me to start, Mr. Buchanan?" The inflection she put on Buchanan's name was a bit barbed. In Keats opinion, for her to be sarcastic or flippant at that particular moment was just plain stupid. But it didn't seem to faze Buchanan.

He simply said, "Call me Tony. You always have, Elizabeth." He hesitated a bit then said, "People are dying. I want you to tell us who's doing the killing. Tell us why this is happening. Start right there." Buchanan showed no emotion whatsoever when he'd said that.

Elizabeth said, "I heard you say David killed a woman. You said he did it in self-defense. I stabbed a woman. She could be dead. I shot at several other individuals. Some were men, some were women. I only know one of the women. And she died. I'm not sure about any of the others. But everything I did, I did in self-defense. Just like David." She paused then added, "I'm not quite sure I know why this is happening."

"So with the exception of one woman, you didn't know any of these individuals personally?" Nate Davenport was doing the asking now. The way he'd asked the question sounded strangely matter-of-fact. It sounded like a simple inquiry, like he was asking her what she'd eaten for dinner or what kind of day she'd had or some other trivial bullshit like that.

Elizabeth considered his question.

Keats started thinking about Nate Davenport. Obviously he and Buchanan had a history together. Angie and Elizabeth were friends or at least acquaintances. What was their connection? Keats had a multitude of questions, but this didn't seem like the right time for him to be asking anything. He decided to stop thinking. Decided he needed to be listening. He stared at Elizabeth. She looked terrible. She was chewing on her lower lip. She was obviously having trouble finding a way to say what she was going to say next. Finally she took a deep breath and answered her grandfather's question.

She said, "Yes, I knew one of the women." Keats could tell that what she was about to say was going to upset her. She was becoming teary-eyed.

She said, "The woman David found lying on the beach was my friend, Trish Compton. I shot and killed her. All the others were complete strangers."

Keats decided to chime in at that point. He asked, "Elizabeth, did you take a shot at me?"

Elizabeth said, "No. I didn't. But I did shoot Trish." She started fidgeting again. Then she added, "David, I shot Trish because I believed she intended to shoot you. But that's the only reason I did it."

"You claim Trish Compton was you're friend," asked Keats. "She worked with you, didn't she?" Elizabeth nodded her head, *yes*.

He asked, "In what capacity?"

Buchanan was getting tired of the back-and-forth questioning. He returned to one of his initial questions. "What's this all about, Elizabeth? There's a lot more to this than what you've told us."

Keats watch Elizabeth's demeanor shift. He watched her hands began to shake. He could tell there was a lot she was withholding. He noticed the only person not asking any questions at all was Angie. Angie hadn't said a word and didn't look like she intended to. She was just sitting there, listening attentively, calmly taking small sips of coffee from her cup.

Elizabeth asked, "How much do I tell them?" She was addressing her Grandfather again and her voice was becoming increasingly shaky. Keats opinion, she was about to go to pieces.

"Start at the beginning," said her Grandfather. "Like I said, they've got to hear all of it. I mean that. You're going to have to answer whatever questions you're asked. And your answers are going to have to be candid. You cannot hold anything back. Not now. That's not an option."

Elizabeth cleared her throat, drew a deep breath, and started talking.

# CHAPTER THIRTY-ONE

"About three years ago a feeble looking little man showed up at my front door. I looked at him through the peep hole in my door. He looked harmless enough so I opened the door and asked him if he needed help. He said he didn't. Said he was my grandfather's friend. Told me it was imperative that I call him right away. I didn't know what to make of that. I decided the man had to be mistaken and asked him who he thought I was. He called me by name and said that Nate Davenport was my Grandfather's name. I asked him if he was alright. He said he was fine. But that I should call him as soon as possible. Then he turned around and walked off. This was strange. I went straight to my study and made the called."

At that point Elizabeth paused. Stared at the SAT phone in the middle of the table. Keats thought she was waiting to see if Nate Davenport wanted to embellish what she'd said so far. But he remained totally quiet. So she continued to talk.

"When I got my Grandfather on the phone, he told me to get a pen and a tablet and tear off a single sheet of paper. He gave me a phone number and told me write it down. He told me to commit the number to memory then destroy the piece of paper completely. He told me to keep calling the number until someone answered then identify myself. He said to tell the individual who answered I wanted to speak to someone with the Resurrection Initiative. He said the person would say I had the wrong number and hang up on me. He told me not to call the number again. He told me to wait until someone contacted me. He said he didn't know how I'd be contacted, didn't know when, or by whom. He refused to answer any of my questions and simply told me to do it. So I did. And it happened, just the way he said it would. I waited for ten or twelve days. Nobody called, nobody came. So I forgot about it. Then one day I woke up at about seven in the morning and smelled coffee brewing. I went into the kitchen to see where the smell was coming from and found a middle-age woman sitting on a stool at the bar in my breakfast room. She was dressed in a business suit, reading a newspaper, and drinking a steaming cup of coffee. I could see she'd brewed the coffee in my kitchen. I thought maybe I'd left my apartment door unlocked overnight and assumed she'd simply entered by mistake. She looked harmless enough so I didn't get overly excited. I simply told her she'd made a mistake. Told her she was in the wrong apartment. She didn't say anything. She didn't even take her eyes off her newspaper. I asked her how she'd gotten into my apartment. She told me she'd used *her* key. She still didn't take her eyes off the newspaper. She was completely lackadaisical. I told her whatever key she'd used belonged to me. I insisted that she give it to me. She folded her newspaper in half and laid it on the bar. Then she told me she was with the Resurrection Initiative. She asked me take a seat at the bar. I didn't have on much and I didn't really want to do that, but I did it anyway. After I was sitting down she got up and walked into the kitchen, grabbed the coffee pot from the counter, refilled her cup and poured me one. Then she added the correct amounts of sweetener and creamer to mine, just like I would have. She returned to the bar, set my cup in front of me, and took a seat. I took a sip or two of the coffee. I told her it had been quite a while. I asked her why it had taken so long for someone to get back to me. She didn't answer the question. She simply said what she'd come to say.

It was something like this, *"If you like your life the way it is I'll finish my coffee and leave. Or you can make a significant contribution to 'the greater good'. Think about that. Take your time. Take all the time you need."*

Then she stopped talking completely. Took another sip of her coffee and went back to reading her newspaper. I waited, thinking she might explain what she meant by *'the greater good'*. But she didn't, she just went on reading the newspaper and taking tiny sips of her coffee. I asked her if my Grandfather had sent her. She looked up and told me he had not. But that he knew about it. She said he'd told her Superior he'd support whatever decision I made. I asked her if I could call him. She offered me her cell phone. I thought about it then I told her I didn't need to. I told her I wanted to know more. She told me to take a shower and get some clothes on. Told me someone else would have to explain things. I showered, got dressed, and we left.

# CHAPTER THIRTY-TWO

At that point Nate Davenport cut in. He said, "Things have gotten lethal, Tony. Angelique and this Keats fellow have gotten caught up in this mess. Now you're involved. Whether we like it or not, the ball is in our court. I say we pool our resources. I can give you an '*insiders*' perspective. Clear up a few things. Expedite what needs to happen next. I'll touch on the relevant points then let Elizabeth continue. She can start with when and where things began going wrong."

Nate Davenport was a manipulative bastard. His offer put a sneer on Buchanan's face. Keats didn't know enough about him to have an opinion. Angie showed no emotion whatsoever. But Elizabeth looked relieved. Keats could tell Buchanan was considering the man's offer.

Buchanan looked at each individual person sitting at the table and asked, "Is that agreeable to everyone?" No one said anything to the contrary so Buchanan gave Davenport permission to get on with his explanation.

"Splendid," said Davenport. Then he proceeded to enlighten everyone.

"I'll start with the morning Elizabeth discovered the woman sitting in her kitchen having coffee. I knew she or someone just like her would eventually show up. I knew that the individual would invite Elizabeth to join a highly select cadre of professionals; professionals who were willing to provide specialized behind-the-scene support for certain clandestine activities of our Federal Government and those of some of our Allies. You might want to know which specific Agencies Elizabeth was being invited to serve. The answer is an amalgamation of them all, but none of them in an officially recognized capacity. The activities of everyone involved in this endeavor were sanctioned to be conducted outside the purview of any Governmental control. Those directly engaged in clandestine operations anywhere in the world acted with total autonomy. No one in the Governmental ranks had the authority to dictate to this group of professionals what they could or couldn't do. And like Elizabeth said, the effort was given a name. It was called The Resurrection Initiative. I wasn't directly involved in field activities until about five years ago. But I'd known the Initiative had existed for nearly fifty years. What I was initially told about it came straight from the horse's mouth. President John F. Kennedy himself told me. He told me in private briefing at the Whitehouse four weeks before he was assassinated. At the time he was very vague about everything. He simply asked me to cooperate fully with anyone who ever approached me and said they were with The Resurrection Initiative. He said they'd tell me they'd been sent by *'Jack Hobbs'* and provide me with an appropriate identification protocol. I gave JFK my word. Agreed to provide whatever I was asked for and swore an oath I'd keep everything a secret. And like I said, five years ago I was finally visited by someone who said they'd been sent by *Jack Hobbs*. Three and a half years ago, I was informed that Elizabeth was about to be contacted and told what her role would be. My contact gave me a lengthy explanation. Here it is in a nutshell. Outside professionals, the *'best-of-the-best'* were being used in the effort. That included surgeons with specialized skills, scientists, soldiers of fortune, and for the lack of a better term, a few Independent Contractors. The Resurrection Initiative definitely had need for the services of a Plastic Surgeon, someone who was new to the trade. The person selected had to be relatively unknown and extremely competent. Obviously Elizabeth fit the bill. I was told if she agreed to do it, she would understand that no participant would know the actual identity of any of the others. She would be called upon to perform a myriad of functions, all with total autonomy. And at some point in time her services would be terminated.

What prompted all this? Here's what my contact told me. For the prior four and a half decades, a highly classified multinational pruning process had been used to eliminate certain covert assets. That included actual people and a lot of other things. The various elements of those assets were labeled *Dead Wood*. After *pruning*, much of the *Dead Wood* was methodically obliterated. But the residual, what was left and considered potentially useful at some point in the future, was given the code name, *Compost*. It's my understanding, that from day one, those charged with the responsibility of doing so were given the task of recycling some of the *Compost*. I don't know why that was being done or what it involved. My role in the effort has always been simple. Provide whatever intelligence was needed whenever it was asked for. That's been my only part in the effort. That's all I know. Elizabeth will have to take it from here." Davenport stopped talking.

# CHAPTER THIRTY-THREE

All eyes shifted to Elizabeth. She was leaning forward now and appeared to be much more relaxed. She said, "I think I'm ready." Buchanan gave her the go-ahead nod and she started talking again.

She said, "I volunteered because I thought it sounded exciting. And at the time I thought it was the right thing to do. If I'd only known how things would ultimately end, I'd never ever have gotten involved."

Nate Davenport interrupted. He said, "Damn it, Elizabeth. Just tell us what the hell has happened. That 'in hind sight' crap is totally unnecessary. Get down to the meat-of-the-matter. People are dying."

Elizabeth stared at the bullet hole in the conference table. Looked like she was reorganizing her thoughts. Angie hadn't said a word since she'd returned with the coffee. Keats figured she was just as much in the dark as he was. They both simply continued staring at Elizabeth. But not Buchanan, he looked like he knew a lot more about this than he'd let on. And his eyes were on the move. He'd look at Keats, then at Angie then back at Keats again, then at Elizabeth, and so forth and so on. The man looked like he was reading everybody's mind. Finally Buchanan's eyes stayed with Elizabeth. And he asked her another question.

"You say you killed Tricia Compton. What was she, a Plastic Surgeon? Or was she a Surgical Assistant? Or what?"

"She was a peer. You might say she was my partner."

"Your business partner?"

"No, Tony. We partnered during surgical procedures. Some of them, but not all. Definitely not the ones connected with the Resurrection Initiative. I valued her opinion. She felt the same way about me. Trish was a gifted Plastic Surgeon and we helped each other achieve extremely desirable effects. Tony, plastic surgery is an art.

We both considered the end result of any surgical procedure a work of art. But you wouldn't understand that."

Nate Davenport intervened again. He said, "Cut the crap, Elizabeth."

Elizabeth began to tear up. Her Grandfather's interruptions were upsetting her. Buchanan told Davenport to stop interrupting and gave Elizabeth a little time to pull herself together.

# CHAPTER THIRTY-FOUR

Elizabeth took several sips of her coffee then said, "This is probably all my fault. I told Trish entirely too much. I should never have told her about the flash drive. Trish insisted that I show her what was on it. She asked me if she could borrow it. She said she wouldn't show it to anyone else, that all she wanted to do was look at it. I explained that everything on the flash drive was highly confidential. She wouldn't stop insisting. I finally let her look. I didn't give the flash drive to her, but I did show her what was on it. That was a terrible mistake. I found that out today when she and two male thugs attempted to abduct me in a hotel parking garage. They were going to get their hands on the flash drive one way or the other."

Davenport interrupted again. He said, "I think I already know the answer to this question, but I'll ask it anyway. What in the hell was on the flash drive, Elizabeth?"

She said, "Photographs of about two dozen of my Resurrection Initiative clients. After I sedated them, I took pictures. After I altered their appearance surgically I took follow-up pictures."

Davenport's reaction was extremely profane.

Buchanan said, "Shut up, Nate. It'd be in your best interest not say anything else. Not unless I say you can." He looked back at Elizabeth. He said, "Settle down. Take a few deep breaths then get on with what you were about to tell us. I know there's a lot more we need to know."

Elizabeth took another sip of her coffee and said, "Today, I'd driven to a hotel parking garage near the Kemah Boardwalk to meet a Resurrection Initiative courier. That's the way I'd always received the instructions for each new assignment. When I got there and parked, I found the courier in his car, bound and gagged and unconscious. I should have left immediately. But I didn't see anyone anywhere in the vicinity so I began removing the bindings from his wrists. He immediately started to stir. Then he began struggling with me. He had this terrified look in his eyes. Within a few seconds I understood why. We were not alone in the parking garage. By the time I realized what was happening an SUV had pulled up behind my car, barring any possibility of escape. Two men bailed out of the SUV and began running in my direction. Just before the bigger of the two men reached me, I dropped and rolled. The largest man's reflexes were really bad and he tripped over me and fell. Then he got up and ran head long into the other man. I was on my feet and running immediately. I ran between two adjacent cars. My intention was to take their SUV and escape. As I approached the SUV, I narrowly avoided colliding with Trish. She was getting out of the back seat of their SUV. When she stood up I smacked her in the face. Then I grabbed her by the blouse and jerked her out of the way. She fell onto the concrete and she didn't get up. I jumped into the front seat of their SUV and slid across to the drivers' side. The driver had left the vehicle running. I immediately shoved it into drive and stomped on the accelerator. The other man, the smaller of the two, tried to get to me. But I was already underway. He ran into the rear fender of the SUV and fell as I drove off. I think I ran over him." She paused, grimaced like she was re-living the experience. Then she went on. "One of the men had left a cell phone on the front seat. I kept it. That's the cell phone you found in my purse, David. Anyway, I drove the SUV to the Cruise Ship Terminal, entered the parking lot, got out and started walking. As I approached the entrance to the lot a late model Cadillac sedan was turning into the lot. There were only two occupants inside the car, an elderly man and a woman about the same age. They were looking for a place to park. The lot was almost completely full. I stepped in front of their vehicle. The car slowed then stopped. I walked around to the driver's side window. The man lowered the glass. I told them the lot was full and asked if they'd left their luggage at the dockside turnaround. He said they had. I offered to park their vehicle. He put his car in park, left it running, opened his door, got out and went around the rear of the vehicle to the other side and helped the old woman get out. They were both smiling and waving at me as I drove off." She paused. There was a momentary look of remorse on her face. Then she continued talking. "I parked old couple's car in the lot in front of Willie G's Restaurant, got out and started for the sidewalk café. Within a block or two I ran into Trish again. She was with another woman and the bigger of the two men from the parking garage. The smaller guy wasn't with them anymore. That's what makes me think I ran over him. It's a good possibility he's dead." She paused and reflected for a few seconds then said, "Trish was the first one to spot me. As soon as she saw me, she broke into a dead run. I waited for her to reach me and this time I really punched her. I guess I knocked her out because she went down and stayed down this time. Then I ran for all I was worth. For almost half an hour I ran up and down back streets and allies, playing *cat-n-mouse* with that big bastard. The other woman couldn't handle the pace and eventually stopped running. But no matter what I did, I couldn't shake the man. That's why I ended up sitting on the concrete bench across the street from the café, David. I never intended to get you involved in this. But I didn't know what else to do."

Keats said, "You had a gun in your purse. Why didn't you use the damn thing? Where'd you get it?"

She didn't tell him where she got it. She simply said, "I was afraid I might hit an innocent bystander." Then she paused. After a moment she added, "I guess I should have used it. That was dumb, wasn't it?"

Keats ignored her question. He said, "You were no longer armed after you left your purse with me. Yet you say you shot Trish and several others. How'd you manage that, Elizabeth? You had to get another gun from somewhere. Where you get it?"

She said, "After I ran from the café, I returned to Willie G's parking lot, got in the Cadillac and drove it to Tiki Island. I went inside your condo and borrowed several of your guns. I used one of them to shoot Trish. The other guns should still be in the trunk of the old couple's car."

"Where's the car right now, Elizabeth?" asked Keats.

She said, "It's about a quarter of a mile from here. It's parked bayside." She paused and thought a second or two then corrected herself. She said, "It's not really parked. It's actually stuck in the sand."

# CHAPTER THIRTY-FIVE

Davenport cut in. "Wait one. Someone just laid a note on my desk. Let me read it." Things remained quiet around the table while he read it. Finally he said, "I'll get right back to you." A conversation ensue in the background. Not a word of it was discernible, because Davenport had the mouthpiece covered with his hand. Within a couple of minutes he was back on the line.

He said, "In two or three minutes a black BMW is going to arrive at your front gate. As soon as the car clears the entrance the driver is going to flash the vehicle's headlights on and off twice. As the car approaches the Bay House the driver will flash the lights again, the same sequence. There'll be just one person in the car, a woman. Tony, meet her outside at the bottom of the steps. Go alone. This is the same woman who spoke to Elizabeth on that first day, the one who recruited her. I'm told the woman is privy to everything that's been said around your table this evening. She'll need to ask Elizabeth some questions. They'll talk inside her car. Give them total privacy. And Elizabeth, you be perfectly candid with this woman."

There was a brief lull then Davenport redirected his comments. He said, "Keats. I was just told about your checkered past. You and I need to talk privately, but not right now, later." At that point Davenport stopped talking. Keats had been watching Elizabeth while her Grandfather was explaining what was about to happen. Her eyes had remained downcast the entire time.

Then Davenport started talking to someone on his end again. Everyone at the table tried to hear what was being said. But Davenport had obviously covered the mouthpiece of the phone with his hand and not a word of what was being said could be understood. This muffled conversation went on for maybe a minute then Davenport came back on the line.

"Keats," said Davenport. "You're a College Professor. Where? And what do you teach?"

"I teach at UTMB Galveston," said Keats. "I'm in the Psychology Department." He did more than just teach, but Keats left it at that. He had questions he wanted answered.

"Look," said Keats. "I'm convinced you're actually Elizabeth's Grandfather. And from what I've witnessed so far, you almost have to be high-ranking Military, or perhaps Secret Service, or FBI, or something along those lines. But then again, I have no way of really knowing that or much of anything else about you. However, your people obviously know a great deal about me. Because of that, and a few other reasons, I'm assuming it's OK to talk to you." Keats paused, looked at Buchanan then added, "How can I be certain about that?"

Buchanan responded to Keats question. He said, "If you want to call someone and verify a few things, I have a secure line you can use. You can call anybody you think you need to."

Keats thought about that for a moment then decided he'd not call anyone. Not yet. He thought about asking Davenport another question. But he decided against that too. No one said anything else and in about ten or fifteen seconds the SAT phone went dead.

Buchanan stood up immediately, motioned to Elizabeth and the two of them walked out of the room together. Buchanan took the SAT phone with him when he left. That left Angie and Keats sitting alone in the conference room.

# CHAPTER THIRTY-SIX

"Want more coffee?" asked Angie.
"Yes," said Keats.

He started to stand when she did, but she told him to keep his seat. So he did. And in less than a minute she was back with the coffee. It was entirely too hot to drink and Keats left his sitting on the table. Angie raised her cup to her face, pursed her lips and blew on hers. He began toying with his cup. They sat there for quite a while without talking. Keats was lost in thought, allowing his imagination to run rampant. But not Angie, she had an, *I'm-reading-you're-mind*, look on her face. Finally she broke the silence.

She said, "My grandparents were Montagnard. They were members of the Degar tribe and made their home in the Central Highlands of Vietnam. During WW II all the women in my mother's village were abducted by the Japanese, taken back to their encampment and used for sex. With the help of a kind Japanese Soldier, my mother and two of the other women managed to escape. They returned to their village, told the men their story then led a band of Montagnard Warriors to the Japanese Encampment. The Montagnards waited until after dark then slipped into the encampment, slaughtered all but one of the Japanese soldiers, and freed the women. They took the lone Japanese Soldier with them when they left and allowed him to wait the War out in their village."

Keats didn't say anything, but Angie could see he wanted to know more.

She said, "My father wasn't Vietnamese. My father was a French Legionnaire. He and my mother met during the French occupation of Indochina. At the time of my conception my mother was twenty years old and I'm told my father was about twenty-three or twenty-four. They never were never married. They say he was killed somewhere in Laos two months after I was conceived." At that point she paused. Keats assumed she was waiting for him to ask her a question. He didn't have one to ask. She could see that and went on.

"French is my dominant language," said Angie. "I'm also proficient in English and Mon-Khmer. I understand a little Malayo-Polynesian, but can't speak it very well." She paused, looked at Keats for a few seconds then added, "I was born in 1964. Buchanan and my father were friends. Buchanan took me and raised me. He's the only father I've ever known."

Keats had been studying Angie while she was talking. Her birth year surprised him. He did the math in his head. Angie was fifty-two years old now. He and she were about the same age. She didn't look anywhere near that old. As a matter of fact, she looked like she was no more than thirty or thirty-five. He started to ask her about that, but she stopped him.

She said, "That's all you need to know about me. I already know more about you than I should so it's better if you don't tell me anything else." She took a big sip of her coffee and added, "The others will be arriving soon. She looked down at his coffee and said, "I think you can drink that now."

Keats picked up his cup and tried it. It was still too hot to drink.

He said, "You said *others* will be arriving soon. Who are they?"

She said, "I'm not sure. We can probably watch some of them arrive if you'd like. I think I can manage that."

Keats gave her a positive nod and Angie retrieved the tablet she used to control the three overhead monitors.

# CHAPTER THIRTY-SEVEN

Buchanan re-entered the conference room shortly after *the others* started arriving and took a seat back at the table. He could see the questioning look on Keats face.

He said, "Elizabeth left with the woman in the BMW. She's created one hell of a problem for everybody, especially for you, Keats. But this is bigger than you. No record of anything connected with the Resurrection Initiative clients was to be made or retained by her. If that flash drive containing photographs of those clients falls into the wrong hands, the lives of at least a dozen deeply embedded covert operatives will be compromised. The impact that would have on world peace could be absolutely devastating. There's more. But you'll have to hear the rest of it later. Let's watch this right now."

Buchanan and Keats redirected their attention to the activity on the three monitors. There was a good bit of it going on out back. People and vehicles had been coming and going while Buchanan had been out of the room and they still were. It'd been a little hard to garner much detail because it was so dark, but they'd managed to see quite a bit of it. There'd been two late model nondescript passenger cars that had simply picked some people up and left as fast as they'd gotten there. There'd been several ATV's, some street legal, some not. And there'd been four motorcycles. One was probably a Harley. But Keats had never seen anything quite like the other three. There'd been no illumination at all during the coming and going. No headlights, no brake lights, no running lights or interior lights, no flashlights, no illumination whatsoever. The most interesting transients came at the very end. Last to arrive had been several water craft. There'd been three of them. They'd come up the canal from

West Galveston Bay. One was definitely amphibious, but the other two didn't appear to be. The watercraft, or boats, or whatever they were, quickly took people and stuff on board and left the way they'd come, via the canal in back of the Bay House. After the third watercraft had come and gone, that was the end of it.

# CHAPTER THIRTY-EIGHT

Buchanan turned, faced inward and squared himself in his chair. Angie and Keats followed suit.

"Angelique, you take the *Stryder* to South Shore Harbor and leave it in the Marina," said Buchanan. "Keats, you'll be meeting her there later, but for the time being, you're going to stay here with me."

Then Buchanan slid two picture IDs in their direction. As he did it he said, "These are your new identities. Angelique, when you get inside the hotel, you show this ID to the woman at the front desk and tell her you have reservations for the suite on the top floor, south side. She's one of us. She's only been partially briefed so you tell her you'll require two key cards, one for you and one for a companion. Tell her to hold your companion's key card. Tell her he'll be joining you later. The woman is supposed to get inquisitive, and when she does, you tell her the individual isn't your husband, he's your protégé. That'll be Keats and he'll be using his new picture ID when he checks in. Be sure to give her his new name. And say it correctly. If anyone else shows up and asks any questions, she'll tell them nothing. She'll wait until they leave then call the suite and hang up after one ring. If that happens, you will immediately take evasive action."

Then Buchanan addressed Keats. He said, "Once you get to the suite you let Angelique make all the decisions. You follow her lead, Keats. You do it to the letter. What you need to be doing between now and then is memorizing everything on both sides of your new picture ID and studying the dossier I'm about to give you." He tossed a manila envelope containing the dossier on the table. Then he said, "And get used to being called by your new name. It may be only temporary. But, for the time being, be sure you can react to the sound of this particular name instantly, like you would if it was your own. To do otherwise, could prove to be fatal." Buchanan paused, waited to see if Keats was going to ask any questions. But he didn't.

So Buchanan continued talking. He said, "You need to look exactly like the picture on the ID. That means you're going to lose half of your facial hair and some of what's on top of your head before you leave here tonight. Angelique will help you with that in a few minutes. You let her do it her way. The woman knows what she's doing."

Buchanan pushed back in his chair and thought a minute. Then he said, "That's about it for now. Angie, when you get to the suite at South Shore Harbor wait for further orders. Either one of you got any questions that have to be answered right now?" Keats didn't know enough to ask anything. But Angie did have a question.

She asked, "Am I dressed appropriately for what's going to happen later on tonight?"

"We won't know that until later. For right now, you're good. Keats will change into something else before he leaves here. Whatever else you two might require later on tonight or tomorrow morning is already there or it'll get delivered to the suite later tonight."

Buchanan looked at Keats again. He could tell the man had a multitude of questions so he gave him the go-ahead. Keats started with the two questions that were of the most importance to him.

"Do I have any say in any of this?" asked Keats. "And is Elizabeth going to be with us later tonight?"

"No, to both your questions," said Buchanan. "If you want to live through the night, you'll simply do what you're told. I'll tell you this much. Elizabeth left with that woman because she's being escorted to a safe house. You don't need to be worrying about Elizabeth. It's your ass that's in a sling now; yours, mine, Angelique's, and a multitude of others." He hesitated then added, "And Elizabeth is the reason for that."

Angie and Keats exchanged quick glances then looked back at Buchanan. Buchanan nodded at Angie. She got up and left the room. Buchanan watched her walk through the door then indicated that Keats should follow her. He did. And that's when he found out there was a lot more to the Bay House than he'd imagined.

# CHAPTER THIRTY-NINE

Keats and Angie passed the large room with the high ceilings and exposed timber first. The next room they entered was a little smaller. It was a sitting room and it was furnished with period pieces from a multitude of Asian cultures. Most of it looked to be centuries old and probably priceless. But Keats didn't know enough about Asian antiques to really judge. For all he knew, some of the furnishings could've been high-dollar reproductions. But it all looked very impressive.

The third room they entered really grabbed him. It was obviously a study and very nicely appointed. Angie invited Keats to sit so he settled into a chair that was sitting at one end of an ornately carved teakwood desk. Then she left the room.

The chair Keats was sitting in was remarkably comfortable. The character of the leather was absolutely fascinating. It was thick and supple and had a texture similar to that of a soft leather glove. He looked at all the things that were hanging on the wall in front of him. There was a shadow box there, dead center. It contained a set of gold Naval Aviator Wings surrounded by an impressive collection of military service medals. There was also a gold-embossed name patch from a flight jacket in the shadow box. The name on the leather patch read, *Commander Anthony T. Buchanan.* Keats looked at the service medals one by one. The only ones he recognized were the Viet Nam Campaign and Service medals and a Purple Heart. There were a number of pictures and plaques and squadron patches surrounding the shadow box. And there was a multitude of framed documents bearing all sorts of official-looking seals hanging on the wall. There were also several diplomas from various institutions of higher learning there. They all belonged to Buchanan. The two that captured and held his attention were the *United States Naval Academy* and the *Naval War College.*

Keats scrutinized the chair sitting behind the teakwood desk. *Gulf of Tonkin Yacht Club* had been tooled into its leather back and it looked as though it'd been upholstered using the same leather as the chair he was sitting in. He was busy admiring the leather on the arm of his chair when Angie re-entered room and saw what he was doing.

She said, "That leather was made from the hide of an Asian Water Buffalo. It's quite nice, isn't it?" Keats nodded his head 'yes' and continued to admire it.

She said, "Those animals were the most valuable thing most of the peasant farmers of South Viet Nam possessed. There's no way to know how many of the animals were slaughtered during the wartime strafing of the rice paddies."

Keats left the leather alone and looked at Angie. She'd entered the study carrying an ornately carved teakwood box containing a set of unusual looking grooming implements. He assumed she intended to use them on him and he was correct about that. She placed the box on the desk and went right to work cutting his hair. Neither he nor she spoke while she did her work. Not while she was cutting the hair on his head or grooming his beard.

Keats enjoyed Angie's technique. Her touch was as light as a feather. And like he'd been told to do, he let her have her way with him; offered no resistance whatsoever. He actually enjoyed the entire experience, especially when she worked on his face. While she did that, she stood directly over him. That gave him a chance to focus on her facial expressions. He tried to get a feel for her personality type, but he couldn't get much from her. While she looked like she was oblivious to what he was attempting to do, she wasn't. He could tell that.

Finally he asked, "How'd you get to know Elizabeth?" Angie heard his question. But she didn't bother to give him an answer. She simply continued to do what she was doing. Keats refrained from asking her anymore questions.

When she was done, she removed a small mirror from the teak wood box and handed it to him. He took a look at himself. He compared what he now looked like with the photo on his new picture ID. It was a perfect match. Buchanan was right. Angie knew her business.

Keats watched her put everything back into the teakwood box and clean up the stray hair clippings. When she was done she left him sitting alone in the room.

# CHAPTER FORTY

Two minutes later Buchanan walked into the study and settled into the leather chair behind the desk. At first he didn't say anything. He just sat there, looking past Keats. There was a large plate glass window directly behind the chair Keats was sitting in and he turned to see what Buchanan was looking at. There was no moon and it was black as pitch outside. Keats couldn't see anything. No silhouettes, no shadows, no nothing. Buchanan must have realized that, because he explained what he was doing.

He said, "I'm watching while Angelique leaves in the *Stryder*." The *Stryder* was the boat Keats had seen in the boathouse that afternoon.

Keats said, "I can't see anything out there." He paused, concentrated for a few more seconds then asked, "Can you?"

"No," said Buchanan. "That's the whole point. I don't want anyone to see her leave here."

Keats understood that, turned back toward the glass and resumed his watch.

After about five minutes Buchanan said, "She's gone now."

Keats didn't know how the hell Buchanan knew that, but obviously he did. Buchanan began rummaging around in one of the desk drawers and turned to face the desk again. Buchanan started laying some documents he'd removed from a drawer on the desktop and spreading them out. While he was doing that Keats looked at the pictures hanging on the wall behind him.

He asked, "Is there a picture of Nathanial Davenport back there?"

"Yes there is," said Buchanan. But he didn't indicate which one it was. Instead, he leaned across the desk and shoved an envelope in Keats direction. The envelope had an official looking seal on the outside, but the seal itself had been broken and the envelope opened. Keats took the envelope from the desktop and examined the outside of it. He read what was imprinted on the seal, the top half first. It read, *'Chief Intelligence Officer'*. He looked back at Buchanan. Buchanan urged him to go on. Keats read the bottom half. It read, *'The White House'*.

"Is this authentic?" asked Keats.

"Open the envelope," said Buchanan. "Remove the document that's on the inside and read it."

Keats removed the document and unfolded it. It was an official memorandum from POTUS, *The President of the United States*. It began, *To Whom It May Concern*. Keats looked back at Buchanan.

"Read the whole thing," said Buchanan.

So Keats read it. He actually read it twice. Then he thought about what he'd just read. It was more than a simple memorandum of understanding. It was a top secret contractual agreement. Keats was beginning to understand what the Bay House actually was. He understood it in a very vague way. He took another look at the document, scanned the signatures at the bottom of the page. Then he refolded the memorandum, put it back into the envelope and returned it to Buchanan. He didn't completely understand the full implications of what he'd just read, but he decided he'd not ask any questions until he heard more from Buchanan.

"I'm offering you an opportunity," said Buchanan. "I'm officially inviting you to join us. What do you say to that?" Keats didn't give Buchanan an immediate answer. He was trying to assess the implications.

Buchanan said, "This isn't your first rodeo, Keats. A lot of lives are hanging in the balance here. That includes yours, big man. Give me an answer. Are you coming to work for me or not?"

Keats said, "If that document is authentic the initial arrangement began the year Kennedy was assassinated. His signature appears first on the list. If everything is what it appears to be, you've had a contractual agreement with every Commander-in-Chief since that time."

"That's correct," said Buchanan. "And I have the authority to invite you to serve with me. There are no limitations on the type of activities we're able to engage in. Absolutely nothing we do is subject to oversight."

"So your people are above the law?" asked Keats. "They're exempt from prosecution?"

Buchanan didn't answer either of Keats questions. He simply cut to the chase. He said, "At least five people have died on Follett's Beach this evening. You'll probably be number six if you don't agree to come on board, at least for the time being. I can offer you sanctuary and provide you with an assumed identity that you'll be able to keep for a while. I don't know how long you'll be able to do that, or who the hell you're going to be down the road, or what you're going to be asked to do in the future. It's still entirely too early to know any of that."

"What are my odds if I decide to go it alone?" asked Keats.

Buchanan responded. "What's your opinion?"

The two men locked eyes for a few seconds then Keats said, "I wouldn't bet any money on the opposition."

That put a hint of a grin on Buchanan's face. He said, "I would." Then he pressed Keats for an answer. He asked, "Are you coming onboard or not? Do we have a deal?"

"Absolutely," said Keats.

Buchanan offered Keats his hand. They shook. Then Buchanan got up and walked out of the study. Keats got up and followed him.

# CHAPTER FORTY-ONE

They ended up back in the conference room. The oldest of the young men from the Pawn Shop was there. The guy was sitting in the same chair Angie had been sitting in and using the same tablet she'd used to manipulate the three live satellite feeds. At that exact moment he was tracking three different vehicles.

It looked like all three of them were somewhere on Galveston Island. One of the vehicles was a pickup truck. It looked exactly like the Dodge Ram Keats had seen on Follett's Beach earlier that evening, but he couldn't tell for sure. And it was definitely too far away to tell if there was still a corpse in the bed of the truck. The other two vehicles being tracked were both SUV's. As far as Keats knew, he'd not seen either of them before.

The three men sat there watching the activity on the three monitors without talking. This went on for maybe ten minutes before they were joined by another of the young men from the Pawn Shop. This new guy walked into the conference room and took a seat next to Buchanan. He'd walked in carrying another tablet with him and he laid it on the table. His tablet was identical to the other one. It also positioned itself automatically for use.

More silent sitting and vigilant watching followed. Keats was fascinated by the way the two young men worked together. The movement of their eyes was strange; it was rapid and jerky, almost bionic looking. Up, down, side-to-side, away then back. Everything these two guys did was perfectly synchronized.

Suddenly all three monitors changed to split screen displays and there were nine vehicles being tracked. Buchanan said, "Those three vehicles on the far left and across the top are theirs, but the others are ours. One of the things we're after are decent photographs of their faces. Profiles are useful, but profiles have their limitations. Full-face images are a hell of a lot better."

Buchanan went on to explain that any photograph they managed to obtain could be used to identify the individual with extreme accuracy. He said they used a process he called *reverse facial recognition*. He said from that, all their personal data could be redacted. He said they'd know who the individual was, who they'd ever said they were, and what they'd used as an address both present and in the past. They'd be able to obtain pictures of their family members and friends, the names and addresses of any social media contacts, personal banking information on everybody, the make and model of every electronic device they ever owned, and the locale where each of the devices had been used within the last year maybe even two. From that they'd gain comprehensive access to all their correspondence. He said everything could be done at damn near the speed of light. After Buchanan's explanation ended, things got quiet again.

After about five minutes the oldest computer tech said, "Standby." Everyone leaned forward. All four had their eyes glued to the same monitor. The Dodge pickup truck had pulled to the side of the road and stopped. Whoever was at the wheel had lowered the front driver-side window. Within a second or two an elbow protruded through the open window. Evidently the driver then tossed a lighted cigar butt through the window, because something collided with the pavement next to the truck and a shower of sparks skittered across the roadway. One of Buchanan's vehicles, a long gray SUV, had been following the truck. It slowed to a crawl and passed the truck. As it passed, a woman's arm shot out of the front window on the passenger-side of the SUV.

"Loretta's shooting him the finger," said one of the young men. He added, "Get ready."

A head immediately protruded from the open driver-side window of the Dodge. The man in the pickup truck had countered with his own 'high sign'.

"Got it," said the same young man, "a full face photograph."

Buchanan said, "Outstanding, gentlemen. Now it's game time."

Buchanan stood up and said, "Let's go get these boys some coffee, Keats." Keats stood like his legs were spring-loaded and they left the room together.

# CHAPTER FORTY-TWO

The trek to the coffee room was quite convoluted. They turned several corners, walked down several short hallways with closed doors on either side then climbed two flights of stairs. The coffee room was on the left at the top of the second set of stairs.

The coffee room itself was rather small. But it opened into two larger sitting rooms with plate glass windows on three sides.

As Keats and Buchanan entered the larger of the two sitting rooms Buchanan said, "Sit down and get comfortable. I'll fix the coffee."

They'd passed a large Avantco coffee urn on the way in and the coffee was already brewed. Buchanan drew three cups, returned to where Keats was sitting and handed him a cup.

He said, "You stay put. I'm going take the others a cup of coffee. When I get back you can tell me what you think about what you just saw. You might even get a few questions answered." Buchanan was smiling the whole time, talking to Keats like they'd been friends or neighbors for years. Keats was actually beginning to feel quite relaxed around Buchanan. He continued thinking about him after the old man was gone.

There was no way Keats could really get a valid 'read' on the guy. It was like he had multiple personalities. But he didn't. He simply had this amazing capacity to act the part of different characters. One minute he acted like a cranky old character from a 1940's western movie. Then the next, he had the traits of a character John Wayne had played in a WW II movie, a Navy Captain named Rockwell Torrey. And just then, as he left the coffee room, he'd taken on the persona of a friendly next door neighbor. Keats was convinced Buchanan was such a convincing actor he could easily fool a seasoned interrogator. He was beginning to believe he could probably beat a polygraph test. Keats was wondering who the hell Anthony Buchanan really was?

# CHAPTER FORTY-THREE

Keats was toying with his coffee when Buchanan returned. Buchanan drew himself a cup, entered the sitting room, sat down across from Keats and took a sip of his coffee. Then he nodded, giving Keats the go-ahead. Keats asked his first question. He asked about the men who were operating the monitors in the conference room. Here's what Buchanan had to say about them.

"They're called *Bricoleurs*. You ever heard the term?" Keats shook his head *'no'*. Buchanan said, "That's what they're being called out in the cyber world. The label is a derivative of the French word, *bricolage. Bricolage* is a type of contemporary methodology being used in many different fields of endeavor; higher education, philosophy, critical theory, computer and software design, fine arts, etcetera."

Buchanan paused, checking Keats for understanding. Keats told Buchanan he thought he'd heard the term used before, but said he couldn't actually recall when or where and he certainly didn't understand its actual meaning. It was his admitted uncertainty that compelled Buchanan to give him a detailed example.

"Take fine arts," said Buchanan. "The gifted artist steps away from the canvas and looks at his work. Then he contemplates a bit, studies the character of the paint he's using, looks at form and texture, and returns the brush to the canvas. It's those in between times, those frequent and sometimes lengthy pauses between the strokes of the brush that guide him in his work. So there you have it. The *Bricoleur* is merely a highly skilled techno-artist. He uses contemporary technology know-how like an artist. He pauses between keystrokes. He does everything 'on the fly' and in fractions of a second. He instantaneously envisions a myriad of unique ways to address almost any issue. And there are damn near no limitations, no barriers, and seldom does he do things the same way twice. He continuously throws 'the book' away, uses inconsistency like a tool or a weapon. And, most of them have the requisite intellectual capacity and cutting-edge techno skills to make things happen. These *Bricoleurs* are the next step in human evolution, Keats. They're more evolved than either one of us could ever be. They're as different from you and I as Neanderthal man was from Cro-magnon."

Buchanan stopped explaining, once again, checking Keats for understanding. Keats didn't give him any feedback. But Buchanan must have decided Keats had gotten the basic gist of the concept, because he curtailed things at that point. He waited for Keats next question, but he didn't get to ask one. His next question was preempted by the vibration of his personal cell phone. He looked at it then showed the face of the phone to Buchanan. It was a text message from Elizabeth. Buchanan read it just like Keats had. It read, *I'm sorry, David.* That's all she'd typed. The two men looked at one another simultaneously.

Keats said, "I can't respond to her, can I?" He'd posed that as a question. But it wasn't a question at all. It was merely an affirmative statement. He knew Elizabeth had no idea Dr. David Keats would soon cease to exist.

Buchanan had a look of uncertainty on his face. That's because he didn't know if he and Keats were actually on the same wave length. So he stated the facts…made everything regarding Elizabeth perfectly clear.

He said, "Keats. You put all of us in peril if you ever attempt to communicate with her again. As far as anyone's concerned, Dr. Elizabeth Davenport no longer exists. She won't die in a fiery car collision like you're about to. She'll simply disappear into oblivion. And she'll be gone for good. Perhaps you're asking yourself whether or not the two of you will ever get to see one another again. I seriously doubt it. But if the two of you want it badly enough I imagine someday you'll figure out a way to make it happen. Who knows, with the passage of time and given totally different circumstances, anything's possible."

Buchanan studied Keats for a moment or two then asked, "Want me to take care of the text message?"

Keats nodded and handed Buchanan his cell phone. Buchanan put Keats phone on the floor, placed the heel of his boot on the phone and crushed it. There was no aggression in the way he did it. He simply converted the cell phone to useless debris. Keats regarded what Buchanan had done closely akin to an act of euthanasia. Elizabeth Davenport was history.

A few more seconds passed then Buchanan gathered the remnants of Keats phone in his hand, wrapped them in a napkin, got up and carried them out of the room.

Keats remained seated in the coffee room. Suddenly Keats heard some sort of strange sound. It sounded a lot like a *general quarters alarm* signifying a condition of battle readiness aboard a U.S. Navy Warship. Keats had no idea what was going on or what he was supposed to do about it. So he waited where he was. Within a minute Keats heard footfalls in stairwell.

One of the *Bricoleurs* stuck his head inside the entrance to the coffee room and said, "We have an unidentified intruder inside our perimeter. The intruder is equipped with state-of-the-art *ECM*." Keats was familiar with the term, *ECM*. It was short for *Electronic Counter Measures*. "Buchanan wants you to stay put while the intruder is being confronted," added the *Bricoleur*.

Keats knew how to follow orders and stayed right where he was. He wanted to know what was happening and tried looking through every window in the vicinity of the coffee room. But he couldn't see a damn thing. He couldn't hear anything either.

Resigned to the fact, Keats drew himself another cup of coffee then took a seat in one of the chairs. He kept his back to the wall and watched the reflection of the landing at the top of the staircase in the glass of the window across the way. He took his handgun out and kept in his right hand. He held the cup of coffee in the other. Keats had been a Navy Seal and deployed to Afghanistan. He was not a novice. But this was a totally new ball game. He knew his lack of understanding could endanger everyone and continued to wait where he was.

# CHAPTER FORTY-FOUR

In about ten minutes Keats heard the same young man yell at him from downstairs. He told Keats the intruder turned out to be one of their people, said that Buchanan wanted him back in the conference room. Keats took another slug of his coffee, wiped his mouth, stood and headed downstairs. When he got to the conference room he found a third young man sitting next to Buchanan. He settled into the same chair he'd been sitting in and Buchanan started explaining.

He said, "Two yet-to-be-identified white males drove a Transit Van onto the tidal flats at San Luis Pass and set up at the entrance to the bridge. They stopped and confronted the young man sitting next to me, thinking he was you. That's understandable. He was driving your car. When they realized he wasn't you, they insisted that he tell them where you were. Of course he wouldn't do it. They decided to leave and take him with them. That was a fatal mistake on their part. He killed them both. Then he loaded their bodies in the van and brought them here. We'll have them identified shortly."

But that's where the rhetoric ended. It ended because some new activity was unfolding on one of the three monitors. What looked like the same Dodge truck Keats had seen on the beach earlier in the evening was approaching the San Luis Pass Causeway from the east. It began to decelerate then slowed to a crawl. But it didn't proceed onto the Causeway. It left the highway just short of the approach to the bridge and drove out onto the tidal flats. And that's where it stopped. About a hundred yards from the water. Two men immediately bailed out of the front seat of the truck onto the beach and started looking around. Within four or five seconds a firefight appeared to ensue. Both of the men who'd gotten out of the truck went down within the first two or three seconds. It looked like they'd been caught in a cross-fire and once they'd fallen to the ground, they stayed there.

Everyone in the conference room continued watching and at exactly the one minute mark, two more men got out of the truck. Both men had been sitting in the back seat. Keats didn't understand exactly what happened after that and asked Buchanan to explain it. Buchanan said he'd let one of the others do it later. He told Keats to remain quiet, told him to keep his eyes on the monitors.

After a few seconds Buchanan pointed at yet a different monitor and said, "That car right there belongs to the elderly couple from the Cruise Ship Terminal parking lot. That's the car Elizabeth commandeered. We recovered it and when the authorities find it, they'll also find your weapons in the trunk."

Keats wanted to ask Buchanan why. But he didn't. He just continued watching the monitors like he'd been told.

After another minute or so Buchanan said, "I'm sure you recognize that vehicle." He was pointing at yet a different vehicle. That one was being tracked on a different monitor.

"That's my car," said Keats. "Who's driving it?"

"You are," said Buchanan. "You're headed west on Highway 265. You're trying to get the hell out of Matagorda County. But you're not going to make it. That's because you'll be dead within fifteen or twenty minutes."

Then Buchanan explained exactly how Keats was going to die. Told him why his body would never be recovered. Keats didn't understand where this was headed. But, he refrained from asking any more questions. He'd be told later and he knew that.

The five men continued watching the monitors for another minute or so then Buchanan told Keats they needed a pint of his blood. The young man who'd arrived in the Transit Van drew the blood, put it in a small cooler, and took it with him when he left.

After he was gone, Buchanan told Keats one of the men from the Transit Van would be found inside his car. He said the man would be armed and there'd be spent shell casings all over ground and even more inside the car. He told Keats the blood he'd just given the young man would be found in and around both vehicles. He said the local Crime Scene Investigators would take samples of the blood found at the scene. He said they'd find tire tracks matching the tread on his vehicle's tires nearly everywhere another dead body turned up. Keats realized he'd be the primary person of interest in several slam dunk homicides cases. The preponderance of evidence alone would convict him. Couple that with the fact that he had no job, no permanent credentials, no home, no money, and no clothes except the ones he had on his back;

and things were looking pretty grim. Keats realized he couldn't even contact a family member or friend. Anyone he tried to communicate with would have to turn him in. If they didn't they'd be found guilty of 'harboring and abetting' a fugitive. Keats was in one hell of a quandary.

# CHAPTER FORTY-FIVE

Keats looked at Buchanan and asked, "Is something like this going to happen to Elizabeth?"

"Forget about Elizabeth," said Buchanan. "She's going to be fine."

Keats was trying to come to grips with the concept of *'no more Elizabeth'*. Buchanan could see that.

He said, "Here's what I think, Keats. Somebody has handed you a shit sandwich. Take a bite of it, spit it out, then wash the taste out of your mouth and get on with your damn business. That's what I do."

*There it is again*, thought Keats, *the Cap'n Rockwell Torrey persona*. He was thinking about that when Buchanan pointed at the monitor on the far left. Keats looked, but couldn't make out what he was looking at. Buchanan told the young man controlling the monitor to enlarge the image. Finally Keats could tell what it was. It was a boat. It looked like it was somewhere out in the Gulf of Mexico. And it was moving at a high rate of speed.

"That's the *'Catch-o-the-Day'*," said Buchanan.

The image continued to grow larger. Keats could see more detail now. He could tell it was a large high-dollar motor yacht. He cast a questioning glance in Buchanan's direction.

Buchanan saw him do it and said, "It belongs to us. That's where you're going to be living for a while."

"That's interesting," said Keats. "Where's the boat going?"

"It's headed for Clear Lake," said Buchanan. "It's in the Gulf right now, about half an hour out. It'll be moored in the Marina at the South Harbor Resort later on tonight. The approximate time of arrival at the Resort should be between twenty-two and twenty-three hundred hours. Angelique should get there about the time the boat arrives. But if she isn't, she won't be far behind."

"And?" asked Keats.

Buchanan said, "I'm going to drive you there right now." He paused and reflected for a moment then added, "If you're ready to go, we'll leave."

Keats shot Buchanan a thumbs-up and they left.

# CHAPTER FORTY-SIX

Ten minutes later, they were headed east on Highway 265. Buchanan had his attention focused on the road. But not Keats, he was ignoring everything around him, he was inside his head, totally engrossed in thought. He wondered if he'd finally gotten a glimpse of the real Buchanan tonight, the man's true persona. He still wasn't sure. And then there was Elizabeth. He'd not even suspected she was involved in anything like this. Buchanan interrupted Keats train of thought.

He said, "Elizabeth is the only reason you got caught up in this mess, Keats. She's the reason Linda Cunningham enrolled in your program at the University. She's the reason you had to kill the woman." He hesitated for a moment or so then added, "Elizabeth may be intelligent, but she hasn't got an ounce of common sense. She's a hazard to herself and everybody around her. Because of her, you can forget about the world of academia. I'm privy to your past. In my opinion you've got some extremely appealing options. Are we on the same page here?"

Keats nodded his head '*yes*'.

Buchanan continued to talk. He said, "When we get to South Shore Harbor, you and I are going to do a drive by. Make sure the '*Catch of the Day*' is moored in the Marina. Make sure there's nothing suspicious looking in the immediate area. If everything looks copacetic, I'm going to drop you off in front of the hotel. You're going to go in, go to the front desk and find out if Angelique has arrived yet. All you need do is mention her first name. If she's already there you'll be given a key card. If not, you'll be told where to wait. The person at the front desk is one of us so do whatever you're told."

"Will we be there alone?" asked Keats.

"For a while," said Buchanan. "But there's going to be others. The first to arrive should be two other women. They're supposed to be all dolled up like high dollar hookers. But they're not hookers. They're seasoned combat veterans, skilled martial artists. Both are excellent boat handlers. Angelique and the two women will probably be your companions in the days to come. There's a high probability that you'll be posing as a wealthy entrepreneur on an Intracoastal Canal poker run from New Orleans, Louisiana to Key West. If that's what's finally decided, you're going to be doing that in the *'Catch-o-the-Day'*. That's why the boat is about to be moored in the Marina at South Shore Harbor. There may be more than just the four of you on board the *Catch*. That's also yet to be determined. I've been told you can you handle yourself at a poker table. Is that right?"

"I've gambled a little bit," said Keats. "And I'm familiar with the poker runs. I've never been directly involved in any of it, but I've watched some of the boats pass while I was eating in a restaurant on the Intracoastal Canal. I learned to play poker at Harrah's Casino in New Orleans, there, and Beau Rivage in Biloxi."

"Good enough," said Buchanan. "Get comfortable around Angelique. You may end up having to pretend you're married to the woman. If that's the case, you'll need to assume the role of a typical inattentive husband. Can you handle that?"

"I think so," said Keats. "It's the *Catch* that concerns me. I've never driven a boat like that."

Buchanan said, "I've already told you the women can handle the boat. Angelique definitely knows what she's doing. As a matter of fact, she's a licensed Marine Pilot. She'll show you how to operate things as soon as you get on board. You just make damn sure you know how to handle all the technology, especially the weapon systems."

"You bet," said Keats.

"Get as much sleep as you can when you get to South Shore. Get it whenever you can," said Buchanan. "If the *Catch* stays moored in the Marina tomorrow, you'll be getting out on deck real early. Angelique always does a little yoga first thing in the morning. The woman has zero inhibitions and won't be wearing very much. You're going to be out there having your morning coffee. You're going to have to ignore her *expose'*. We want to turn everybody else's head in the vicinity, not yours. You're going to have to look totally detached. You'll be pretending you don't see a damn thing that's going on around you. Read your *Wall Street Journal* or *Forbes* or whatever the hell else you can find to read. Meanwhile, we'll be discretely photographing the faces of any voyeurs. You can help us accomplish that by letting Angie wait on you whenever and however she wants to. You can even handle her a little bit. But don't overdo things."

Buchanan glanced at Keats briefly to see if he understood that part. He must have been satisfied with what he saw, because he continued to talk.

He said, "The two of you may be eating breakfast inside the hotel tomorrow morning. If you do, you'll probably eat the buffet at the Paradise Grill. Don't be surprised by anything Angelique does. You just be amused if she acts like a bitch. You let her do whatever she decides to do. You, yourself, keep things very low key. You get my drift?" Keats nodded that he did.

Buchanan went on talking. He said, "We'll be conducting a discrete photo shoot inside the restaurant while she works the crowd. There isn't any way of telling what might happen after you leave the restaurant. We'll have to play it by ear. This isn't the first time Angelique has done something like this, so you simply stay alert and follow her lead. Are you clear on all that?"

Keats said, "I hope so."

"I know you have a lot of questions," said Buchanan. "I can't answer most of them right now. When I know more, you'll know more."

"I do have a question I think you can answer," said Keats. "Mind if I ask it?"

"Shoot," said Buchanan.

# CHAPTER FORTY-SEVEN

"Angie told me you were her stepfather," said Keats. "Is that true?"

There was genuine surprise on Buchanan's face. He asked, "When did she tell you that?"

Keats said, "She volunteered the information while we were alone in the conference room. I have to admit it, I was wondering about you and her, what brought the two of you together." Keats saw a crooked little grin creep across Buchanan's face again.

"I don't mind telling you," said Buchanan.

Keats added, "I'm also puzzled about Nate Davenport. What's the connection between you and Davenport?" Buchanan's grin began to wane a bit, but it didn't dissipate completely.

"Why not, we have a little time," said Buchanan. "But understand this, I don't want you to divulge one word of what you're about to hear to anyone. Can I depend on that?"

"You have my word," said Keats.

"Also," said Buchanan, "when that SAT phone rings the chit-chat is over. As soon as that happens, you get your mind back on our mission and forget about all this other drivel." He shot Keats a stern look.

"Understood," said Keats.

Then Buchanan proceeded with an explanation.

# CHAPTER FORTY-EIGHT

Buchanan said, "Nate Davenport and I have been on a destiny-driven collision course for most of our adult lives. We both graduated from the Naval Academy, me, three years ahead of him. After graduation and being commissioned I went to Flight School in Florida and was trained to be a Navy Fighter Pilot. Same thing happened to Nate. I met him for the first time at Miramar Naval Air Station in San Diego. He got assigned to the same F-8 Squadron I was in. I was the Squadron XO at the time. A year and a half earlier, during my first combat deployment to Nam, I'd been credited with five MIG kills. I was a Navy Ace. But Nate was a rookie in every sense of the word. And he turned out to be one of the most reckless accident prone son-of-a-bitches I've ever met."

Buchanan paused. He looked like he was rethinking everything he'd just said, recalling some of Davenport's most prominent screws ups. Keats thought of a couple other questions he wanted to ask. He thought maybe he needed to steer Buchanan away from the Davenport issue. But he held his tongue and in about a minute Buchanan began talking again.

Buchanan said, "We deployed to Southeast Asia on board the USS Hancock in late April 1969. That was about a year and a month after the Tet Offensive. Things were really heating up in Nam about that time. We'd been on Yankee Station for about a week. Nate and I were flying escort for half a dozen A-4 Fighter-bombers. Around noon on a Thursday Nate Davenport got my ass shot down. It happened near the Mu Gia Pass on the South Vietnamese-Laotian border. I intentionally put my aircraft between Nate and an 'Atoll, air-to-air missile that a MIG 17 had fired at his aircraft. The stupid son-of-a-bitch had no idea he was about to get his ass shot down. But I knew it and I made a snap decision. I decided my chances in the jungle were a lot better than his were and I took the missile meant for him right up the ass end of my

F-8. I managed to eject an instant before the missile hit my aircraft. Later that day, in the jungle, I decided I was going to kill Davenport if I ever got half the chance. I'm still waiting for the opportune time."

Buchanan cut his eyes toward Keats. Keats eyes were wide with amazement. Buchanan burst into laughter. About that time the SAT phone sounded off. Before Keats could blink an eye Buchanan had the phone pressed against the side of his head.

"Speak," he said. Buchanan listened to whoever was on the other end. He cut his eyes toward Keats several times while he was listening. But he didn't say anything. The person on the other end was doing all the talking. Buchanan finally looked out the window to his left. Then he said, "Confirm that. Then get back to me."

Buchanan terminated the call. Keats expected some kind of explanation, but Buchanan didn't say anything about what he'd just been told. Instead he said, "You look concerned. Don't be. The body count just went up, that's all. Their body count, not ours."

That meant someone else was dead. Evidently the discretionary the use of deadly force was business as usual for Buchanan's crew.

"When will I be briefed on the actual rules of engagement?" asked Keats.

"The rules of engagement are simple," said Buchanan. I'll do that for you right now. I'm giving you license to kill anyone who looks suspect. You can do that anytime you think you should. I don't take orders from anyone. And your orders come directly from me, or from my designee. Do you understand? I'm giving you license to do whatever you have to do. I'll handle any repercussions."

"You're serious about that, aren't you?" said Keats.

Buchanan affirmed that with a nod and said, "Deadly serious. And before you ask, I know you're in the dark regarding who our adversaries are. We already know quite a bit about our adversaries, but our *intel* is still fragmented. What we do know is we're headed in the right direction. To draw any final conclusions at this point would be premature. But it won't be that way long. We'll know exactly who it is we're up against and why. We'll have access to photographs of our adversaries, their rank and file, their wrap sheets, where they are, what they're all about, etcetera. We should have most of it by the time you finish breakfast tomorrow morning." He paused then asked, "How do you feel about all this?"

"It's a bit much," said Keats. "But you have my back, right?"

Buchanan said, "That's affirmative. And you have mine."

"What am I supposed to call you?" asked Keats.

"You can call me Tony," said Buchanan. "And don't worry about what's in store for you. You'll have no regrets when all this is over."

"When am I going to have a name that's going to stick with me a while?" asked Keats.

"That'll have to come from someone else." said Buchanan. "As we speak, consideration is being given to several names, very common names that used to belong to real people." He hesitated then asked, "Do you think you could put a little 'New Iberia, Louisiana twang' in your voice?"

"Maybe a little," said Keats.

Buchanan looked at him and smiled then looked back at the road. They could both see the bridge at San Luis Pass up ahead.

Buchanan said, "The other end of that bridge is where our adversary's body count just went up. They sent someone to look for their people, the one's that had gone missing in that vicinity within the last hour or so. That cost the guy his life. That brings their body count on San Luis Island and at the Pass to six. Those six are in addition to the woman you killed and the other two or three Elizabeth may have killed."

"So we haven't lost anyone yet?"

Buchanan didn't give him an answer.

# CHAPTER FORTY-NINE

Keats and Buchanan crossed the bridge at San Luis Pass unmolested. By then it was about 10:00 pm and the wind had died down almost completely. The clouds had scattered, and for the most part, the sky was clear and the moon full. An open beach ran along the right side of the road. Keats looked out into the Gulf. The surf was completely flat and the seawater looked as slick as glass.

Up ahead the beach houses on both sides of the road were spread out and most of the property values fell into the seven digit category. It wasn't about to be bedtime yet, but almost all the houses were totally dark. That seemed a little strange to Keats. He turned his head and looked at Buchanan. Buchanan was looking at the beach houses too. Keats figured their minds had to be running in the same track.

Buchanan confirmed that when he said, "People who have an ungodly amount of money don't seem to get much benefit from what they own, do they?"

"It certainly seems that way to me," said Keats. "I'm wondering, what made you say that?"

Buchanan smiled at him. He asked, "Think I read your mind?" Keats didn't give him an answer.

Buchanan said, "I'm not a mind reader, Keats. But you have to assume some of the people we're up against might possess special intellectual propensities. That's why you can't afford to be *you*, pretending to be *someone else*. You cannot afford to let anything you do raise their suspicions. You have to be totally convincing when dealing with the opposition. You're a *'shrink'*. You know exactly what I'm talking about?" Buchanan stopped talking and waited for response from Keats.

Keats said, "I guess I do."

Buchanan looked back at the road. He said, "When we get to South Shore Harbor you're going to have to start acting like the character you're supposed to be impersonating. Tonight will be like a dress rehearsal. You have to become this other person. You have to be comfortable in your new role. Don't let anything get you off track. Take everything in. Soak it all up. Play the part to perfection. You think you can do that, Keats?"

"I'll do my dead-level best," said Keats.

# CHAPTER FIFTY

They traveled maybe another quarter mile without speaking. Keats, he was busy rethinking everything Buchanan had already said to him. Buchanan decided Keats had had enough time to think about things and said what he needed to say next. And he made damn sure he had Keats undivided attention before he said it.

"Clear your head and listen to me," said Buchanan. He waited until he was certain he had Keats' undivided attention then said, "You're not going to like what I'm about to tell you. But, understand this. At the time and in light of your circumstances, I'd have done exactly the same thing." Buchanan's tone made Keats uneasy.

"The person you knew as Linda Cunningham," said Buchanan, "She's done contract work for the CIA. There's a possibility she wasn't there to do you any harm. But that hasn't yet been substantiated. It'll be a while before we really know." Buchanan stopped, waited for that to sink in.

Keats was too dumbfounded to say anything, his thinking dominated by disbelief.

Finally, he got himself together and said, "She had me convinced she intended to ambush me. I don't know what to think."

Buchanan said, "She was an accomplished assassin. That's a fact. But you may not have been her target. We have reason to believe she'd been ordered to see that you got back into your vehicle and safely on your way without being captured."

Keats skin began to crawl. He asked, "How long have you known about this?"

"I was told that a few minutes ago," said Buchanan, "When I took that last call. We're trying to substantiate things right now. We know Linda Cunningham wasn't the woman's real name. We're still trying to identify her. We suspect she may have enrolled in your Program at the University to protect you."

"Was Elizabeth aware of this?" asked Keats.

"I have no idea," said Buchanan.

Keats said, "I may have killed the person who was sent to protect me. Shit."

Somehow he knew it was true. She'd been intentionally obnoxious so she wouldn't have to deal with anyone trying to date her or make friends with her. That made all kind of sense.

"Now what happens?" asked Keats.

"Get over it," said Buchanan. "You were not informed. That's the only reason it happened the way it did. You or I would've handled things a whole lot differently if we'd been calling the shots."

"Who in the fuck is behind this fiasco?" asked Keats.

"We don't really know yet," said Buchanan. "But I'm about to find out. Hand me the SAT phone."

Keats handed him the phone. Buchanan switched it to Bluetooth and placed a call.

# CHAPTER FIFTY-ONE

As soon as someone answered Buchanan said, "Put Davenport on and don't give me that *wait one* crap." Davenport must have been standing right next to the individual who'd taken the call, because he was on the line within two seconds.

"Tony?" said Davenport. "What's wrong?" The apprehension in his voice was more than obvious.

"You need to tell me who's behind this crap. You need to tell me that right now."

Davenport said, "I'm going to have to take this call in my office." He'd said that to someone on his end, probably whoever had answered the phone the first time he called.

Davenport said, "Don't hang up, Tony. I'll hurry."

Keats heard someone in the background say, "Who the hell is Tony Buchanan?" Whoever it was didn't get an answer, at least not one that Keats could hear.

Davenport was in his office and back on the line in just a few seconds. He said, "They have me grazing in a mighty small pasture these days, Tony. I hope you have adequate clearance to hear what I'm about to tell you. I assume you're alone right now. Is that correct?"

"No. There are other ears here. And you don't need to be concerned about my clearance to hear any damn thing you have to say. Here's all you need to be concerned about. One of my people has probably killed one of the Agency's people tonight. Matter of fact, there are about ten confirmed fatalities at this time. We haven't lost anybody yet and we don't intend to. Now either you get me on the same page with what's going on or more Agency people may come to no good end. You better tell me exactly what this is about. You read me, old man?"

Davenport didn't answer Buchanan's question. Instead he asked a question. He asked, "Is Elizabeth alright, Tony?" Buchanan terminated the call without giving him an answer.

They drove for a while without talking. Keats was mulling things over in his mind, asking himself some questions. Things like, *who in the world was Anthony Buchanan?* Keats was beginning to wonder if the man feared anybody or anything. He wondered how much stroke Buchanan actually had with the upper echelon. He'd just told Davenport someone had killed a CIA Field Officer. Hell, he was the one who'd killed Linda Cunningham. Keats was wondering just how much trouble he might be in? He thought about the Memorandum of Understanding from the Chief Intelligence Officer at the White House. Maybe that was his 'get-out-of-jail-free' card. He certainly hoped the damn document was legit. He thought about Elizabeth. She was a non-entity now. That didn't seem to bother him as much as it had earlier. Neither did the fact that he'd killed Cunningham with his bare hands. He realized his capacity to empathize was beginning to evolve. It wasn't at all diminished. If anything it was enhanced, just more selective. He realized he was resurrecting a 'no holds barred' mentality. That part of his psyche had been buried for years. What was most amazing was he wasn't really worried about any of it. Keats realized he'd passed through a mysterious portal. The transition was complete. He'd entered the clandestine world of espionage.

# CHAPTER FIFTY-TWO

The SAT phone sounded off again. Buchanan snatched it off the seat, had it switched on and pressed to the side of his head in less than a heartbeat.

"Speak," he said. But this time he didn't switch the call to Bluetooth.

The conversation lasted about ten minutes and it was completely one-sided again. Once during the call Keats heard Buchanan utter something or other, but he couldn't make it out. When whomever Buchanan was listening to was done talking he simply switched the SAT phone off and laid it back on the seat. He didn't bother to volunteer any information. Keats didn't ask him for any either.

Within two or three minutes the SAT phone sounded off again. Buchanan picked it up again, listened intently for maybe thirty seconds then terminated the call. This time he'd not uttered a single sound. Again, he gave Keats no immediate feedback.

Finally he nodded in Keats direction and said, "The two women I told you about are on their way to the Resort. When you get to the suite you're not to interfere with whatever it is they're doing or intend to do. Not for any reason. You may feel like you're being placed in an extremely vulnerable set of circumstances. But you'll not be vulnerable at all. There are sentries in place to insure everybody's safety. They're just not detectable. They'll preclude any possibility of an armed incursion." Buchanan paused. Keats took his cue and responded to what he'd just been told with an affirmative nod.

Then Buchanan continued. He said, "That may not be the case tomorrow morning. Things could turn to shit early on. If that happens, we'll have adequate back up in place. You just remember this. Your three lady-friends have been schooled in every imaginable form of martial arts. They're highly proficient martial art eclectics and they'll not require your protection.

"Let me ask you a question," said Keats. "Who the hell are you?"

Buchanan looked Keats squarely in the face and smiled. He said, "I'm Anthony Ambrose. I'm with MI6 British Intelligence. My immediate Superior is Sir Francis Maude, Cabinet Level Minister for MI6."

Keats was astounded. The man sounded so damn British.

The rhetoric continued. "Sir Francis answers directly to Jon Day, Chairman of the Joint Intelligence Committee of the United Kingdom."

He went on to tell Keats that they were headquartered at 70 Whitehall in London and shared a few other choice tidbits of information. Keats was utterly amazed. His British accent was absolutely flawless. There was nothing indicating he was lying. No 'tell' in his demeanor whatsoever. Keats decided there was no way that could be faked.

"Well at last you're being truthful with me," said Keats.

"And you believe me. Don't you?" Again, his British diction was totally uncontaminated. That had not been the case with some of the other personality traits he'd witnessed Buchanan exhibit.

Keats told him he was totally convinced.

"Keats. It's all bullshit. I got that crap off the internet. Listen to me. Hitler played the part of *Mein Fuhrer* to perfection. He was such a convincing actor he damn near conquered the World when he did it. That's because he became the person he wanted everybody to think he was. You're going to get a new persona tonight. You may have to become a wealthy Cajun asshole. And you better be damn good at, because if you're not totally believable some of the wrong people are going to die. And you'll probably be first to go."

# CHAPTER FIFTY-THREE

"When are we going to know something more definite?" asked Keats.

"Soon," said Buchanan. Then Buchanan asked Keats a question. "Is there anything in your home or your office that has to be removed, anything that might cause us problems down the road?"

"I'm not sure," said Keats. "I'd have to give that some thought."

"Well you better think about it fast," said Buchanan. "We don't have that much time."

Keats agreed with him and began taking mental inventory of his home. Then he thought about his office at the University. Buchanan stayed real quiet while he did it.

Finally Keats said, "There's a file folder at the house and another one in my office at University. Elizabeth asked me to hold some folders for her. I did. I have no idea what's in them. They were sealed when she gave them to me and that's the way they stayed."

"You're sure that's all there is?" asked Buchanan.

"That's all I can think of right now," said Keats. "Something else may come to me later."

Buchanan said, "Understand this. Whatever you have that could be problematic for anybody must be recovered. We can't let anything of a sensitive nature fall into our adversary's hands. So you think real hard. Be sure that's all there is."

Keats reflected for another minute or so then said, "There are two more things that could be a potential problem."

"Tell me what they are," said Buchanan.

"I have photographs of two men I served with in the Hindu Kush," explained Keats. "The photographs were taken five days after they were declared dead. I'm holding a newspaper and their picture is on the front page. The cover story depicts how they died earlier in the week. They're standing right next to me, big as life. I don't know where they are or what they're doing now. But that could be a problem for them."

"Holding a newspaper with a cover story like that proves they weren't actually dead." said Buchanan. "Wasn't that clever? Can you think of anything else?"

Keats said, "I have a personal item one of my team members removed from the body of a dead Pakistanis. The man was killed the last night we were in the Hindu Kush Mountains. It's also in my office."

"You say it's a personal item, what is it?" asked Buchanan.

"It's a photograph," said Keats, "a picture of the dead Pakistani with his wife and two children. I promised the man I'd return it to his wife if anything ever happened to him. He died helping us escape that night. He's the only reason we survived. Someday I'm going to try to return the photograph to his widow or one of his two kids if I can find them."

Buchanan looked back at the road. He said, "None of that bodes well for you or anyone else connected in any way with those photographs. We'll remove Elizabeth's folders and the other stuff from your office first. Then we'll go to Bolivar. I have to make a quick stop at an abandoned lighthouse near the Ferry Landing. After that we'll ride the ferry back to Galveston and head for the mainland. We'll go to your place, get Elizabeth's other folders and whatever else you mentioned then head on over to South Shore Harbor."

# CHAPTER FIFTY-FOUR

Keats told Buchanan things on campus were usually very relaxed on Friday afternoon. However, going back to his office this particular Friday evening might get a bit tricky. He said Campus Security could be an issue. He shared the Linda Cunningham encounter with Buchanan. Told him exactly how the Security Officer had responded to his call. Buchanan asked Keats a few questions then told him how they'd handle things.

In a few minutes they reached the west end of the Galveston Island Seawall. The esplanade between the eastbound and westbound lanes of the San Luis Pass Road disappeared and the two lanes converged at the entrance to Seawall Boulevard. At that point the elevation of the roadway increased to about thirty-five feet above sea level and they were driving along the top of a seawall that ran from one end of Galveston Island to the other. As they continued traveling east they passed a few small motels and some convenience stores and a bar or two. That was all on the left side of the road. On the right there was a wide elevated sidewalk bordering a narrow stretch of beach then nothing but the open waters of the Gulf of Mexico beyond that. The number of people walking on the sidewalk increased geometrically as they continued traveling east.

Finally the traffic flow in the street slowed to a crawl. That's because there were a lot of young women walking along the sidewalk. Most of them were wearing very skimpy beach attire. More than just a few were wearing thong bikinis. The result, there were swivel-headed passengers in nearly every vehicle. They all had their eyes glued to the pedestrians. Buchanan decided there was no way they could afford to stay hung up in that mess for long so he took a left at the first side road they came to.

Within four or five blocks Buchanan pulled into the parking lot of a large hardware store and parked. He killed the engine, got out and went inside by himself.

Keats looked a lot different than he had earlier in the day. Neither he nor Buchanan thought anybody would recognize him back on campus. But they needed a change of clothes and some cosmetic alterations to the vehicle. Then they could go anywhere they needed to on campus.

Buchanan was back in about ten or twelve minutes and he'd purchased everything he thought they needed to pull off the ruse he had planned. He showed Keats two identical magnetic signs. They read, *Asbestos Disposal Inc*. He slapped a sign on each side of their SUV then climbed inside. He'd bought both he and Keats a pair of oversized coveralls, an industrial safety helmet, and a shoulder-slung utility bag. Inside each bag were leather work gloves, razor box-cutters, two rolls of duct tape, and a box of form fitting face protectors. They both donned a pair of coveralls. Buchanan gave Keats a-once-over glance, told him he looked the part. Then he started the SUV and drove out of the parking lot.

Ten minutes later they pulled into an auxiliary parking lot at the University. They got out, grabbed their stuff and headed for the Psychology Building. There were a few students still on campus, but no onsite Security Personnel visible anywhere. Nobody they passed even bothered to give them a second look.

When they got to the Psychology Building they rode the elevator to the third floor, got out, and walked directly to the Office Complex. Keats realized there was someone in his office, standing in front of his desk. Buchanan waited at the door while Keats went in.

The person in Keats office was a man and he had his back was to the door. Keats managed to get right behind him before the man realized someone was there and turned around.

The man was startled. He said, "Who gave you permission to enter this office?"

Keats didn't give the man an answer.

"Give me your name," said the man. Keats still didn't respond.

They stood there for a moment, each staring the other in the face. Neither man knew the other. But Buchanan knew exactly who he was. Buchanan knew the man's last name. He was someone Buchanan had met in Moscow years ago, a member of the Soviet KGB. Back then he'd spoke only Russian. But he spoke damn near perfect English now. Any linguist worth his salt would have immediately recognized what they were hearing in this man's voice. Buchanan knew exactly what the Russian had done. He'd obviously used recorded audio programming to learn English. His brain had become hard wired to the tempo of the audio program and his speech had some of the elements of a percussionist's drumming. There was a definitive rhythm or meter to the flow of his discourse, each word standing alone, each slightly separated from the others and spoken a bit too succinctly. Buchanan had considered killing the bastard years ago in Moscow. He hadn't done it back then. But now seemed like the opportune time.

Buchanan immediately entered Keats office. He stopped and stood toe to toe with the guy. The old man recognized Buchanan immediately. Keats could see the recognition in his eyes. He could also see the man's apprehension. The guy tried to go for his weapon, but his fingers never even touched the butt of his gun. That's because Keats pinned his hand against his chest.

At that exact moment Buchanan stepped forward, pressed his Beretta into the man's middle and pumped two 9mm rounds into the left side of his abdomen. The guy stood there for a second or two, grimacing, and clutching the front of Buchanan's coveralls. They could both tell he was getting a *dead man's thousand yard stare* in his eyes. Buchanan didn't wait for the inevitable. He raised his weapon to the Russian's chin and pumped a third round into him. Bullet number three entered his soft palate then traveled at a forty-five degree angle through the center of his brain. The result was instantaneous cardiac arrest. The Russians knees buckled and he collapsed on the floor in front of Keats desk.

They stood over him for several seconds watching the blood pool on the floor behind his head. Then Keats looked at the ceiling. There was a hole in the ceiling above his desk and the area around the hole was one hell of a mess.

Keats looked back at Buchanan. He asked, "Who was he?"

"His last name was Petchenko," said Buchanan. "I don't remember his first name. At one time the man was a Soviet KGB Agent."

Then Buchanan looked at Keats and said, "Get what you came for."

Keats pointed at Petchenko. He asked, "What about him?"

Buchanan said, "Linda Cunningham killed him. That's what Campus Security will believe. That's what they'll tell the authorities."

Buchanan told Keats to ransack his office. He told him to avoid getting blood on his shoes or hands, but not to worry about leaving his fingerprints anywhere. It was his office and the authorities would expect that. As soon as Buchanan was satisfied with what Keats had done, they left.

# CHAPTER FIFTY-FIVE

After leaving the University Buchanan took a convoluted route through Old Town to get to the ferry landing. The traffic in that part of town was fairly light and they made real good time. In ten or twelve minutes they were approaching the ferry landing on the extreme east end of Galveston Island. As they got to the end of the boulevard they entered one of the three feeder lanes and pulled up behind several other vehicles already waiting in line to board the *Robert C. Lanier.* The *Lanier* is one of five ferries owned and operated by the Texas Department of Transportation. Buchanan stopped behind the last vehicle, shifted into park and killed the engine.

They'd arrived just in time to see the oldest ferry in the fleet, the *Gibb Gilchrist,* depart from the starboard side docking basin and begin an East Bay run to the Bolivar Peninsula. In less than a minute the other ferry collided with the pilings lining the docking basin on the port side. As soon as the *Lanier* was secured to the pilings a deckhand dropped the ramp and started directing vehicles off the boat. There were quite a few motorcycles parked on the bow and they were gone within ten seconds. Offloading the cars, trucks and SUV's took a little longer, maybe five or six minutes. Keats and Buchanan watched the entire offload in silence.

As a Coast Guard Inspector approached their vehicle, Buchanan lowered the window glass on driver side. The Inspector stopped, eyed the interior of their vehicle then moved on to the truck parked right behind them. He performed cursory inspection of the interior of that vehicle then sauntered down the long line of vehicles piling up behind them.

Buchanan raised the glass in his window. About the time he got it up his SAT phone sounded off again. He picked it up, looked at who was calling, switch to Bluetooth, made the connection and laid the phone back on the seat. He looked at

Keats and mouthed, *"Don't say anything."* The two men sat in silence for maybe a full minute. Finally the caller spoke.

"How goes it, Buck?" said the caller. The voice belonged to a male. It was unusually high pitched for a man. For some strange reason the voice sounded vaguely familiar to Keats.

Keats looked at Buchanan. Buchanan grinned.

"Somebody is trying to get into the middle of my business, Buck. You got any idea who it might be."

"Maybe," said Buchanan. There was no audible reaction from the other end.

Buchanan inserted the dead Russian's name in a question. He asked, "Does the name Petchenko ring a bell? I ran in to him at UTMB not thirty minutes ago. Do you think he could be part of your problem?"

The other man didn't answer Buchanan's question. Instead he asked a question.

"Buck, are you alone right now?"

"No," said Buchanan. "I'm with a friend. Until this evening he called himself David Keats. But now he doesn't have an identity."

"Is Keats the only other person there?" asked the caller. "And do you trust him?"

"Yes, to both your questions," said Buchanan.

There was silence for a moment then the other man said, "Mr. Keats, I'm thinking back to Tibet. I'm remembering a man I met in Nepal. He was named David Keats. Might you be that same man?"

Nepal, Tibet had been Keats avenue of escape after completing his final mission in the Hindu Kush Mountains of Afghanistan. The Kathmandu University in Nepal had been where the members of his team had been told to go for extraction. He'd been the only member of his squad to make it out of mountains and into Tibet. He'd met a man there who'd given him what he needed to get out of Asia. That's why this man's voice sounded familiar. This was the very same man. Now some things were starting to fall into place.

"I remember you," said Keats. You're the English Professor."

Buchanan had a quizzical look on his face. Keats shot Buchanan a *'thumbs up'*. Buchanan's eyes narrowed.

"It's good to hear your voice again," said Keats. "I'm sorry, but I can't remember your name."

"My name changes constantly," said the caller.

Then he addressed Buchanan. He said, "Buck, the Russian Federation has been trying to catch and kill Petchenko for more than five years. He's been near the top of Russia's Foreign Intelligence Service hit list since 2013. What do you think Petchenko was doing at UTMB?"

"I'll let Keats answer that question," said Buchanan.

"I'm just guessing," said Keats. "But I think he was trying to get his hands on an envelope a friend of mine had asked me to keep in my office. It was sealed and I have no idea what was inside it. I also kept a photograph of a Pakistani man I met years ago in the Hindu Kush. He died helping me get out of the Mountains. His first name was Dipesh, but I forget his last. In the picture he's standing by his wife and two children."

The man said, "If it's the same Dipesh I know, he was wounded but didn't die in the Mountains. He was a Russian collaborator. They rescued him. He's fine. He now works for the Russian Federation Internal Intelligence Directorate in Moscow. He's coordinating the manhunt for Petchenko. Tell me who gave you the sealed envelope and asked you to hold it?"

Buchanan interrupted. He said, "Let me answer that one, Keats. The woman's name is Elizabeth Davenport. I think Petchenko was after the envelope she asked Keats to hold. She's a Plastic Surgeon and the envelope may have contained the photographs of about two dozen of Davenport's clients. We have reason to believe she took before-and-after photographs of each client. These people are very special. She was not supposed to do that. The reason is quite simple. They were all getting new faces because of the kind of work they do. Some are professional assassins, some are provocateurs, probably a few of them are moles, and who knows what else. The pictures of these individuals could be sold on the foreign market for millions."

All three men sat there in silence for maybe two minutes before anyone said anything else. The caller finally spoke. He asked, "We need to talk face-to-face, Buck. Where can we meet?"

Buchanan said, "Wait a minute."

A Coast Guard Inspection Officer was trying to get Buchanan's attention. He was trying to get him to drive forward. Buchanan turned the key in the ignition, shifted the SUV into drive, and drove on board the *Lanier*.

Keats looked at Buchanan. He asked, "You want me to look at what's in the envelope?"

Buchanan was concentrating on getting parked and didn't give him an answer.

Once parked, he asked the man on the phone another question. "Where do you propose we meet?"

The caller said, "I think you're somewhere in Galveston County right now. If I'm right about that, I'll come to you."

"That's not where we are," said Buchanan. "But we're not that far away. Tell you what I'll do. I'll call you back at about twenty-three hundred hours. Then we'll decide where we'll meet."

"I'll configure my SAT phone to take the call," said the caller. "Don't keep me waiting."

The line went dead.

# CHAPTER FIFTY-SIX

"You lied to him," said Keats. "We are in Galveston County. You don't trust him?" Buchanan said, "I trust him. I'm simply being cautious."

Then Keats and Buchanan sat there quietly, watching people get out of their vehicles and walk around on deck. Some of them were walking forward and standing near the bow. A lot of people were lining up to climb the stairs to the second level observation deck. Everybody seemed to be enjoying the boat ride. Keats was primarily watching the goings-on in front of them. Buchanan had his eyes on the side and rearview mirrors. He was watching the activity behind their SUV.

Keats finally said, "Don't you think we better meet this guy somewhere soon? I think the three of us need to get on the same page."

"I agree with that," said Buchanan. "But here's my dilemma, do we finish what we've started before we meet with him? Or do we meet with him first?"

Keats said, "I'm not in a position to even have an opinion."

Buchanan thought for a few more seconds then he picked up the SAT phone again. He placed a call and switched to Bluetooth. Plenty of time passed. But there was never a connection. No sound whatsoever. Buchanan finally terminated the call. Then they sat in silence.

# CHAPTER FIFTY-SEVEN

They reached the Bolivar Peninsula Ferry Landing in about ten minutes. The SUV lurched forward as the bow of the *Lanier* collided with the pilings at the Ferry Landing. The SAT phone rang about the time that happened, but Buchanan ignored it.

"Aren't you going to answer that?" asked Keats.

"Not yet," said Buchanan.

After the tenth ring Buchanan picked up the SAT phone and answered it. He said, "Be on the next ferry."

Evidently the caller told him he'd do it, because Buchanan said, "Good. When you get over here we'll be waiting for you at the first convenience store on the right." Then he terminated the call.

"What kind of game is this?" asked Keats. "You knew the caller was in our vicinity. I don't get it."

Buchanan said, "Listen to me. This man and I understand one another completely. We both use contradiction as a deceptive tool. If you skirt the issue while at the same time understanding one another perfectly, you confuse any eavesdropper. The sooner you learn how to do that the better off you'll be."

Buchanan looked at Keats for maybe five more seconds then he returned to looking straight ahead. Within a few seconds a deck hand was directing them to drive forward.

# CHAPTER FIFTY-EIGHT

Their vehicle was one of the first to cross the ramp and begin traveling east on Highway 87. But they only drove a short distance before Buchanan pulled to the side of the road. He waited until he had an opening then made a u-turn.

"What are you doing?" asked Keats.

"Sit tight," said Buchanan. "I'm returning to the Ferry Landing." He looked at Keats and added, "That's what he expects me to do."

"I don't understand," said Keats. "I was listening to what was being said the entire time and I never heard anything said that would make me think that."

Buchanan said, "Listen to me. He was giving me the opportunity to make sure we weren't being followed. Well, we're not."

"So now we're going to meet the guy somewhere back on Galveston Island?" asked Keats.

Buchanan didn't say yea or nay. Now Keats was more confused than ever. He decided he'd not ask Buchanan any more questions for the time being. And he was glad Buchanan decided not to volunteer anything. Five minutes later they were back on board the *Lanier*.

Buchanan rolled to a stop, turned the engine off and set the parking brake. Then he grabbed his SAT phone. He placed another call, switched to Bluetooth again and laid the phone on the seat. Someone answered immediately.

Keats studied the character of the other person's voice. The gender of the person doing the talking was indistinguishable. It could have been a woman, could've been a man. What the person said was fundamentally nonsensical to Keats. From what little he could ascertain he assumed their vehicle was displayed on one of the satellite tracking monitors at the San Luis Bay House. Maybe there was a young *bricoleur* he'd not yet met. But whoever it was told Buchanan they were no longer being followed. He said their *tail* had been handled. Finally the person on the other end stopped talking. Buchanan thought a moment then asked several cryptic sounding questions. He was given one word cryptic answers. Not a single word of it made a damn bit of sense to Keats. There was more silence. Then Buchanan terminated the call. Buchanan didn't volunteer an explanation of any kind and Keats didn't ask him any questions.

Finally Buchanan looked at Keats and said, "You can relax."

Keats nodded and went back to people-watching. After a moment or two Buchanan told him he had to use the *head*. He told Keats to slide behind the steering wheel after he got out and stay put. Then he got out of the SUV and disappeared inside the Ferry's superstructure on the starboard side. There were a lot of other people coming and going through that same entryway. Keats watched the people come and go. Buchanan returned to the SUV in about eight minutes. He opened the passenger side door, slipped inside, hit the door locks and started talking.

"There's a problem on the Galveston side. We may have to lay off shore for a few minutes while the Coast Guard gets things resolved." Keats had a questioning look on his face so Buchanan added more. "I was told there was a fight next to the restroom in the parking area. Four or five people got injured and there are several ambulances en route."

In less than fifteen seconds there was a light rap on the SUV's starboard side rear window. Buchanan unlocked the door and someone slipped into the back seat.

Keats turned and looked at the individual sitting in the back seat. He looked back at Buchanan and asked, "What the hell's going on here?"

# CHAPTER FIFTY-NINE

The man in the rear seat said, "When you sat down at the table that day in that little ramshackle café on Bautoom Street in Nepal, what were the first words out of your mouth?"

Keats thought about it. He remembered everything he'd said and done that day. He remembered it in detail. But he didn't give the guy an answer.

The man answered for him. "You said, *'Is that a Coca Cola you got there?'* Isn't that exactly what you asked me, word for word? Do you recall what I said in return?"

"Why don't you tell me," said Keats. Then he looked at Buchanan. Buchanan had a big shit-eating grin on his face.

The guy in the back seat supplied the answer. He said, "I didn't say a damn thing, did I? I just shoved the bottle of Coke in front of you. Then what'd you do? You pushed the bottle back in front of me, didn't you? Then you said, *'I hope you're as good at what you do as I've been told you are'*. Those were your exact words. Were they not? You think about that. If I wasn't the man who helped you get out of Tibet, how the hell would I know any of that?"

"I am clueless," said Keats. "But you sure as hell don't look like yourself. You would have to be at least seventy years old by now. You don't look anywhere close to seventy. You look like you're in your mid forties."

"Early fifties," said the man.

Buchanan cut in. He said, "The man in the back seat has a special appliance or device or whatever the hell you want to call it surgically implanted behind his ear. The man you met in Nepal that day is feeding him the information through the device. *'Remember that day in Nepal'* and all the rest of it. That shit is coming straight from the old man himself. The man you met in Nepal was named Jack Hobbs. The Jack Hobbs you met in Nepal is waiting for us in the parking lot at the Galveston Ferry Landing."

That made all kinds of sense to Keats.

Buchanan went on. He said, "But understand this, the man ashore isn't the only man named Jack Hobbs. The *original* Jack Hobbs died at Pearl Harbor during the Second World War. He's still entombed inside the USS Arizona. The man in the backseat is his great grandson. The man you met in Nepal was his grandfather."

# CHAPTER SIXTY

When they got to the Ferry Landing parking lot the old man was waiting for them. Just like Buchanan had said he would be. He was standing near the entrance to the restrooms. He had his arms folded and appeared to be watching the women line up and wait their turn to go in. As is usually the case on the men's side, there was no line.

Buchanan got Keats attention and told him where to park. He parked and turned off the engine and waited. Keats expected to hear more from Buchanan. And he did start talking immediately. He told Keats and the guy in the back seat to stay in the vehicle. Then he got out. He walked across the parking lot and entered the men's restroom. He walked right in front of Keats *long lost* friend from Nepal. But the two men ignored one another. The guy in the back seat and Keats didn't say a word to one another either. They just waited and watched.

When Buchanan came out of the restroom he stopped and stood next to the other man and they stood there, side by side, watching the women come and go. They talked a little, but not very much. That went on for maybe ten or twelve minutes. Then they shook hands and Buchanan returned to where Keats and young Hobbs were waiting. He opened the passenger side door of the SUV and slid inside. He immediately started issuing orders.

He told young Hobbs to drive Keats to his condominium on Tiki Island. Said Hobbs was to go inside and recover the photographs he'd been saving all these years, the photograph of Keats and the other two guys who were with him in the Hindu Kush. Then he told Hobbs to drop Keats off at the South Shore Harbor Resort and return to the San Luis Bay House. He instructed him to remain there and wait for further orders.

Buchanan said he and the other man, the older Hobbs, would make sure things were secure around the Marina at the South Shore Harbor Resort. He said the 'Catch-of-the-Day' was now moored there. He said they'd get that done before young Jack got there. He didn't tell Keats what he and the older Hobbs were going to do after that. His orders were to get his key card and join Angie on the top floor. He said the other two women who were supposed to be waiting in the suite with Angie would probably be gone. Buchanan said those two women were going to be used in a different way than he'd been originally told. However, he didn't say how.

# CHAPTER SIXTY-ONE

Buchanan got out and walked across the parking lot and stopped next to the restrooms. The older Jack Hobbs was still standing where Buchanan had left him. In a few seconds the two men walked off together. Keats and young Hobbs left as soon as they lost sight of the other two men.

Keats was driving. Hobbs was talking. He didn't say much of anything Keats wanted hear so he wasn't really listening. But he patronized the man by nodding every now and then. Hobbs stopped talking while they were crossing the Galveston Bay Causeway. He was watching two ships that were crossing East Galveston Bay. Keats was looking west toward Moody Gardens. All he could see was the glass Pyramid and a lot of lights. He checked the time. It was well after 10:00 pm. It was late, but still early enough they'd missed the heavy traffic that's always headed back into Houston on a Friday night.

They reached the north end of the Causeway in three or four minutes and took the first feeder road on the right. They crossed under I-45, stayed on the feeder and drove a short distance then made another right turn. Hobbs asked Keats to stop at the convenience store at the foot of the two lane bridge that crosses the narrow canal at the entrance to the Village. They drove past Fat Boys Bait and Tackle and stopped in front of the convenience store. Keats was more than just a little curious as to why Hobbs had wanted him to do that. So he questioned him.

"Why are we stopping here?" he asked.

"I'm going inside to buy some beer," he said. "And while I'm in the store you need to slide over so I can do the driving when I come out." He reflected for a moment then he said, "If we accidentally run into anyone, you remember to call me *Jack*. Hopefully that won't happen."

Keats could tell he wanted some kind of affirmation so he nodded. Then he said, "*Jack* it is. Tell me why you want to do the driving now."

"When we get to your place I'm the only one who's going to get out and go in," he said. "The glass in this vehicle is heavily tinted. No one will be able to tell you're still inside. And that's the way it has to be. Ok?" Keats didn't understand why he wanted to do it that way, but he nodded 'ok' anyway.

"You like Bud Lite Lime?" asked Hobbs.

"Why are you going to buy beer?" asked Keats.

"I have my reasons," was his only answer.

"My next door neighbor is nosey. Her name is Denise something or other. What'll you tell her if you run into her?"

"I'm going to tell her you've gone abroad for a few weeks and you left the keys to your place with me," he said. "I'll tell her you told me I could stay there while you were gone."

"What if she notices the beer and wants to share it with you?" asked Keats. "She's bad about that."

"I'll ask her to join me."

Keats said, "You're going to be sorry. She's a party animal. Like a piece of gum on your shoe. You're going to have a hard time getting rid of her."

Hobbs grinned, got out and went in. Keats slid over. He came out five minutes later, got behind the wheel, and set the beer on the seat between them. He had two new t-shirts wadded up in one of his hands and he placed them on top of the beer. Keats wondered what he was going to do with the t-shirts, but he didn't ask.

# CHAPTER SIXTY-TWO

Jack pulled out of the parking lot and drove across the bridge. Then he slowed to a crawl. Both men looked to their left. There were three people on foot at the kayak landing. They were walking around carrying flashlights. Two of them handed their flashlights to the third guy. Those two started unloading three kayaks from the bed of a pickup truck while the third man watched. Number three cast a fleeting glance in the direction of the SUV then looked back at what his buddies were doing. The other two ignored their vehicle completely. Jack drove on, past Admiral Circle and Windward Way. He was driving at a snail's pace. They pulled to a stop at the intersection of Tiki Drive and Lokai Avenue.

"What's that up there on the right?" asked Jack. He was looking at the large metal building fifty yards or so up the road. There were no exterior lights outside the building so he couldn't read the signage. Keats wondered why he was asking.

"The building belongs to Legends Saltwater Charters," said Keats. Then he asked Jack why he wanted to know. Jack didn't answer his question. He asked Keats another question.

"You ever charter a boat from them?" he asked.

"Nope," said Keats. "Why?"

"No reason." That's all the answer he gave. The guy was starting to aggravate Keats again.

Keats said, "Let's get on with this, Jack. Quit messing around."

Jack shot Keats a sardonic grin and pulled away from the intersection. Then he drove at a reasonable rate of speed all the way to the end of the road. As they approached the intersection Keats told him to turn right. He did. That put them on Isles End Road. Keats place was several houses down the road, on the left, at the entrance to the cul-de-sac. When they reached the fork in the road, Jack went straight then pulled up on the grass in the middle of the cul-de-sac.

Then he turned and looked at Keats. "Where does Denise live?" he asked.

Keats pointed at her place. It was next door to his.

"Do you think she's home?" he asked.

"If her lights are on she's home," said Keats. "And they're on. There's no other car parked in the driveway so she's probably alone. If you make the slightest sound when you go up the stairs, she'll be right behind you. I can promise you that."

Jack nodded. He didn't ask anything more questions. He just got out of the vehicle, marched straight across the street, up on to Denise's porch, and rang her damn door bell. Keats wanted to get out and go after the goofy son-of-a-bitch, but he didn't. He was thinking, 'this guy has got to be nuts'.

Denise opened the door almost immediately. Keats lowered the glass in the window on the driver's side a little and listened. The crazy son-of-a-bitch told her his full name. Then he told her Keats had left the country. And finally he told her he'd be staying next door indefinitely. Then he offered Denise a beer. She hesitated for maybe a microsecond then invited Jack inside and closed the door behind him. That came as no surprise.

In less than a minute Jack opened Denise's front door. He motioned for Keats to get out and come on in. He had a big shit-eating grin on his face. That was just plain nonsense to Keats. It blew his mind completely. But he got out and hurried across the street anyway. He slowed down as he approached Denise's front door. Jack motioned him inside and he went on in. Jack's grin disappeared as soon as he closed the door behind Keats. Keats looked for Denise. She was there alright. She was sprawled on the kitchen floor at the end of the island. He looked back at Jack.

"What the hell did you do to her?" he asked.

"I subdued her," said Jack.

"Bullshit," said Keats. "You knocked her ass out."

Jack said, "Strip her and then put one of these t-shirts on her." Keats looked at the man like he was crazy.

"Do it," said Jack. "She's one of them. She'll be harder to strip if she comes around before you get that done." Keats stood there and just stared at him. He thought, *"You are one crazy son-of-a-bitch."* Then he said it, word-for-word.

Jack said, "You didn't suspect a thing. This bitch works for Petchenko. She used to work for Russia's external intelligence agency for civilian affairs, the SVR. That's how she met Petchenko, in Moscow while he was still an active GVR Field Agent. His expertise was military affairs."

Jack could see the skepticism on Keats face. He added, "You didn't know any of that shit, but now you do. I speak the truth and you better listen to me."

Keats could see something in man's eyes now that he hadn't seen there before, something cold and calculating.

"When you get her bra off, lift her left breast," said Jack. "You'll see a tiny scar there. They always implant a tracking device just beneath the skin right there. That's what they do to all the females. Check it out."

Keats did. Jack was right. The scar was there. He got busy following his orders while Jack went through every drawer in her kitchen. He was selecting all kinds of utensils. For what reason, God only knows. Jack finished what he was doing before Keats did.

When he saw Keats was done with Denise he said, "Drag her over here to the island, stand her up, and bend her over. I want her face down over the sink."

Keats did everything exactly the way he was told to do it. Jack gathered up all the utensils he'd selected and carried them to the island. He laid them on the granite surface next to the sink. Then he pulled Denise's arms across the sink and used two electrical ties to bind her arms together at the elbow. He used two more ties to anchor her elbows to something inside the garbage disposal. Keats was amazed. He was so damn methodical about everything he did. Keats could see this man was no neophyte.

When Jack was done with that he said, "Get some paper towels and stuff them into her mouth." Keats did as he'd been told.

Jack said, "Stand behind me where she can't see you." Keats moved around behind him.

Jack pressed his groin against Denise's bare butt. He slapped her on the butt, on the right cheek, one time, real hard. He did it a second time. She stirred a little. He switched hands and slapped her a third time on the left cheek. Then he did it again. She squirmed and whimpered a little. He bent over and whispered something into her right ear. Then he stood up and laid a butcher knife on her back, he put it right between her shoulder blades. He picked up a second knife and tapped the blade on the granite surface next to her head, right in front of her eyes. She stopped squirming and stared at the blade. Jack slowly removed the paper towels from her mouth and let them drop into the sink.

He said, "That feels better, doesn't it?" Denise nodded her head 'yes'. He said something else to her, but this time he spoke Russian. She answered him in Russian. A conversation ensued, every word of it, in Russian. That went on for maybe ten minutes. Of course Keats didn't understand a single thing they said to one another.

Finally Jack turned to Keats and said, "Come around here Keats and stand where she can see you." Keats did that.

Jack spoke to her again, this time he used English. He said, "You tell David everything you just told me. And you better not leave one damn thing out." She threw a quick glance in Keats direction.

She looked down into the sink again. "That's not David," she said. The new look Angie had given Keats had done the trick. Denise didn't recognize him.

"Look again," said Jack. She looked at Keats again.

Keats said, "Hello Denise." She could tell from the sound of his voice it was actually him. They could both see the recognition in her face.

Denise looked back into the sink. Keats could only see her profile, but he could sense the hardness in her demeanor. She didn't intend to tell him one damn thing. But then Jack began tearing strips of material from the bottom of the t-shirt she was wearing. He tied several large knots in the material. Then he showed her his handiwork. He picked up another knife and tapped it on the granite surface. Then he laid it on her backside, right where her two butt cheeks converged. She immediately started talking. Keats found some of the things she told him hard to believe.

She looked back at Jack when she was all done. She obviously wanted his approval.

He said, "You left out part of it, but that's good enough."

# CHAPTER SIXTY-THREE

Jack produced a handgun and laid it on the granite surface next to Denise's head. He'd had the weapon concealed on him the whole time. Keats didn't know that. Denise took a quick look at the gun lying beside her head then looked back into the bottom of the sink. She didn't bother to look in Keats direction at all. He'd stopped looking at her too. He was staring at the weapon lying on the granite countertop. It had a silencer installed on it. He recognized the gun. He'd used a newer version of it himself. His had been a Sig Sauer P226-9-NAVY. This one was also a 9mm, but a much older version. It'd been manufactured by Smith & Wesson during the Vietnam era. Navy Seal Teams had used the weapon in Southeast Asia to silence any enemy watchdog that might potentially compromise an operation. The Seals had nicknamed the weapon the *Hush Puppy*. The sound the gun produced when fired was practically nil.

Jack looked at Keats and said, "You go recover the photograph from your place then bring it back here and show it to me. When we're both satisfied, I'll do what I promised Denise I'd do." Keats figured he already knew what that was, but he asked Jack anyway. Jack was more than happy to enlighten him.

He said, "I told the woman if she'd cooperate, I'd kill her quickly. I promised her there'd be no pain. She left that part out when she'd told you what she'd said to me in Russian. But that's Ok. I'm a man of my word."

That was perfectly clear to Keats. He nodded, turned and left to go next door immediately. He was back in less than five minutes. Jack was still standing right where he'd been when Keats had left him. Jack had his arms folded and looked like he was in a quasi-meditative state. Denise was also waiting calmly.

As Keats walked through the door he said, "My place has been ransacked." Jack looked him in the eyes and smiled a knowing smile. Denise was staring at Keats too.

The look on her face was also quite telling. What Keats just said to Jack was definitely news to her.

She looked down into the sink again. She said, "Now I'm really fucked." She said that very succinctly.

Keats motioned for Jack to come closer to him so Denise couldn't hear what he had to say. He walked to where Keats was standing.

"They didn't find the photograph," said Keats. "I have it. I locked it in the SUV."

Then Jack did something Keats never dreamed he'd do. He walked back to the island and picked up the knife resting between Denise's shoulder blades and laid it on the countertop. He used the other knife to cut all of her bindings. Denise slumped onto the floor. Jack laid the knife down, picked up the *Hush Puppy* and put it back into his waistband where he'd taken it from.

"You can help her up now," he said. "She didn't know the photograph was missing. Petchenko double crossed her, David. I'm prepared to make her an offer only an idiot would turn down." Denise was staring exclusively at Jack. Keats could see the lie he'd told was taking effect.

"They've implanted a tracking device under my left breast. You need to remove it before we go anywhere. You can use one of those things." Denise was referring to the knives Jack had piled on the granite countertop.

She looked at Keats and said, "David, are you going to help me up or not?" Keats nodded and helped her get on her feet.

Jack asked Denise a question. "Do you have any hard liquor in the house?"

She nodded her head 'yes', walked over to a cabinet and removed a bottle of vodka. It was a two liter bottle of Russian vodka, the brand was *Absolut*. She carried the bottle of vodka to the island and set it down.

Jack said, "You have excellent taste. Do you have any zakuskis?"

Keats wondered what the hell that was. Denise knew. She told him she didn't have any zakuskis, but she did have some lemons.

"They'll do," said Jack. "Get the lemons and four glasses and bring everything over here."

Keats only understood bits and pieces of what was going on between these two. But Denise obviously understood everything Jack was talking about. Keats wondered who the fourth glass was for. Denise had a questioning look on her face.

Jack knew what she wanted to know. He said, "Make them all doubles, Denise."

"You want all four to be doubles?" she asked.

Jack said, "No. Go easy on number four."

"That's what I thought," said Denise. That part was also totally *Greek* to Keats. What the hell was going on between these two? Denise poured the vodka.

Jack looked at Keats. He said, "David, I'm going to ask you to lift Denise's left breast while I remove the tracking devise." Keats nodded 'ok'.

Then Jack looked at her and said, "Get rid of the t-shirt, Denise. And I think you might need to sit on your hands." She agreed with him and so did Keats.

Jack looked around the room. He said, "David, drag that bar stool over there, over here."

Denise shed the t-shirt she was wearing and spread it out on the seat of the bar stool. She didn't have a damn thing on, but her nudity didn't seem to bother her at all.

Jack handed Keats and Denise each a vodka-filled glass. They all three emptied their glasses. Jack and Denise emptied theirs in a single gulp. Keats drank his a lot slower. Jack sliced the lemons while Keats finished his vodka. Then he handed both of them lemon wedges, two each. Keats watched Denise bite into both of hers. She squeezed them into her mouth, sucked and swallowed the juice. It looked rather ritualistic to him. He followed her lead and stuck a wedge in his mouth. She watched him do it. She gave him an approving nod. She explained that the lemon was an acceptable substitute for zakuskis. She explained that zakuskis was a type of Russian appetizer. She told him the consumption of the appetizer during a drinking bout was an age-old Russian tradition. It was intended to neutralize the alcohol after each shot.

Keats looked at these two characters. They fascinated him. They were both so calm. She was just standing there, buck naked, instructing him in the proper technique for consuming vodka, and Jack? He was all about his business, selecting a suitable cutting blade. He finally interrupted the drinking instruction.

He said, "That's enough, Denise. Come over here and sit on your hands." She did exactly what Jack told her to.

He said, "David, you get behind her, stand a little to the right of her midline, and give me your left hand. Denise, you put your head back and rest it against David's left cheek." They both followed Jack's instructions to the letter.

Keats reached around Denise. Jack took his hand and placed it under her left breast. Then he repositioned everything; Keats hand, her breast, his make-shift surgical instruments, the fourth glass of vodka, and the leftover lemon wedges. He put everything right where he needed them to be during surgery.

Then he said, "Take a deep breath, Denise." She did, and so did Keats.

Jack used his left index finger to thump the surface of her skin right over the scar under her breast. He thumped her skin three or four times really hard. Denise closed her eyes. She squeezed them tight while he did cut her. The entire procedure was over in less than three seconds.

"All done," said Jack. Denise's eyes popped open.

She moved Keats hand out of the way, lifted her breast and took a look at the surface of her skin. Keats snaked his head around Denise and looked too. Where there'd been a scar, there was a small incision and just a trickle of blood. They both looked back at Jack. He had a big smile on his face and he was holding the tiny tracking device between two of his fingers. He laid it gently on a piece of paper towel. He offered Denise another piece of paper towel.

He said, "You might want to clean the incision with this then dab a little vodka on it. Put a piece of gauze and some tape over the incision. I'll help you pick out some clothes."

Denise took the paper towel, did what he'd suggested then grabbed her clothes and hurried out of the room. Jack followed her out. Keats sat there, looking around the kitchen. His eyes finally settled on the bottle of vodka. He grabbed the bottle and a glass and poured himself another double. Then he sat down on the bar stool and began mulling things over. He sipped the vodka while he did it.

Finally he looked into the bottom of the empty glass. He thought, *"Vodka is nasty tasting shit."* He picked up a lemon wedge and bit into it. He did that twice. The lemon juice made no damn difference at all.

# CHAPTER SIXTY-FOUR

In about ten minutes Jack and Denise walked into the kitchen. Denise was wearing street clothes. Everything she had on was dark, neat and clean. Jack was trailing a couple of steps behind her. He still looked a bit rumpled up. But he had washed his hands.

Keats was thinking, *"You are one unpredictable son-of-a bitch."* He opened his mouth to say that, but Jack preempted him.

"Petchenko double crossed Denise," said Hobbs. "She's switching sides. If some of the things she just told me can be verified, she is about to become one hell of an asset."

Keats looked at Denise. The woman looked livid. He sure hoped the son-of-a-bitch knew what he was talking about.

Jack immediately started rifling through Denise's kitchen cabinets again. He came up with something to write on. He found a pencil. He laid everything on the granite countertop. When he'd returned to the kitchen he'd been carrying a box containing two handguns, several tasers, and some other stuff. He'd set the box on the countertop next to the bottle of vodka. He started looking at the stuff in the box. He stopped doing that and started staring at Denise.

Jack must have made her nervous, because she grabbed an empty glass and poured another double shot of vodka. She started looking for some unused lemon wedges. There weren't any left. She looked at David and smiled. She gathered a handful of used wedges and squeezed the residual juice out of them into an empty glass. Then she downed the vodka and chased it with the lemon juice.

Jack had laid his cell phone on the granite countertop. He picked it up and placed a call. Someone on the other end picked up immediately. He started talking to the other party.

"I'm switching this phone to speaker mode, sir." he said. "Am I correct in assuming you're not alone?" The voice on the other end belonged to Buchanan.

"That's correct," said Buchanan. "I'm in the company of one other person. Who is this?" Buchanan said it like he didn't know it was Jack, but he knew. What he didn't know was who else was listening to the conversation.

"This is Jack Hobbs. Do you remember me?" Keats thought, *"These two guys are unbelievable."*

"Hello Jack," said Buchanan. "My brother is with me. You remember him, don't you?" Jack told him he did.

"My brother is here for the annual family reunion," said Buchanan. "The rest of the family is waiting for us to arrive."

Keats was following all the double speak with no problem at all. It sounded like Buchanan and the older Hobbs were still on their way to the Marina. And it sounded like Buchanan had a team already there and in place. He and Jack went on with the ruse.

Jack said, "I have a close friend who is having some difficulties. His name is David Keats. He's a tenured Professor of Psychology at UTMB Galveston. Perhaps you've heard of him?"

"Can't say that I have," said Buchanan. Jack went on with the ruse.

"David Keats has a friend, a Dr. Elizabeth Davenport," he said. "She seems to be the focal point of David's difficulties. She's a Plastic Surgeon in the Kemah area. Maybe you've met her?"

"Can't say I've ever had the pleasure," said Buchanan. "But that doesn't matter, Jack. Any friend of yours is a friend of mine. Go on."

"David Keats is here with me now, sir. He's listening. There's also a woman who's first name is Denise. She's Keats neighbor and she's listening too." It was easy to see Denise was falling for their routine. Her face reflected her naivety. Jack continued.

"Denise has a serious problem, sir. I believe her life may be hanging in the balance. I'm most concerned about my friend, David. But I'm thinking helping her may help my friend. I've explained that you have influence with the right people, that you might be able to do something for her. If I'm correct in saying that, she's agreed to be totally open and candid with you."

"I'm listening," said Buchanan. "What's her problem?"

Jack and Keats were both staring at Denise. She was biting her lower lip. She looked rather teary eyed.

Jack said, "Give us a moment, Sir." Jack walked around the bar, stopped and stood in front of Denise. He took both her hands in his, looked into her eyes and said, "I believe this man will put you in touch with individuals who can provide you with proper sanctuary. He has connections. Without his help, you're dead or even worse. We both know that. You tell this man who you are and who you work for. You tell him what this is all about. You tell him what you're willing to do if he'll put you in touch with the right people."

Denise said, "Alright, David. I will." She took a deep breath and started talking.

"At one time I was an Intelligence Agent for the Russian Federation," she said. "I made a big mistake. I shared classified Intelligence with an outside entity, a private contractor. I left Russia before I was found out. I've never returned. I went to work for the contractor. His last name is Petchenko. He was a KGB Field Officer at one time. I've been unsuccessful in finding some photographs he instructed me to obtain. I'm convinced Petchenko already knows I've failed to obtain the photographs. He'll come for me and if he manages to find me, he'll kill me. If you can put me in touch with the right people and they'll hide me from this man, I'm willing to become an *Agent-in-Place* or an *Agent of Influence* or whatever. I have nothing to lose, sir. Without your help, I'm as good as dead."

Buchanan reiterated everything Denise had just said. Then he asked, "Are you sure you want to do this?"

"I'll do it," said Denise. "Without your help, I'm a dead woman."

Buchanan said, "I can put you in touch with someone from the American Intelligence Community, someone willing to guarantee you immunity and sanctuary in exchange for what you know and are willing to do. That's what you want me to do?"

Denise said, "That's exactly what I'm asking, sir."

Buchanan said, "The Russians will burn you alive too if they ever get their hands on you. You are aware of that?"

"I am," said Denise. "And Petchenko will kill me if they don't."

"Tell me your name. Your actual name," said Buchanan. "And tell me what your standing is in Petchenko's Chain-of-Command. Then I want everybody's name, from top-to-bottom. I'll have to share the information with the right person before anyone will be willing to give you sanctuary."

Denise told Buchanan everything he'd asked for and more. Buchanan peppered her with a multitude of other questions. She gave him an answer for everything he asked. He finally told her he'd heard enough.

"Jack?" said Buchanan.

"Yes Sir," answered Jack.

"Do you have a way to stage this woman's suicide?" asked Buchanan. "Something others will believe?" Jack was eyeing the box containing the handguns and tasers and stuff.

"I think so," said Jack. He hadn't gotten that out of his mouth good and he tacked on, "Yes sir. I certainly do."

Watching Jack come up with a plan was like observing a nuclear chain reaction. He immediately cut to the chase and explained in detail what he had planned for Denise's feigned suicide. Buchanan listened to every word Jack said.

"Good," said Buchanan. "You need to do that as soon as you can. Make a big-to-do about it with the neighbors. Make them believe she isn't going to make it. Better yet, make them believe she's actually dead. Tell the neighbors that her friends or relatives may show up before long. Tell them it's important that they share what they witness with whoever shows. Think you can make that happen, Jack?"

"Can do," said Jack. "Then what do I do, Sir?"

"The reunion is where we usually have it," said Buchanan. "Bring her there." Then he asked Denise a question. "This may not be painless, young lady. Can you handle that?"

"I have to," she said. "I have no other option." She added a 'thank you' as an afterthought.

Jack was staring at Keats. He was waiting to see if Keats had any questions or wanted to add anything. Keats didn't have a thing to ask or add.

"I guess that's it," said Jack. "Thank you, sir."

"See you soon," said Buchanan. Then he terminated the call.

# CHAPTER SIXTY-FIVE

"Keats, see who's at home in the cul-de-sac," said Jack. "But don't disturb any of your neighbors yet, just take a look outside."

Then he said, "Finish the bottle of vodka, Denise. Drink every last drop of it." She reached for a glass. He put his hand over hers and said, "No no, you drink straight from the bottle. Finish all of it right now." He looked at Keats and said,

"Do what I asked you to do, David."

Keats turned around, walked to the door, stepped outside, took a quick look around the cul-de-sac then looked the other way, down the street. There were several neighbors at home down the street, but only one in the cul-de-sac. He stepped back inside. Denise had the vodka bottle upended. Jack looked at Keats and Keats gave him a thumbs-up. They both waited and watched Denise finish the vodka. Jack looked back at Keats as soon as she set the bottle down.

"Are any of your neighbors Physicians or Pharmacists?" he asked.

"Not on this street," said Keats.

"Good," he said. "Then I'm a Physician."

"You are?" asked Keats.

"No, I'm not. But that's what you're going to tell your neighbors. Now go into the bathroom and get every bottle of prescription medication you can lay your hands on and bring them all in here."

Keats did that. Jack selected a few of the pills and scattered them on the floor. He dropped two or three empty bottles on the floor, crushed one or two with his foot. He put the rest of the bottles containing the balance of the pills into a quart size Ziploc storage bag. He had Keats wrap the storage bag in a dish towel and stomp on it until the bottles were all thoroughly crushed. Then he told Keats to go behind the house and throw it all in the canal. Keats did everything he was told.

When he got back to the kitchen Jack was telling Denise what he was about to do to her. She was well on her way to getting sloppy drunk and seemed to be ok with everything he said. There was a single writing tablet still lying on the granite countertop. Jack told her to scrawl, *I'm a wretched failure,* on the top line of the first sheet of paper then break the pencil into three or four pieces. He had her hold the pieces a foot above the countertop and let them drop. The *Absolute* was really starting to take effect. He told Keats to help him get her on her feet and keep her standing. Keats helped him do it. Then Jack sprinkled a few drops of water on the piece of paper. He told Denise to smear it around, make a real mess of it. He explained he wanted it to look like there were tears on the paper.

"Are you ready?" asked Jack. Denise smiled nervously and shook her head 'yes'.

Jack crossed his wrists in front of her throat and gathered her blouse in his fists. He tightened the collar of the garment around her throat and squeezed off the blood supply to her brain. Within ten or fifteen seconds Denise lost consciousness. He lowered her gently to the floor.

He looked at Keats and said, "Let's mess this place up a little. Knock a few things off the lamp tables, a crooked lamp shade or two is a good touch, and randomly scatter the chairs around the room. Wash all but one of those glasses. Leave three in the sink and break one. Leave the broken glass in the sink. Take two or three cold things out of the refrigerator and set them on the countertop under the cabinets. Leave all the knives out, but put the other utensils back in the drawers they came out of."

Jack removed several pills from a plastic container he had in his pocket and put them in the glass still sitting next to the empty vodka bottle. He shook the last few drops of vodka from the bottom of the bottle into the glass and saturated the pills with the liquor. The pills immediately began to disintegrate. Keats had a puzzled look on his face and he was told they were 'bad-ass narcotics'.

He slid the box in Keats direction and said, "Slip outside and hide the stuff in this box somewhere inside the SUV. Make sure nobody is watching before you go out into the street. When you're done, lock the vehicle and come back here." Keats headed for the door with the box.

# CHAPTER SIXTY-SIX

As Keats walked back through the door he could see Denise was lying on the floor having what looked like a myoclonic seizure. The shock-like muscle contractions were affecting her entire body; her arms, her legs, her facial muscles, every muscle in the woman's body. Thank God she was unconscious. He stood there next to Jack, quietly watching and waiting until she settled down. Then Jack explained what they were going to do next.

He told Keats what he was supposed to do twice. Keats must have had a skeptical look on his face, because he said, "Are you sure you can do your part? We can't afford any mishaps." Keats told him not to worry about him, just make sure he could handle his end of the deal. That made Jack grin.

Jack said, "Pick a neighbor and make it happen." Keats turned around and walked out the front door.

Two women lived across the street. They were the only ones in the cul-de-sac with their lights on. They'd have to do. He thought about the two women. One of them was a notorious busybody. She wrote editorials for a gossip column. The other woman referred to herself as a real estate mogul. Keats thought she probably was. They lived in about a five thousand square foot Bay House.

Keats approached the front of the house, walked up the stairs and stood on the stoop. He pounded on their front door. Both women are rather large so it's understandable that it would take a little while for one of them to get to the door. Keats waited patiently. The *journalist*, her name's Margaret, was the one who finally showed up at the door and opened it. She still had on her street clothes.

"David? Is something wrong?"

Keats said, "You need to come with me, Margaret. It's Denise. Something terrible has happened to her."

Margaret turned her head to the side and yelled, "Lucille, come here, quick. It's David. Something's happened to Denise."

Lucille was there in half the time it took Margaret to get there. Keats immediately turned around and hurried down the stairs and into the street. The two women were right behind him, they matched him step-for-step. In no more than ten seconds, they were all three standing in Denise's kitchen.

"I think Denise tried to kill herself," said Keats. "She's obviously swallowed a lot of prescription medication and she may have consumed that entire bottle of vodka on top of the pills she swallowed. Luckily my friend, Jack, is a physician. We noticed Denise's front door was ajar when we drove up and I thought I'd better check on her. This is the way we found her." Keats noticed Margaret was reading Denise's *suicide note.*

"Poor thing," said Margaret. "I knew she had serious problems. I tried to get her to talk about it, but she was such a private person. I couldn't get a damn thing out of her. What a tragedy."

"Be still Margaret," said Lucille. "What are her chances, Doctor?"

"Slim to none," said Jack. "She's had two seizures since I got here. Her heart started fibrillating, but I did manage to stop that and get her heart beating at a constant rate again. We don't have time to wait for an ambulance. David and I are going to leave with her right now and try to get her to a private medical emergency center. There's one not too far from here. Earlier in the day she'd told David she was expecting guests later tonight."

Jack placed his fingers against the side of Denise's throat and checked her carotid. He was very convincing, displayed all the earmarks of a real physician.

He looked up at Lucille and said, "She may not make it, ladies. Will you please watch for her guests to arrive and tell them exactly what happened here?"

Margaret was wringing her hands and saying, "Why do these kinds of terrible things have happen?"

"Shut up, Margaret," said Lucille. She added, "We'll handle things here, Doctor."

The two men scooped Denise up and rushed out the door with her. They had her in the backseat of the SUV within ten or twelve seconds and Jack was all over the woman. He was checking her carotid again and pounding on her chest. Keats slid behind the steering wheel. Lucille shut all the doors.

Jack said, "I'm afraid we're going to lose her." He started pounding on her chest again. He sat back on his heels and said, "Damn it, she's gone. Drive, David."

Keats could hear Margaret saying, "Why, my God? Why?"

He heard Lucille say, "Shut up, Margaret," as the last door slammed shut.

Jack said, "Get the hell out of here, David." Keats could hear Jack slapping Denise in the face as he drove off.

Keats hadn't driven more than fifty feet when he heard Jack say, "That's my girl. You're going be just fine." Keats heard Denise mumble something. It was unintelligible, but that really didn't matter. At least she wasn't dead.

"There's another tracking device," said Denise. That gave Keats pause. He looked back at Hobbs.

Hobbs said, "Don't worry about it. We'll take care of it in a few minutes."

# CHAPTER SIXTY-SEVEN

Jack said, "When we get to Legends pull between the boat slips and the main building. Park in the shadows then sit tight and wait. Somebody will come out of the building and whoever it is will help me get Denise out of the SUV. We'll take her inside the building. Once we have her inside you head on over to South Shore Harbor."

"I'll be driving there alone?" asked Keats.

"That's right," said Jack. "You do know what to do when you get there?"

"Sure," said Keats.

Denise mumbled something else.

"What is it, Denise?" said Jack.

She said, "I'm sorry, David."

"Be quiet," said Jack. "We know."

When they reached Legends, Keats parked in the shadows. They both detected movement in the shadows. Hobbs had a pistol in his hand. They watched two men from the building approach the SUV. Jack opened the rear door of the SUV on his side and got out. He and the other two men huddled in the shadows for just a moment. Then one of the men helped Jack get Denise out of the back seat. Keats was only able to catch a glimpse of the other man before they carried Denise away.

Jack stuck his head back inside the vehicle and said, "Better be on your way." Then he slammed the door shut.

Keats watched Jack disappear into the shadows. He assumed they'd all gone inside the building.

Keats started the engine, backed up, shifted into drive, and drove off. Three or four minutes later he was back on the Gulf Freeway, headed north toward Kemah. His head was spinning, his mind cluttered with one erroneous thought after another. He looked at the clock on the dash and 11:11 pm glared back at him. The colon between the elevens was pulsating and the effect was almost hypnotic. He needed to clear his head, stop thinking and give his mind a little time to rest. He settled on a suitable mental mantra. He used the rhythm of the pulsating pairs of numbers as a mantra and silently repeated the numbers; *eleven, eleven; eleven, eleven; eleven, twelve; eleven, twelve* and so-on. And it worked wonders. By the time he reached the League City exit he'd calmed down and thoroughly cleared his head.

He took the proper exit, stayed to the right on the feeder road, slowed to a crawl at the first intersection, veered right onto Hwy 518, and headed for South Shore Harbor Resort. He drove through an older part of League City first then on toward Kemah. In about eight or nine minutes he reached the Resort at South Shore Harbor.

# CHAPTER SIXTY-EIGHT

Keats decided he'd try to get a look at the 'Catch-of-the Day' before he checked in and took the ramp that led down to the Boat Basin. He drove from one end of the Marina to the other and on the second pass he spotted it. He pulled into the nearest parking space and killed the engine. The 'Catch-of-the Day' was one hell of a motor yacht. Definitely a live-aboard boat. Outfitted to go the distance. He looked at all the other boats moored in the Marina. South Shore Harbor was definitely high-roller country.

His curiosity satisfied, he hit the ignition, backed up and headed for the parking garage. He found the garage packed to capacity. Parking availability topside wasn't much different so he drove to the end of the block, parked in front of a Randall's Grocery Market and returned to the hotel on foot. He stopped at the front desk and showed the woman on duty his picture ID. She gave him a key card, with no questions asked, and directed him to an elevator that would take him to the top floor.

There were only four suites on the fourth floor and the one they'd be using was on the southeast side, overlooking the Boat Basin and Marina. He stood at the door to the suite and listened. Total silence. He inserted the key card into the indicated slot and when a green light came on, went in. The entire suite was the epitome of luxury. He walked through all three bed rooms, checked the bathrooms then returned to the sitting room. He walked to the far end of the room, stopped at the glass doors to the balcony and that's where he found Angie, sitting cross-legged on a chase lounge. She was still wearing the same clothes she'd had on earlier. He opened the sliding glass door, stepped out onto the balcony, closed the door behind him and walked to the railing. Nearly every boat in the Marina could be seen from where he was standing. He lingered there for a moment or two looking at the boats. Then he turned and looked at Angie. She looked like she was meditating. There was a chase lounge adjacent to hers so he took a seat and waited.

Finally she spoke. She said, "How long has Denise been your neighbor?"

"Who told you about Denise?" asked Keats.

She said, "Buchanan. He said she's a member of a Russian hit squad. Where is she now?"

"I left her on Tiki Island. She's with a man named Jack Hobbs. He took her inside a building that's owned by an outfit called Legends Saltwater Charters. Did Buchanan tell you about the tracking device?"

Angie said, "Yes."

"She told us there was another tracking device," said Keats. "She was extremely inebriated at the time so I don't know if that's true or not." Then Keats changed the subject. Told her he'd like to take a shower and get some sleep.

She said, "Buchanan told me we won't be leaving the suite tonight so you have time to take a shower. But don't go to sleep. There'll be a briefing as soon as the others get here. I've been told there are clothes for you and I in the master bedroom, that's the bedroom on the far left as you enter the suite."

"Good," said Keats. Then he stood and went inside.

# CHAPTER SIXTY-NINE

There were actually two closets in the bedroom, one had clothes in it for a woman, the other contained clothes for a man. Keats looked around the bedroom. The shower and Jacuzzi were practically an integral part of the room, all glass, absolutely no provision for privacy. Only the commode and bidet were in a separate enclosure.

He walked back to the bedroom door, closed it then stripped down to nothing. He left his clothes lying in a heap on the floor, walked to the shower, opened the glass door and stepped inside. He studied the various gadgets on the wall. The standard knobs and levers one usually finds in a hotel suite were not there. Everything operated by simply touching an illuminated keypad. He studied the symbols representing the various functions. They were simple enough to understand and touched the symbol that appeared to control the showerheads. Water came at him instantly from three different directions. The temperature was preset, almost perfect. So all he did was select a pulsating spray that suited him.

He found a bottle of body wash that had been placed in an indention in the wall. He removed it and read the label. It was supposed to be a body wash for men. It smelled nice so he squeezed a generous portion of the gel-like substance into palm of his hand, bent over and set the bottle on the floor. He rubbed his hands together then spread the gel all over himself. He over indulged. It felt really good. After he'd totally saturated himself with gel, he stepped under the pulsating stream of water, rinsed thoroughly then stood there, letting the water hammer him. He did that for quite a while. He'd probably have pulled his head out from under the water and turned around a lot sooner if he'd known he wasn't alone in the bedroom.

# CHAPTER SEVENTY

When Keats finally opened his eyes he noticed a faint shadow on the wall in front of him. The shadow hadn't been there before. He turned abruptly and found Angie standing there, watching him through the glass door. She'd taken off all her clothes and wrapped herself in a towel.

She asked, "Will you be much longer?"

Keats was at a loss for words.

She said, "I can use one of the other bathrooms."

Keats told her that wouldn't be necessary. Told her he was done. Told her it was her turn.

What she did next definitely took him by surprise. She opened the shower door, looked down at the bottle of body wash he'd placed on the floor, bent over, picked it up, and read the printing on the front side of the bottle. Then she reached over, lifted one of his hands and smelled of his skin.

"Smells nice," she said. Then she let go of his hand. She inverted the bottle, squeezed a little of the gel onto her fingers, and rubbed her fingertips together.

Keats said, "I'm sure there's something for women in one of the other bathrooms. I don't mind taking a look."

"Don't bother," she said. "I'll use this. The texture is a little heavy, but its fine."

Then she began reading the label on flip side of the bottle. When she was done reading, she set the bottle back on the floor. Keats realized the water was still pounding on his back. He turned and shut it off then grabbed the towel that was hanging on the wall and wrapped it around his waist. At that point Angie entered the stall, stopped and stood there. He stepped to one side. She slipped by him, turned and nodded. He assumed she wanted him to get out. He stepped outside the stall, turned around and stood where she'd been standing.

She removed her towel and hung it on the wall then turned toward him and closed the glass door. She gathered up about half her hair and pulled it around in front, looked at the keypad, made her selections then moved directly under the showerhead. Rivulets of water began coursing through her hair and cascading down her back.

She asked, "Are you still there, David?"

He said, "Yes."

She place both of her hands on the wall in front of her, look up, leaned farther in and allowed the pulsating stream of water to strike her full force in the face. The water cascading down her back converged into a single stream and Keats followed the flow all the way to the floor.

She turned her head to the side and said, "I made us both a cup of tea. I don't take anything in mine so I didn't put anything in yours."

"That's fine," said Keats.

She turned and faced him again, bent over and picked up the bottle of body wash, up-ended the bottle and let the gel drizzle across her chest from the tip of one shoulder to the tip of the other. The gel began a slow descent between her breasts and down the front of her torso. She squeezed additional gel into the palm of her hand then placed the bottle back on the floor.

She looked past him and said, "Your tea is sitting on the desk."

Then she began rubbing her hands together. She applied some of the gel to her face and neck and spread the rest of it on her body, first over and around her breasts and finally down the front of her abdomen and onto her thighs.

Keats turned his back on her, pulled his towel off, patted himself dry, dropped the towel onto the pile of clothes he'd left lying on the floor then walked to the bureau. He found a pair of boxer shorts in the bureau and put them on. He then selected a pair of casual slacks from the closet and slipped them on. He walked to the desk, picked up his cup of tea and carried it out onto the balcony. He stopped at the railing and stood there, looking across the lake. There was a full moon out now and the water in Clear Lake looked as slick as glass. He set his cup of tea on the ledge in front of him, crossed his arms and leaned against the wall on his left.

# CHAPTER SEVENTY-ONE

Keats had consumed about half his tea when he heard the patio door slide open then close again. Angie joined him at the rail, stopped and stood next to him. He didn't look directly at her, but he could tell she'd wrapped herself in a towel again. He could tell her hair was still wet and that she had the bulk of it hanging between her breasts.

She said, "That wasn't easy, wasn't it?"

He didn't comment.

She said, "You and I are probably going to be used to bait a trap. We are going to have to act like we're married. Think you can do that?"

Again, Keats made no comment. She changed the subject.

"Denise was telling the truth," said Angie. "Buchanan said there's almost always a second tracking device." She hesitated momentarily then added, "But that's no longer an issue."

"Where was the other device?" asked Keats. He was wondering if it had to be surgically removed like the first one.

She didn't give him an answer.

He turned his head to the side and looked directly at her. Started to repeat his question, but then decided against it. He looked back at the boats moored in the Marina.

"Denise should be quite an asset," said Angie.

"Do you think the woman can ever be trusted?" asked Keats.

"Not really," said Angie.

An extended period of silence followed.

Angie was first to speak again. She said, "How do you feel about what's happened between you and Elizabeth?"

"I honestly don't know," said Keats. Then he asked, "Were you and Elizabeth friends?"

She said, "No."

They heard a knock on the bedroom door. Angie turned and walked back into the bedroom. Keats followed her in.

She said, "We'll be out in a few minutes." She'd said that to whoever was standing on the other side of the door. Then to Keats, she said, "Get dressed."

She walked into the bathroom, stopped and stood in front of the wash basin, undid the towel she had wrapped around herself, and let it fall to the floor. Keats stopped and stood by the bed. She saw his reflection in the mirror and told him he needed to get dressed. He continued to stand there, watching her blow dry her hair.

When she finished her hair she walked back into the bedroom, stopped and stood in front of the bureau, selected some undergarments, turned and tossed them onto the bed then walked to the closet and began choosing the other things she intended to wear. She turned to Keats again and told him what he needed to put on.

He went to his closet and did what he was told.

# CHAPTER SEVENTY-TWO

Keats and Angie walked through the sitting room and into an adjacent room. It looked like a typical corporate board room. There was huge table centered in the middle of the room. The chairs were all leather. And one entire wall was glass. All in all the room looked exactly like Keats had imagined it would. Angie settled into the chair next to Keats. Denise was sitting right across from her. Keats took the seat next to Buchanan. Young Hobbs was sitting at the far end of the table. The elderly Hobbs was sitting next to the younger man.

Keats turned to Buchanan, told him what Denise was willing to do.

Buchanan listened, but made no comment.

At that exact moment everyone started looking at the two satellite surveillance monitors mounted the walls. Everyone watched Keats kill Cunningham. Denise appeared to be unaffected.

"You knew that woman, didn't you?" asked Buchanan.

"She called herself Linda Cunningham, but her real name was Tiana Petchenko."

"What's your real name?"

"Rebecca Wainwright. My friends call me Reba."

"Where'd you meet Tiana?"

"Bruges, Belgium."

"What were the two of you doing in Bruges?"

"When I've told you everything you're going to kill me, aren't you?"

"That all depends on whether what you tell us is compatible with what we already know."

It looked like Reba was thinking about that.

Buchanan said, "Refocus, Reba. Tell me what happened in Bruges."

"Tiana and I were members of a terrorist sleeper cell. Bruges is where we went to meet our handler. Should everyone in this room be hearing this?"

"That's not you're concern."

Buchanan slid two photographs across the table. "Do you recognize either of these individuals?"

She pointed at one of the two photographs and said, "That's Alrik Didrikson."

"Where does he fit into the scheme of things?"

"He's a member of a Russian hit squad. He's actually the team leader."

"Are you able to get in touch with Alrik?"

"I have his cell phone number. I can give it to you."

Buchanan slid a note pad and a pen across the table and told her to write his number down. As soon as she was done one of the Bricoleurs retrieved the note pad and left the room with it. Angie got up and went to get coffee for everyone. Buchanan turned to Keats, asked him if he had any questions.

"Just one," said Keats. "Did Linda Cunningham, or Tiana, or whatever her name was have orders to kill me?"

"Yes."

"Why?"

"I don't know."

Buchannan pointed at the other photograph lying on the table and asked, "Is this man your handler?"

Reba nodded *yes*.

"And what's his name?" asked Buchanan.

"Boris Petchenko. He's Tiana's father. Buchanan placed several more photographs on the table in front of Reba.

"Do you recognize any of these men?"

"I do. I've met them all. They're members of a Russian hit squad and they're on their way to New Orleans right now with orders to raid the corporate offices of a private business concern in Federal City. It's a fusion center for gathering and disseminating intelligence and they're going to kill everyone who works there."

"Why?"

"I wasn't told why," said Reba.

# CHAPTER SEVENTY-THREE

Angie returned with the coffee then immediately left the room again. In less than a minute she was back. She had two large Hispanic males dressed in dark suits with her. The taller of the two asked Reba to stand. He cuffed her while the other read her her rights. Buchanan explained that the two men were Federal Marshalls and that they were going to turn Reba over to Homeland Security.

Buchanan looked at the two policemen and said, "Look. If you two don't want to be present when she gets around to telling us what we need to know, you can wait in the hall. But we're going to get to the truth before she leaves here. There are too many lives hanging in the balance."

"That door right there is the only way in and out of here, right?" The taller of the two Marshalls had asked the question.

Buchanan said, "Correct."

"We'll wait in the hall," said the Marshall. "Do you think this is going to take very long?"

"It shouldn't. But you might as well make yourself comfortable. Take a couple of these chairs with you."

Angie got up and walked to the door and opened it. The two men grabbed two chairs and carried them out into the hall. Angie closed the door behind them, bolted it, and returned to her seat.

"Alrik is going to find me and kill me," said Reba. "Or Boris will."

"Boris Petchenko isn't going to kill anybody" said Buchanan. He's dead. I killed the son-of-a-bitch myself, tonight."

"You did what?"

"Angie, get the cuffs off her," said Buchanan. "I killed Petchenko, Reba. He's dead. What were your orders?"

Reba looked shocked. Angie produced a set of tools designed for picking locks and had the cuffs off in a matter of seconds. Reba rubbed her wrists then leaned forward.

She said, "I was supposed to find the photographs Elizabeth left at Keats house, kill Keats then drive to Federal City."

"Where's Federal City?" asked Buchanan.

"Across the Mississippi River from New Orleans," answered Reba.

"When? Tommorrow?"

"I'm supposed to be in New Orleans by 11:00 am the day after tomorrow." She pointed at one of the photographs lying on the table. "I'm supposed to meet this guy there then drive him to Federal City and help him get into the office building. I used to work there and know the gate code. I still have a key card that will get us inside the building. These other four," she pointed at the other four photographs still lying on the table, "they'll be waiting for us."

"And what happens when you get there?" asked Buchanan.

"I don't know."

"That's bullshit," said young Hobbs. "She knows these guys are human traffickers."

"Reba, I can't believe you're involved in this," said Keats.

Reba said, "I grew up on the street on the streets of New Orleans, worked the paddleboats, prostituted myself and made damn good money at it. I got involved with all the wrong people." She thought for a moment then added, "I fucked up, Ok? So get off my ass."

Everyone ignored her rant.

"Who are our adversaries, Reba?" Buchanan was doing the asking.

One of the Bricoleurs responded to Buchanan's question. He said, "Ramon Luis Ibarra is the team leader. He's the *money man*. He's on the CIA's list of the ten most wanted. We've got the rest of the hit squad identified. We managed to do that with reverse facial recognition and redacted data."

The kid was grinning from ear to ear. Buchanan urged him on.

"Alrik has been in touch with the five guys using his cell phone. That's enabled us to track them using satellite surveillance. Hell, we know where they are right now. They're on IH-45 headed north." The Bricoleur reflected for a moment then added, "And they know about Petchenko. They know about Tiana or whatever her name is. What they don't know is that they're being tracked."

"Five guys and Alrik, that's all there is?" asked Buchanan.

"No," said the Bricoleur. "Alrik has others working with him. We don't know how many of them there are."

"This is a problem that needs to be addressed immediately," said Buchanan. "I have a friend somewhere in the Hill Country who's running a human trafficking interdiction program. His business is intercepting traffickers who are bringing in girls from Mexico. This falls in his *bailiwick*." Buchanan turned to Angelique and said, "Bring me the SAT phone."

The rooster-tail of sand and caliche gravel behind the rear wheels of the Jeep Wrangler collapsed as the vehicle ground to a halt on the plateau. Anticipating the inevitable assault of a trailing cloud of dust, both the driver and his passenger shielded their eyes. The older of the two men had been doing the driving. He cast a fleeting glance across the expansive ravine in front of the Wrangler.

He said, "The Mexicans call that thing the Arroyo del Diablo. Be a bitch to drive through, wouldn't it?"

The other man peered into the ravine. He said, "From the looks of those tracks I think our man tried it." The driver of the Jeep agreed with what he'd said.

Both men grasped the Wrangler's roll-bar and dismounted. The driver reached behind his seat and retrieved two plastic bottles of water. He tossed one of the bottles to the other man and they both rinsed and spit.

"We'll cross the arroyo about a quarter mile south of here," said the older man. "That's where things flatten out a bit. Then we'll see if we can pick up his tracks on the other side." He wiped his mouth on the sleeve of his shirt then gestured at the barren area to the north.

He added, "There's a deer proof fence where the clear-cut begins. He'll have to cut it to get through."

Earlier in the day the two men had seen a plume of smoke in the distance. Assuming the individual they were tracking had built a fire during the night they'd spent a couple of hours looking for the origin of the smoke. The jeep was parked a few yards from the source of the smoke. The younger man retrieved a stick from behind the passenger seat and approached the pile of smoldering ashes. A quick stir of the ashes exposed an inferno of glowing coals. He tossed the stick aside. The older man approached, stopped and stood there. The two men waited in silence as the volume of spiraling smoke rapidly increased. The fresh air had fanned the coals. A small piece of partially burned mesquite ignited. Flame replaced the smoke.

The older of the two men squatted down next to the fire and recovered the stick. He removed his hat and began unconsciously tapping on a piece of volcanic rock nestled in the sand. The other man appeared to be oblivious to the sound. His attention was fixated on the horizon to the west where the crest of the distant mountain range had been set ablaze by the setting sun.

The older man looked up. On the far side of the arroyo, maybe a hundred yards to the north, a bird from a swirling column of turkey vultures collided with the ground. The late-comer was joining more than a dozen of his quarreling cousins as they waited for an injured animal to die so they could devour its carcass. The obnoxious looking birds captured the older man's attention. He squinted, attempting to watch the developing spectacle. Deciding he needed to take a closer look, he retrieved a pair of binoculars from the Wrangler. The glasses put him right in the middle of a potential feeding frenzy. The squabbling birds were impatient. They repeatedly approached the object of their desire then retreated. The lopsided limp characteristic of the vultures was a morbid thing to watch. Not quite able to make out what kind of animal was about to become a feast for the birds, he sharpened the focus of the glasses. That's when he saw the boot.

Within less than a minute the fish-tailing Jeep Wrangler plunged into the arroyo. Because it was so late in the afternoon, the blanket of shadows within the ravine made navigating the terrain extremely difficult. As the Wrangler descended toward the bottom, mesquite brush and the low hanging branches of scrubby oak trees viciously thrashed the windshield and body of the careening Jeep. The trip up the far side of the ravine was a lot slower than the descent, but it was equally punishing. Weightlessness followed by a terrific concussion replaced the chaotic assent as the vehicle cleared the lip of the ravine and went airborne. The Wrangler slammed into the flat ground of the plateau then skidded to a halt.

The two men were on the ground and into the brush instantly. They had their guns in hand. They made their way through the meandering chaparral along the rim of the arroyo, and within a few seconds, burst into the clearing. They fired their weapons into the air as they rushed the throng of ravenous vultures. The gunfire startled the birds, evoked panic, and caused a helter-shelter departure.

The two men stood where the birds had been standing. The boot the older man had spotted with the binoculars was on the right foot of the man they'd been tracking.

The man was a gory mess. His clothing had been ripped to shreds, was blood-soaked and matted with pieces of debris and grit. There were puncture wounds and deep lacerations all over his body and his left foot was mangled. He was still alive, but he was totally incoherent. They could both see it wouldn't be long and he'd be dead.

The younger of the two men had been was carrying a SAT phone. He had it in a pouch hanging from his belt. The phone began vibrating. He answered it.

He offered it to the older man and said, "It's for you, Sergeant Major." Then he mouthed, "Buchanan."

The old Marine accepted the SAT phone and said, "Speak to me."

A lengthy conversation ensued. The younger man was only able to hear one side of the conversation. He listened carefully, but bits and pieces was the best he could do.

The last thing the Sergeant Major said was, "We're down in the Valley and I can't give you our exact coordinates until I get back to the Wrangler." He paused momentarily and listened. Then he said, "I'm standing over the body of a dead Mexican. He had a bunch of young girls with him. He was going to sell them as sex slaves. Some of his cohorts are probably holding them in a cave not far from here." The old man paused again and listened. Then he said, "The son-of-a-bitch was alive when we found him, but something had ripped him from one end to the other. It was probably a cougar." He took another quick look at the man lying on the ground. He added, "I think he's dead now." The younger man kneeled down and checked his pulse. The man was definitely dead.

The Sergeant Major continued to talk. He said, "The man's vehicle couldn't be very far from here. I'm guessing it's somewhere down in the ravine we just drove through. The girls he was transporting are probably still in the ravine. The thing is honey-combed with caves."

The Sergeant Major stopped talking at that point. He covered the mouth piece of the SAT phone and told his partner to check the dead guy for anything they might be able to use for identification. The younger man did what he'd been told to do. Then he stood, faced the old man and said, "Nada, Sergeant Major."

The old Marine was holding his Beretta in his right hand. He pointed at his companion and fired a single 9 mm round. It struck the younger man in the center of his forehead. The man dropped like a rock.

The Sergeant Major put the phone to his ear again and spoke into the mouthpiece. He said, "Yesterday my young associate asked me if I knew your real name. I told him what you told me to say in the event that ever happened. I also told him he was going to get to meet you face to face as soon as we were done here. He believed me. I'll burn his body with the other one. Now what's this about New Orleans? Sure, I can be there by 11:00 am in the morning. And I'll bring reinforcements."

# CHAPTER SEVENTY-FOUR

"Sounds like the two Federal Marshalls waiting in the hall are arguing," said Angie.

Within two or three seconds they were watching and listening to the two men argue on one of the overhead monitors.

The taller of the two men said, "Kiss my ass," then turned and headed for the elevator. The other man followed him.

"Our people at ground level need to take them down," said Buchanan. "Don't hurt them, just hold them."

Reba said, "I'm getting a text from Alrik. He's threatening to kill me if I expose him."

"Get busy texting," said Buchanan. "Tell him you were arrested by two Federal Marshalls and then released after questioning. Convince him you have not and will not expose him. Then agree to meet him in New Orleans. Young Hobbs will drive you there. He'll see that you're not harmed."

Reba began composing a text message.

Buchanan turned to Keats and said, "You and Angie need to leave for Key West immediately. You'll be taking the Catch-o-the-Day. There'll be two other women on board. They know how to handle the boat. The other boat, the Stryder, will take the lead."

"But we'll be sailing directly into a tropical storm," said Keats.

Buchanan grinned and said, "I thought you were a Navy Seal."

"I was, but my only tour of duty was in the mountains," said Keats. "Remember… the Hindu Kush?"

Buchanan ignored Keats protest, told him a little about the two women on board the Stryder, told him one was an Asian, the other a Filipino, told him both women were seasoned Marine Pilots. He said all they had to do was keep the Catch in the Stryders wake and it'd be relatively smooth sailing.

Keats asked him what was going to happen when they got to Key West.

Buchanan said a Fishing Charter Service operating out of Key West was being used for human trafficking. The owner of the Charter Service lived in Havana. He told him his assignment was to take the man out to sea and dispose of him. He said he'd have his people burn all the man's boats then liberate anyone they were holding captive. Keats looked perplexed.

Buchanan could see that and said, "Angie will tell you everything you need to know later tonight."

Buchanan turned to Angie and said, "You two have got fifteen minutes to get your shit together. There are some problems down on the Marina. The snipers we have stationed on the roof are gonna take care of that. Now go get ready."

Angie got up and headed for the bedroom. Keats followed her.

# CHAPTER SEVENTY-FIVE

In ten minutes Keats and Angie were back.

"Change of plans," said Buchanan. "You'll be riding to New Orleans with Jack and me, Keats." He nodded in the older Hobbs direction as he said it. Then he turned to Angie and said, "Denise and young Hobbs will be going with you. And you'll be going to New Orleans, not Key West. Key West comes later.

At that exact instant there was an explosion outside.

Buchanan said, "That's your cue, Angie. Time to get underway."

Angie got up and left the room with young Hobbs and Denise. Keats got up and walked to the window. He could see a boat burning on the far end of the Marina. He turned and looked at Buchanan.

Buchanan said, "Propane is mighty dangerous. Says so right on the bottle."

"You made that happen, didn't you? Why?"

"Good way to dispose of the bodies. The two men who claimed they were Federal Marshalls were lying. They intended to kill Denise. They work for Alrik Dedricksen."

"So your people killed them and ...."

Buchanan cut him off. He said, "That's all we have time for. Let's go."

# CHAPTER SEVENTY-SIX

They were crossing the Hartman Bridge before anybody said anything.

Leaning toward Buchanan, Keats asked, "What's his story?" He was referring to Hobbs.

Buchanan smiled, tossed a glance in the rearview mirror and said, "He wants to hear your story, Jack."

"Oh he does?" said the old man.

Keats nodded *yes*. Looked at Hobbs then Buchanan. Buchanan was grinning.

"Are you two playing games with me?"

Buchanan said, "No. But you better settle back. This is gonna take a while."

Keats shrugged. He said, "We have the time, right?"

"We gotta stop once or twice. So let's say five hours. By 11:00 am we should be sitting in the Café' du Monde having biegnets with the Sergeant Major."

Keats threw a glance in Hobbs direction. Now the old man was smiling.

"It's gonna be one hell of a reunion." said Buchanan. "How many years has it been since you seen the Sergeant Major, Hobbs?"

"Forty, maybe fifty years; I heard he shaves his head now."

"That's right," said Buchanan. "Get started with your story. I'd like Keats to hear it all."

The old man grinned, nodded then started talking.

He said, "I flew from Bangkok to Manila the third week in August, 1963. The flight was no different from any of the others I'd taken. Like always, same boring food. Same watered-down drinks. Same idle chit-chat. However I had an Interpreter with me this time and that was a first. The woman was Tai by birth. Spoke French and English fluently as well as a wide variety of Austroasiatic languages. It was absolutely essential that no one know we were traveling together so she had a window seat near the front of the aircraft. I took a seat on the aisle, third row from the back.

Because of a significant headwind that afternoon, we landed a bit late. The Interpreter was the first passenger off the aircraft and first to enter the airport terminal. I trailed across the tarmac some distance behind the woman and was the very last person to enter the terminal. Once inside, I kept to myself. I waited until everyone had cleared customs then approached the Airport Security Desk. I handed the Duty Officer my bundle of travel documents and looked on as he scrutinized my papers. The man read my name aloud.

"Jack Hobbs," said the Duty Officer. "We've met before, haven't we?"

I said, "I don't think so."

"We've met," said the man. "You're a pilot."

I lied again and said, "No, I'm not a pilot. I'm a Flight Engineer."

The man looked down again. Peered intently at my papers. He said, "I see you're with Air America. I'm not familiar with that Company."

I said, "I'm sure you've heard of Civil Air Transport. It's the same company."

The Officer nodded. He said he'd heard of 'CAT'.

He asked, "How long will you be in Manila?"

I said, "Overnight. I'm flying on to Hong Kong first thing in the morning. I've got to meet with one of the Company's Avionics Specialists in Kowloon."

"Where will you be staying tonight?" he asked.

I said, "At the Pearl Garden Hotel. I'm sure you know the place, it's on Adriatico Street."

"Never been there," said the man. "The food in the restaurant any good?"

I told him the food was excellent. I invited him to join me for dinner. Told him he could bring a guest if he wanted to. Said I'd put everything on my expense account. He smiled politely, thanked me, but said he couldn't accept my offer. Then the man feigned disappointment. Said his relief wouldn't arrive at the Terminal until sometime after 10:00 pm. The Duty Officer was lying. The guy knew I was with the CIA. He knew I knew that. He took one last dutiful look at my travel documents, stamped my passport, and let me leave the Terminal.

Early the next morning the Interpreter and I flew from Manila to Hong Kong. Again, we maintained our distance. I checked into the Miramar Hotel in Central Kowloon in the middle of the afternoon and after a shave and a shower and a change of clothes headed down to the cocktail lounge. That's where I was supposed to meet an Agency Courier, the individual I'd referred to as an 'Avionics Specialist' the previous day. The man wasn't there yet so I went to the far end of the bar, grabbed a stool and waited.

At about 5:00 pm I had the waitress transfer my drink and a half-eaten platter of appetizers to a table in the back of the lounge. I sat there for another hour and a half. The Courier never showed so at exactly 6:30 pm I left the hotel and walked to the waterfront. I was vigilant on the way there. The fact that the Courier had failed to make connections had me a little concerned. I decided I'd better make sure I wasn't being followed.

I stood on the dock for a few moments then boarded a water taxi. I crossed Victoria Harbor to the Island of Hong Kong proper and rode the tram to the top of Victoria Peak. I made the return trip down the mountain in a cab and got out in front of the Bank of China in the downtown business district. I walked up and down the back streets until I was satisfied I'd not been followed. Then I returned to the Miramar.

Later that evening I had dinner in the rooftop restaurant at the hotel. The Interpreter was my pretentious dinner guest. She and I did a little role playing. She told me all about herself and I pretended to listen with great fascination. About the time our small talk turned to teasing the waiter approached our table and laid the tab on the table. I scrutinized it. The meal, the drinks, everything had cost nine Hong Kong dollars, roughly equivalent to fourteen dollars American at that time. The tab had been marked paid in full. I handed the waiter an American twenty and told him I didn't need any change. He graciously thanked me and left. I picked up the small envelope he'd placed on the table next to the tab. I examined it, front and back. It would've looked like a thank you note to any casual observer, but both the Interpreter and I knew it wasn't. I broke the seal on the envelope, removed a small slip of paper, unfolded it and read what was written on it.

It read, "You're needed at the house. Come home as soon as you can." The note was unsigned. There was no need for me to look around the restaurant. I knew the note was from the Courier. I also knew he'd come and gone. I passed the note to the Interpreter. She read it. Then she refolded it and handed it back to me. I slipped the note inside the breast pocket of my sport jacket, wadded up the envelope, and stuffed it into one of the empty wine glasses. Then the Interpreter and I got up and left. We went to her room and spent the rest of the night there.

By noon the next day I was airborne again, and this time, headed to 'the house'. For the next two weeks I dressed like a tourist. I spent a couple days here, a couple days there. All of it punctuated by reckless abandon. A week and six days after leaving Hong Kong that came to an end. On day fourteen I flew into the Baltimore-Washington International Airport and took the Amtrak into DC. At exactly 9:30 the next evening I was standing at a gate on the west end of the Whitehouse.

The Corporal of the Guard had not been given the prerogative to deviate from the established protocol and asked me the same question for the third time.

"Why would the Sergeant Major expect me to do that, Sir?"

I repeated my initial response. "Ask the Sergeant Major, Corporal."

The young Marine was hesitant. But I could see his level of concern was definitely on the rise.

"Look," I said. "I've got to speak with the Sergeant Major right now. You can trust me. Just make the call. Please. It's urgent."

I knew there was no way this young man was going to yield to a direct order from me or respond to anything else that smacked of an out-n-out challenge. So I hoped the 'urgency' part of my request plus my pleading demeanor would do the trick. And it did. He started scrutinizing my Photo ID again, studying my face, considering what he was reading there. He looked back at me and asked a different question.

"You're actually a CIA Field Officer?" I shot the young man an affirmative nod.

The Corporal held out his hand and the young Private standing at his side handed him a sound powered phone. Then he made the call. The three of us waited. After the fourth or fifth ring someone answered.

"There's a man at the west gate who claims he's Jack Hobbs," said the Corporal. "The man said you'd know who he is and that you'd expect me to notify you of his arrival before I attempted to verify his credentials." The Corporal abruptly stopped talking and started listening. That's exactly what I knew would happen. After a moment or so the Corporal spoke again.

He said, "That's correct, Sergeant Major. I told him he'd be arrested and detained if he was mistaken. The man told me he had absolutely no problem with that."

The Corporal cast a questioning glance in my direction. I shot him a second affirmative nod. He looked the other way. Another one-sided phone conversation appeared to ensue. After maybe a minute and a half of listening, he offered me the phone. I took it from him, turned to the side, and spoke quietly into the mouthpiece.

I said, "It's me."

"Who all knows you're here, Jack?" asked the Sergeant Major.

I said, "Only these two young Marines."

A period of profound silence followed. Finally the Sergeant Major said, "Let me speak to the Corporal of the Guard again."

I handed the Corporal the phone. The young man put it to his ear, listened for several seconds then terminated the call.

The Sergeant Major arrived at the west gate in less than ten minutes. He took the Corporal of the Guard and the other Marine aside, told them something or other then turned around and spoke directly to me.

"Come with me."

The Corporal of the Guard opened the gate and I walked through it. Then the Sergeant Major and I started across the lawn toward the west end of the Whitehouse. The two young Marines remained on guard at the gate. The Sergeant Major took me around the west end of the Whitehouse and we both entered the rear of the building through a service entrance. Once inside, we passed several other individuals, some were uniformed some were not. Not a single word was exchanged with anyone in passing. As a matter of fact our presence wasn't acknowledged by anyone in any way.

Finally we came to the end of a long hallway and descended a single set of stairs. Then we walked down one long corridor after another. We were still descending, but there were no more stairs. There were only downward sloping ramps and hair-pin turns connecting each of the corridors. We finally ended up standing in front of a door to a room that was located in a very out-of-the-way part of the basement. The Sergeant Major rapped on the door a couple of times and whoever was inside told us to enter. The Marine opened the door and we both went in.

The room was small, probably no more than twelve or thirteen feet square. It had a very low ceiling, was dingy and musty and beginning to deteriorate. The paint on the walls and ceiling was gray and splotchy. Most of the finish had been worn off the wooden flooring. The paint on the door was peeling.

There was a worn out leather love seat against the wall opposite the door and two mismatched chairs upholstered in a hideous looking plaid fabric on either side of the room. A lone naked light bulb was screwed into the overhead. And that was it. My best guess, the room hadn't been used for much of anything in years.

President John F. Kennedy was sitting in one of the two plaid chairs. He invited me to sit in the other one. Then he instructed the Sergeant Major to wait outside in the corridor and see that we were not disturbed. The Sergeant Major snapped to, did an about face, and shut the door behind him when he left. Neither Kennedy nor I said anything for probably a full minute. It was the President who finally broke the silence.

He said, "This past February the French Secret service prevented Colonel Antoine Argoud from assassinating President Charles de Gaulle. Yitzhak Ben-Zvi, President of Israel, died April twenty-third. Everyone was told he'd had a fatal heart attack, but the truth is he was assassinated by his attending physician. Last week the British Prime Minister, Harold Macmillan, announced his retirement. He told the press he had inoperable prostate cancer, but the man was lying. He'd had the tumor removed and it was benign. Macmillan knew that before he had the surgery. He also knew he was about to be assassinated. In my opinion, he'd be dead today if he hadn't retired. His successor, Lord Alec Douglas-Home, told me he won't stay on as Prime Minister for long. He said to remain in office would be tantamount to sentencing himself to death."

I was considering the implications of everything Kennedy had just told me when he asked me a direct question. "When is the Diem coup slated to happen?"

I said, "The assassination of Ngo Dinh Diem will take place the first week in November. It'll happen the second week at the latest. If his Generals don't manage to pull it off this time, I'll kill the son-of-a-bitch myself."

"You may have to do that," said Kennedy. "Diem has got to go or we'll lose the entire Indochinese Peninsula to Communism if he remains in office much longer."

Then Kennedy stopped talking, stopped looking at me. He looked down at the floor and began to ruminate about something. I decided I'd fill the void.

I said, "I agree with you completely, Mr. President. Diem is undermining the effort." It didn't look like the man heard me say it. He appeared to be quite troubled. I kept quiet.

Finally Kennedy looked up and said, "I want to talk to you about something else." He hesitated for a moment then he looked me directly in the eyes. He said, "I have reason to believe the Russians are going to attempt to assassinate me. I feel like it's going to happen soon. I can't be certain because our Intelligence is extremely sketchy. That's because they're getting help from someone on the inside, one of our own people. We don't know who the traitor is, who the assassin might be, where it'll happen, or when. But it will happen."

Then Kennedy paused. He started ruminating again. The look on his face was uncharacteristically strange. I thought about what I'd just heard him say.

I asked, "What would you have me do, Mr. President?"

He looked directly at me and said, "If I'm assassinated, I want you to protect Lyndon. And I want his successor protected. Will you do that for me?"

I said, "You can count on it, Sir. But look. I'm here now. Let me protect you. Let me talk to the people you know you can trust. I'll find the traitor. I'll eliminate the son-of-a-bitch."

"No," said Kennedy. "You have to deal with Diem. That's your first priority."

I said, "I understand. But I'm coming back here when I'm done."

Kennedy said, "I'd rather you didn't. I'd rather you consider doing something else. But understand this, it's strictly voluntary. I am not ordering you to do this."

Kennedy paused, waiting for some kind of reaction from me. I didn't give him one.

He expanded on what he'd just said. "You need to know this up front. Volunteering means you'll have to stage your own death. You won't actually be dead, but you can never go back to your old life. As a matter of fact you'll probably never be able to have a fixed identity again."

At that point Kennedy stopped talking. He was obviously waiting for some kind of feedback from me. I had no problem living under false pretenses, but I'm a very cautious and deliberate man. I needed to hear a lot more. Kennedy understood that and he continued to talk.

He said, "This isn't simply my brainchild, Jack. I've discussed the issue with Charles de Gaulle and the two 'new' foreign Heads of State in Israel and the United Kingdom. What I'm talking about is an ultra top secret counterespionage operation. One that will be collaboratively planned and executed by a multinational special-ops team of your choosing. We believe the effort has terrific merit. If you agree to do what I'm asking, you and your team will have our full support." Kennedy paused again, leveled a penetrating stare at me and added, "You'll answer to no one, Jack. There will be absolutely no rules of engagement. No limits whatsoever." He paused for a moment to study me. He could tell I got the point so he went on.

He said, "We've considered several other individuals for this mission, but you're at the top of the list."

Again, he waited for some kind of feedback from me. This scenario sounded extremely inauspicious. I needed to hear something a little more specific.

Kennedy leaned in, narrowed his gaze and said, "I'm can't proceed without some indication of your interest. I'm not asking for a commitment yet. Just talk to me."

Kennedy waited for my response. I thought about it. The only way I'd find out anything of significance was to yield. So I took the leap.

I said, "I'll do it."

JFK did a double take. He asked, "Jack, are you certain?"

I didn't hesitate. I said, "Absolutely."

Kennedy could tell I meant it. A smile bloomed on the man's face. He immediately launched into a lengthy explanation. He talked about the failed attempt to assassinate President Ngo Dinh Diem in 1960, the Bay of Pigs Invasion in '61, the Cuban Missile Crisis in '62, and the ever increasing spread of Communism throughout world. He used the phrase, 'if worst comes to worst' several times. He repeatedly quoted scripture from the New Testament, most of it from the Book of Revelations. He also made references to the game of chess. As a youth, Kennedy had been a member of an elite Chess Club in Hamburg, Germany. The members of the club played a three-dimensional variant of the traditional game called Raumschach. The Club went out of existence with the outbreak of World War II, but the game itself continued. Kennedy knew I played Raumschach and understood the game strategies. As a result, everything the man said made perfect sense to me.

We talked for hours, discussing the 'nuts and bolts' of the operation. We finally wrapped things up a little after 5:00 in the morning and the Sergeant Major escorted me back to the west gate. He and I parted without uttering a single word to each other.

A subsequent meeting took place a week later outside the Continental United States under totally clandestine circumstances. The attendees included me, John F. Kennedy, Charles de Gaulle of France, Zalman Shazar of Isreal, and Lord Alec Douglas-Home of the United Kingdom. Three foreign Special Ops Officers were also there, one from each of the other three countries. All three individuals had been hand-picked by me, personally. At my request, the Sergeant Major was also there. However he didn't participate in the meeting. The man was already in the know. He simply stationed himself outside the building and made sure we weren't bothered.

The eight of us inside the building formed a secret pact. Each individual swore an oath they'd never divulge a single word of anything that was about to be said by anyone. Then President Kennedy and the three foreign Heads of State laid all their cards on the table. Kennedy had assured me 'The Team' would have more than adequate resources at our disposal to finance the effort. With that in mind, I'd formulated a tentative Game Plan, both immediate and long range. I presented the Plan to the other seven. Everybody had their say and after a few minor modifications the four Heads of State approved The Plan. Then 'The Team' was given a free hand to do whatever it took to get the job done. Our operational parameters were quite simple. There'd be no ground rules. No holds barred. No limitations whatsoever.

The meeting ended half an hour before dawn and the four Heads of State left. The Sergeant Major stayed behind with the rest of 'The Team' and we continued planning.

One week later the President of South Vietnam, Ngo Dinh Diem, was assassinated by his own Generals. They managed to get it done without an assist from me. Three weeks after Diem's death the President of the United States, John Fitzgerald Kennedy, was assassinated by Lee Harvey Oswald while the President rode in a motorcade through downtown Dallas, Texas.

I had boots on the ground within a month, and two months later I was killed somewhere in the jungles of Southeast Asia. There were no witnesses to my final demise and my body was never recovered. I simply disappeared and was reported as Missing-in-Action. Like so many others who went missing during the Indochinese crapshoot that followed, I was ultimately and formally considered KIA. The official record at the Bureau of Naval Personnel today reflects my status as Killed-in-Action/Body-Never-Recovered.

Everything went according to plan. The three foreign Special Ops Officers followed suit and staged their deaths. But not the Sergeant Major. That wasn't part of the plan. He simply resigned his post at the White House and accepted an appointment to the United States Naval Academy. Five years later he became a Navy Fighter Pilot. As for the three surviving foreign Heads of State, they never violated their oaths and divulged a single word of the secret they shared. John Fitzgerald Kennedy, being a man of his word, did what he had to do. He established an inexhaustible and totally untraceable source of funding to support our efforts. He managed to get that done one week before he was assassinated. He also set aside an independent trust for the personal needs of each team member, one that has enabled each of us to live comfortably anywhere in the world for the balance of our lives."

"But what was their mission?" asked Keats.

"They became an invisible shield for top level Allied Leadership. Dozens of assassination plots were uncovered and the perpetrators terminated before they could kill anybody."

"And that's the end of the story?"

"No. In August of 1991 a coup d'etat to eliminate Mikhail Gorbachev as President of the USSR failed. We were there. We made it fail. Gorbachev managed to remain in office and four months later dissolution of the United Soviet Socialist Republic was complete. Communism was diminished in that part of the world and The Cold War ended. That's the end of the story."

"You expect me to believe all that?" asked Keats.

Hobbs said, "Sure do. It's the gospel truth."

Keats said, "Sounds far-fetched to me."

Buchanan interrupted. He said, "You two better gets some sleep."

Keats turned to Buchanan and said, "Before I go to sleep, let me get this straight. You say I'm supposed to kill some Cuban named Ramon Ibarra. Tell me why again."

"Because *those are your orders*. Look, Ibarra's people are selling young girls between the ages of thirteen and twenty as sex slaves, Keats. Somebody's got to eliminate the son-of-a-bitch. Listen to me, the enactment of the *Victims of Trafficking and Violence Protection Act* in 2000 established the Department of State's *Office to Monitor and Combat Trafficking in Persons*. The Office publishes a *Trafficking in Persons Report* annually. In 2008 they reported that in excess of 2 million children were being exploited by the global commercial sex trade. Ain't nobody doing anything to stop it, Keats."

"And that's why Angie and I are headed to Key West after we're done in New Orleans? She and I are going to *eliminate* Ibarra."

Buchanan nodded and said, "You and Angie are going to do it together."

"Then what?" asked Keats.

Buchanan showed Keats another photograph. He said, "The two of you are gonna find and kill this man and anybody that's with him."

He told Keats the man's first name was Alrik. Said he had no idea what his last name was. Keats took a good look at the man. He was looking at a photograph of a rugged-looking young Swede, had all the earmarks of a filthy-rich Scandinavian playboy.

Buchanan said, "Look at this next picture." The second picture was of a woman. He looked back at Buchanan.

"We know her nationality," said Buchanan. "She's Latvian. So far that's all we know about her."

Keats took a good look at the woman. She was a real looker, had jet-black hair and a flawless lily- white complexion.

Hobbs said, "Let *me* see what she looks like," and he reached over the seat. Keats handed Hobbs the cell phone.

"She's definitely got that Latvian look," said Hobbs. Then he handed the phone back to Keats.

Buchanan said, "That brings us to Denise. Denise is an assassin, Keats. She had orders to kill you. But now she's changed sides. She says she's going to help us track down this Latvian woman. Says she met her for the first time about a year ago. They were both traveling under assumed names. Neither knew who the other really was. She said they met in Bruges, Belgium. She told me they shared a suite at the Hotel Prinsenhof on Ontvangerstrat. Said they stayed there for two nights and two days. Then on the third day they met with their Russian handler, a man named Boris Petchenko."

The mention of Petchenko's name evoked the image in Keats' mind of the blood spattered mess on the ceiling in his office. Keats would have given a pretty penny to see the face of the Security Officer he'd spoken to earlier that day when the man saw the mess on the ceiling. Keats thought about Denise. *How would she have reacted to the mess in his office?* He pictured Denise in his mind's eye…standing there, mouth wide open, gasping and trying to catch her breath."

*Denise is a fucking animal,* thought Keats. He pictured her and the Latvian woman alone in the hotel room, walking around with nothing on but their bras and bikini panties. Hobbs interrupted Keats' reverie with a question.

He asked, "How does Alrik fit in here?"

"Alrik is the *hit squad* team leader," said Buchanan. "The CIA had detected a mole inside their organization some time ago, but couldn't figure who it was."

"And that'd be Alrik," suggested Hobbs.

"That's ffirmative," said Buchanan.

Keats said, "You're losing me."

"You want me to fill him in?" asked Hobbs. He was addressing his question to Buchanan.

Buchanan said, "It would probably be to our advantage to give him the big picture."

But Hobbs didn't get the chance because the SAT phone sounded off about that time.

Buchanan told Keats to pick it up, see who was calling.

It was Angie.

Angie had been watching a NORAD weather report on TV. She asked Buchanan if remaining in the suite at South Shore Harbor until the weather conditions improved was an option. He told her it wasn't. He said it was absolutely imperative that she get underway as soon as possible. She didn't question her orders. She knew there was absolutely no use. She knew Buchanan couldn't be swayed.

The Stryder was already out in Clear Lake awaiting their rendezvous. Angie could see the boat's running lights from the window. The sight of the lights offered her some degree of comfort, but not really that much. She knew once they cleared the mouth of the channel and got out into Galveston Bay things would get treacherous.

She sighed, terminated the call and headed down to the Marina.

# CHAPTER SEVENTY-SEVEN

The rain was coming down in sheets and there was absolutely no wind. The boat down in the Marina was still burning and the smoke was drifting across the water like a ghost. Those who had fans had turned them on in an attempt to dissipate the smoke, but to no avail. There was a cruiser from the Clear Lake PD on the scene and two Police Officers were questioning everyone in the immediate vicinity. Only one witness had anything to offer and the investigating officer discounted what he had to say. For one thing he was drunk on his ass, and for another, he was very old.

Angie and the other two women made it to the Marina without being interfered with. When they reached the boat they were within earshot of the local TV news crew. The Newscaster was interviewing the old man. The women listened to the interview. The old man told the reporter that he'd seen a streak of light just before the boat blew. He said he couldn't attribute it to anything in particular. Said he'd never seen anything quite like it before.

Angie knew what the streak of light had been. It was a bullet, a tracer round fired from a silenced sniper rifle. That's what had caused the propane tank to explode and the boat to burn.

The reporter saw Angie eavesdropping and called out to her. She responded to him in French.

He smiled politely, looked the other way and told the cameraman, "That's a wrap."

Within thirty seconds the three women had the ropes off the *Catch-o-the-Day*. The *Catch*, a high-dollar motor yacht owned by Buchanan, was the boat the three women were supposed to take to New Orleans. Angie cranked up the engines and slowly backed the boat out of the stall. The smoke from the burning boat made maneuvering inside the Marina a little tricky, but the women did ok. Within three or four minutes they were idling past the lighthouse at the entrance to the harbor. The women on board the Stryder watched the *Catch* clear the entrance to the harbor. As soon as they rounded Lighthouse Point Angie began to pick up speed.

Angie noticed another boat clear the entrance to the harbor within a few seconds of their departure. It fell in behind the *Catch*. She told one of the women to keep an eye on the other boat and tell her if it picked up any speed. Within a minute or two the boat began to do just that.

# CHAPTER SEVENTY-EIGHT

Angie radioed the women on board the Stryder and told them what was happening. The women on board both boats were armed with fully automatic handguns, as well as, saw-off shotguns. All weapons, shotguns included, were equipped with silencers and flash suppressors.

Angie pulled back on the throttle. The *Catch* slowed. The Stryder followed suit. The chase boat slowed. Angie pulled the throttle all the way back and the *Catch* came to a complete stop. The chase boat slowed then stopped. The Stryder idled past the *Catch* and stopped. The six women watched the activity on board the chase boat. They could see several men scrambling for cover.

Angie picked up the SAT phone and called Buchanan. He answered immediately. She told him there was a boat from Legends Saltwater Charter Services following them, but at the moment, they were all dead in the water. He told her to open fire. She conveyed the message to the women on board the Stryder and the six women opened fire…simultaneously. They hammered the chase boat from one end to the other. One of the men on board the boat managed to jump over the side. They watched him flailing in the water. Twice he attempted to swim underwater. Finally he gave up on that and started begging for help. They cautiously approached him, told him to show both his hands. He did it, but when he did, he really had to struggle to keep his head above water. One of the women on board the *Catch* extended a boat hook. He grabbed it and held on. They could all see he was bleeding profusely. Angie asked him in Russian if he was armed. He responded in Russsian. Told her he was not armed. She asked him if he spoke English. He said *yes*, that he did.

Angie picked up the SAT phone and called Buchanan again. She told him they had a live one. He asked her about the boat from Legends. She told him it was sinking with all hands on board, save for one. He asked her if there was any debris in the water. She said there were several life jackets in the water, but nothing else. He asked her what kind of shape the survivor was in. She told him he was wounded, bleeding badly, but still alive. Buchanan told her to take him onboard and see if she could make him talk. She said *"will do"* and terminated the call.

By that time the man in the water was damn near hysterical. He believed he was bleeding to death, told the women that, and said he'd do anything if they just wouldn't let him die. The woman holding the boat hook jerked it out of his hands.

The man screamed, "No. I mean it. I'll do anything. Just don't let me die."

She extended the boat hook again and he grabbed it.

"What's your name?" asked Angie.

He gave her a name.

She said, "Look at me." He did.

She took out her cell phone and photographed his face. Then she forwarded the picture to one of the Bricoleurs. Within a few seconds she got the feedback she needed. The name and the face were a perfect match.

She said, "Bring him onboard."

Pulling the man onboard was tough for the women. He was dead weight, unable to help at all. Soon as he was onboard Angie examined the man's wounds. She was anything but gentle with him, but he didn't complain. She found all his wounds to be superficial, but she didn't tell him that, as a matter of fact she told him he was critically wounded. The fear in the man's eyes spoke volumes.

She asked, "How does it feel to be the lone survivor?"

"Right now I'm in so much pain I'm not so sure I wouldn't rather be dead," said the man.

"Throw him over the side," said Angie.

"No. Wait," said the man. "Please don't do that. You need me."

Angie picked up the SAT phone and called Buchanan again.

When Buchanan answered she said, "He says we need him."

Buchanan asked, "What the fuck for?"

The man overheard Buchanan's question and responded. He said, "I know things."

Angie said, "Here, you talk to him," and handed the man her cell phone.

"I know things," repeated the man.

"Give me an example," said Buchanan.

"Ask me a question," said the man.

Buchanan said, "Give the phone back to the woman."

He handed the cell phone back to Angie.

Buchanan said, "Throw his ass over the side."

Again, the man heard him say it.

"I can give you Alrik," yelled the man.

Buchanan asked Angie, "Who in the hell is Alrik?"

Keats looked at Buchanan. Buchanan knew exactly who Alrik was. Keats realized he was merely playing *cat-n-mouse* with the guy.

Angie interrupted and said, "I've heard he's an assassin."

"That's right," said the man. "And I know where he is."

"One of you women got an iPad with you?" asked Buchanan.

Angie said, "I think so."

Angie looked at the other two women. One of them offered her an iPad. She took it then said, "I have one in my hands. What do you want me to do with it?"

"What do you call it when you can look at one another and talk?" asked Buchanan.

"*Facetime*," said Angie.

"Do I have an App on my cell phone that will allow me to do that?"

"I think so," said Angie. "Ask your young companion. He'll know."

Buchanan handed the phone to Keats. Keats took a look at the cell phone then nodded *yes,* indicating he had the App.

"Make it happen," said Buchanan.

Keats initialized the *Facetime* App then looked back at Buchanan. Buchanan told him to hold the phone at an angle. He said it was imperative that the wounded man not be able to see any of their faces. Then he told Angie to let him see the man's face. Angie made it happen.

At that point the man began heaving, vomited then passed out

"Get a pot of cold water out of the galley and throw it in his face," said Buchanan. They did that, but it didn't help.

Buchanan told them to use electrical ties to secure the man's hands and feet. Told Angie they could question him later. He also told Angie to see to his wounds, not to let him to die. Said they probably needed to know what he knew. Then he terminated the call.

# CHAPTER SEVENTY-NINE

"You better get some sleep," said Buchanan. "I may need you to drive."

Within five minutes Keats was out cold. So was Hobbs.

An hour and forty-five minutes later Buchanan crossed the Sabine River. Once he got off the Sabine River Bridge the highway divided and for ten miles the eastbound and westbound lanes of Interstate 10 were separated by a concrete barricade. At the ten mile marker things changed. A grassy esplanade replaced the barricade. And there were trees. Mostly Evangeline Oaks, but there were a few cedar. The sky was clear. The moon was full. And the traffic was sparse. All things considered, it was a beautiful night for a drive. But Buchanan couldn't have cared less. He was preoccupied, thinking about everything that had transpired.

Buchanan's cell phone began to vibrate. He answered it. It was one of the Bricoleurs. He told Buchanan the Russian hit squad was not more than twenty miles behind him.

"Got a head count?" asked Buchanan.

"Five," said the Bricoleur, "all males."

"How fast are they driving?"

"Fast…at your current rate of speed they'll overtake you in less than an hour."

"Have they stopped anywhere along the way?"

"Not since Baytown."

"Tell me what's up the road."

"There's a Welcome Center right after you cross the levee on the west side of the Atchafalaya then nothing but swamp. Swamp for miles."

"They'll stop at the Welcome Center," said Buchanan. "Give me an immediate heads-up if they do anything unexpected; like stop anywhere else, or speed up, or slow down, or whatever."

He terminated the call.

# CHAPTER EIGHTY

Buchanan continued to drive while the other two continued to sleep. At exactly the forty-five minute mark Buchanan looked over at Keats and said, "Wake up."

Keats opened his eyes, yawned, stretched then exclaimed, "I was having one hell of a nightmare. Dreaming Hobbs got shot and killed."

Buchanan ignored Keats revelation. He said, "In a few minutes we'll be stopping at an Atchafalaya Swamp Welcome Center. When we get there you're gonna have about five minutes to take a leak and splash some water in your face. You need to wake yourself up real good, because when we leave the Welcome Center you'll be driving."

Keats looked at his watch then asked, "Why just five minutes?"

"Cause ten or fifteen minutes later all hell's gonna break loose," said Buchanan.

Keats sat up straight, looked back at Buchanan and said, "I don't understand."

"You don't need to understand," said Buchanan. "You just need to know this, by 11:00 am tomorrow morning you gotta be sitting inside the Café du Monde on Decatur Street having beignets with the Sergeant Major."

"That sounds good to me," said Keats. Then he began nonchalantly looking at the trees in the middle of the esplanade. He yawned again, obviously recalling some of the details of his dream.

Buchanan interrupted his ruminations. He said, "There's more." Keats looked back at Buchanan.

"You're going to be driving the rest of the way to New Orleans by yourself," said Buchanan.

"Why?" asked Keats.

"Cause Hobbs and I've got something to do," said Buchanan.

"What?"

"We have to reduce our adversaries' resources," said Buchanan.

"You're losing me again," said Keats.

"There are five men not fifteen minutes behind us. Hobbs and I are going to stay behind and kill them."

Keats did a double take.

"You heard me right," said Buchanan.

"Why?"

"The five men are members of Petchenko's mob. And after we kill them we're gonna commandeer their vehicle and drive on to New Orleans."

"So that means you won't be far behind me?"

"If all goes well, we should be right behind you."

"And if *it* doesn't go well?"

Keats got no answer. Buchanan was concentrating on the road. At that exact moment Buchanan was driving across the levee and into the Welcome Center parking lot. The time for talking was over.

Buchanan looked around. He said, "There's no one else here. That's good, that way there'll be no collateral damage."

# CHAPTER EIGHTY-ONE

They parked in a space indicated for *The Handicapped,* got out, and entered the men's restroom. There, they found a tall slender black man lying on the floor. Buchanan told the man to get up and get out. The man sat up but he didn't stand. Buchanan asked him if he had a problem. The man didn't answer. Buchanan asked him if he was deaf. He shook his head *no.* Buchanan took a real good look at him. The man was skin and bones. Buchanan asked him if he was hungry. He said he was. Buchanan told Keats go outside and buy him something from the vending machine. Something he could eat. Something he could drink. Keats turned and left.

The man got to his feet immediately and in an instant was embracing Buchanan. Buchanan pushed him away then took a look at his clothing. Everything was a real bad fit. Way too short. Extremely dirty.

Buchanan gave him some cash and told him to buy himself some clothes that fit the first chance he got. Told him it might not be a bad idea if he bathed before he changed. Then he told him to go outside. The man didn't move. Hobbs and Buchanan exchanged glances. Hobbs was starting to grin.

Buchanan said, "Don't say a word, Hobbs." He looked back at the black man and asked, "Now what the fuck's your problem?"

"My father is in Angola Prison," said the black man. "He's supposed to be executed Wednesday morning. I need to get there."

"What'd your father do?" asked Buchanan.

"He killed a man, a very bad man. But he had good reason…the man was abusing my mother."

"What's your father's name," asked Buchanan.

*"Mkombazi."*

"And your name is?"

*"Himaya."*

"Protection," said Buchanan. "Your name means *Protection.*"

Eyes wide with amazement, the black man said, "You understand Swahili."

Buchanan nodded *yes.* Then he retrieved his SAT phone and called one of the Bricoleurs. When the Bricoleur answered he told the young man he wanted to speak to the Warden at the Louisiana State Penitentiary. The young man did as he'd been told and called Angola. Someone at the Prison answered immediately. The Bricoleur transferred the call to Buchanan's SAT phone. Buchanan told whoever answered who he was and asked the person to wake the Warden. The Warden was on the line in two or three minutes.

Buchanan said, "Dan, I need you to release a man you are currently holding on death row into my custody. His son is with me and I have reason to believe the man may be innocent. The man calls himself Mkombazi." Buchanan listened for a few seconds then said, "That's right." He paused, listened then added, "I'll send someone for him."

*Himaya's* eyes were as big as saucers. He asked Buchanan what he'd just done. Buchanan told him for now, his father was safe. Told him he didn't have time to explain and told him to go with Keats. *Himaya* spun around and immediately left the restroom.

Then Buchanan turned to Hobbs and asked, "Do we have a plan of attack?"

Hobbs grinned. Showed Buchanan a Filipino *balisong* knife then began *flipping* it. Buchanan returned the grin and continued watching Hobbs do his *knife thing.*

# CHAPTER EIGHTY-TWO

Five minutes later Hobbs and Buchanan heard the slamming of car doors outside in the parking lot. Then they heard voices. Hobbs continued flipping the knife. Buchanan continued to watch. Four men entered the restroom. The first two stopped and watched while the other two walked to the urinals. A fifth man entered the restroom a few seconds later. He told Hobbs to stop what he was doing and for him and Buchanan to get out. One of the men who'd been standing at a urinal approached the fifth man and said they didn't need to go anywhere. Said he wanted to watch *the old fart* do his *knife thing*. The two men started arguing. The third man left the urinals and walked to where Hobbs and Buchanan were standing and started watching the *knife flipping*. The man standing closest to Hobbs was studying the knife. Hobbs asked the man if he'd like a closer look. The man nodded *yes,* said that he would. Hobbs buried the blade of the knife in the man's belly then turned and slashed the throats of the second and third man. At the very same instant Buchanan drew his Beretta and shot the two arguing men. Hobbs turned, looked at Buchanan and grinned. Buchanan nodded then slipped his Beretta back inside the waistband of his pants. Hobbs leaned over, wiped the blade of his *balisong* on the pant leg of the man lying nearest him then stood up.

"When do we have to be in Key West?" asked Hobbs.

"Six days from now," said Buchanan.

"No pun intended," said Hobbs, "but we do have some *time to kill*…and we are headed for the *Big Easy.*"

Buchanan nodded *yes.*

Hobbs said, "What say we take a day or two and *laissez les bon ton rouler, Mon'Amie.*"

"What say we search these five guys first," said Buchanan, "see what they got on them."

"Good idea," said Hobbs. "Careful not to get any blood on you."

# CHAPTER EIGHTY-THREE

Hobbs and Buchanan searched all five men. Took their cell phones, their wallets, keys, coins, and whatever else they had on them. Then suddenly, both men froze in place.

"Did you hear a car door slam?" whispered Hobbs.

"Game time," said Buchanan. "Get on the floor. Pretend you're unconscious. I'm a Physician. You know the routine."

Hobbs hit the floor. Buchanan knelt next to him. A sixth man entered the restroom. Buchanan ignored him. The man cleared his throat. Buchanan looked up. Alrik Dedriksen was standing there holding an automatic handgun, a gun fitted with a silencer. But that wasn't the only thing he was holding. He was also holding the denim shirt *Himaya* had been wearing in his free hand.

Buchanan ignored the gun. Looked down at Hobbs and said, "Come over here. I need your help."

Dedriksen slowly approached Buchanan then stopped and stood over him. His gun was pointed at Buchanan's head.

"What happened here?" asked Dedriksen. "You know any of these men?"

"No," said Buchanan. "This is the way they were when I walked into restroom. Those five were already dead. But this one has a pulse."

"You have anyone with you?" asked Dedriksen.

"I did," said Buchanan. "My Assistant was with me. But I sent her for help. Listen to me. I'm a Physician. I can save this man's life if we can get him into surgery." He pointed at *Himaya's* shirt and said, "Roll that thing into a bundle and give it to me."

Dedriksen shook his head in disgust, shoved his handgun inside the waistband of his pants, rolled *Himaya's* shirt into a bundle, and handed it to Buchanan. Buchanan placed it under Hobbs head.

"What are you and your *companion* doing in this Godforsaken swamp in the middle of the night?" asked Dedriksen.

Buchanan told him they were on their way to New Orleans. Said he was slated to present at a Physician's Symposium the next day. Just as Buchanan finished saying that, Hobbs opened his eyes. He first looked at Dedriksen. Then he looked at Buchanan. He appeared to be extremely confused.

"What happened?" asked Hobbs. "And who are you people?"

Buchanan didn't answer his question, instead he said, "Someone killed your friends."

"Those men are not my friends," said Hobbs. "I don't know who the hell they are. The one lying over there," he gestured at the man lying nearest the urinals, "he knocked me down as I entered the restroom." He looked the other way then added, "Those three over there were fighting with knives. The other two were watching them fight. Who the hell are you?"

"I'm Dr. Robert Bryant."

Hobbs grimaced, rubbed his head and looking up at Dedriksen asked, "And who the hell are you?"

Dedriksen told Hobbs to *shut up,* told Buchanan to stand up, told him to walk into the nearest toilet stall, told him to go in, lock the door behind him and not come out for any reason.

Buchanan did what he was told, and as soon as he was inside the stall, lowered the toilet seat, climbed up on it and peered over the top of the door. He watched Dedriksen pick up one of the knives and press the point against Hobbs left cheek.

"You're a fucking liar," said Dedriksen. "You know exactly why this happened. You know who these men are." He grinned then added, "The *good Doctor* said you needed surgery. I think I can manage that."

Dedriksen drew the knife blade across Hobbs cheek, slicing his skin in the process. The sight of Hobbs blood was all it took. Buchanan drew his Berretta and fired one round. The bullet entered Dedriksen's head at the base of his skull and made its exit through the lower half of his face. Dedriksen slumped forward, fell to one side, and rolled off Hobbs. Buchanan climbed down off the toilet seat and opened the door to the stall. Hobbs was standing up by that time, staring at what was left of Dedriksen's face.

"I'll get Himaya's shirt," said Buchanan. Then pointing at Dedriksen said, "Get that SOB's keys, his cell phone, and his gun."

Buchanan held up Himaya's shirt. The buttons had been ripped off and it was torn in several places.

"Gimme the SAT phone," said Buchanan.

Hobbs handed it to him. He punched in the number of the cell phone Keats had taken with him. Keats answered immediately.

"You on your way, Keats?" asked Buchanan, "And Himaya…he still with you?"

"Yes," replied Keats. "I take it things went well?"

"Exceedingly well," said Buchanan.

"We now have two more vehicles. I'm taking the one Alrik Dedriksen was driving. I'm gonna drive it to Angola. Hobbs is heading directly to New Orleans in the other one."

Before Keats could ask any questions, Buchanan terminated the call. Then he and Hobbs gathered up all the stuff they'd taken from the six dead men and walked to the parking lot. The keys Buchanan had found in Dedriksen's pocket fit a late model Cadillac Convertible. Hobbs, much to his delight, had inherited a brand new Mercedes-Benz G-Class 4X4 SUV.

Buchanan used the SAT phone and called the Bay House near San Luis Pass. When one of the Bricoleurs answered he told him he was going to give him the numbers to six cell phones and told him he wanted all data associated with the phones redacted. Then he waited.

After three or four minutes passed the Bricoleur said, "I'm ready when you are."

Buchanan said, "I want to know where the phones have been used and what they were used for."

Within three or four minutes the Bricoleur was back on the line. He said, "Houston, Galveston Island, social media mostly; porn, guns, girls…that kind of stuff."

"Any calls to the New Orleans area?"

"No."

"They call any international exchanges?"

"Multiple calls to Cuba, only one phone, called the same number every time."

"Call the number and make the call originate from a convenience store anywhere along Seawall Boulevard in Galveston. Transfer the call to my SAT phone before you make the connection. And record the entire conversation."

"Will do," said the Bricoleur. Then he went off line.

He was back in less than ten seconds. He said, "Bad news. The Cuban knows something has happened to his men. Our intel is still fragmented, but he knows something has gone afoul. There's a good chance there's a mole among us, Sir."

"See what you can determine," said Buchanan. "When you say *Cuban,* you mean Ramon Ibarra?"

"The man himself," said the Bricoleur.

Buchanan said, "Call the Fusion Center at Langley and tell them the offices in Federal City have been compromised. Tell them you're calling for the Sergeant Major. If they act like they don't know who you're talking about tell them to wake the Commander-in-Chief. He'll explain who the Sergeant Major is. Don't identify yourself and make certain your call is untraceable."

"Let me make sure I've got this straight," said the Bricoleur. "You're talking about the offices at the Fusion Center in Federal City, the offices located across the river from downtown New Orleans?"

"Yes. And tell them everyone working there must get out immediately. Tell them if they don't they're going to die. Tell them they must take everything with them when they go and that Homeland Security needs to be notified." Buchanan paused then added, "If you identify our mole don't tell anyone about it. Call me and we'll talk. I intend to use that SOB to our advantage."

Buchanan terminated the exchange then called the Sergeant Major.

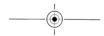

"Where are you, Sergeant Major?"

"I'm at a truck stop between Baton Rouge and New Orleans, waiting on an eighteen wheeler to get here. Could be *liberation day* for about forty or fifty young women, Tony. Gonna be Armageddon day for the driver if that turns out to be the case."

"And the women…what are you gonna do with them?" asked Buchanan.

"Mom's with me," said the Sergeant Major. "She'll handle the women."

"What about the truck?"

"Going to burn it," said the Sergeant Major. "By the way, I know who your mole is."

"Really," said Buchanan. "Who is it?"

"That can wait," said the Sergeant Major.

"You sure about that?" asked Buchanan. But he got no answer. He asked, "Mom in the car with you?"

"No, she's on her Harley," said the Sergeant Major. "She's tailing the tractor trailer rig."

"Wish I was there," said Buchanan.

"Me too," said the Sergeant Major. And he terminated the call.

Buchanan and Hobbs divvied up the stuff they'd taken off the six dead men then walked to the parking lot and found two vehicles, a Cadillac convertible and an SUV. Buchanan opened the trunk of the Caddy and examined the contents; a suitcase, a backpack, several automatic handguns, and a butt load of ammunition. He opened the suitcase and found it contained a woman's clothing and some cosmetics. The backpack contained a change of clothes for a man. Hobbs was rummaging around in the SUV. It had a few empty beer bottles and some trash in it, but nothing else.

# PART THREE

# THE LIBERATION

# CHAPTER EIGHTY-FOUR

The road to Angola was a real piece of shit. Huge Acadian Oaks lined the left side of the roadway. Their ancient root systems had done a number on the asphalt road. It was so rough Buchanan had no choice but to slow down. And an eroded blacktop road wasn't his only problem; feral hogs continually crisscrossed the roadway; big ones, little ones, and everything in between. They'd plowed up every square inch of the levee running along the right side of the road. Buchanan studied the animals. None of the porkers seemed to be bothered by the convertibles headlights, but the lights flashing in the treetops on the other side of the levee made them extremely nervous. Buchanan assumed the lights were coming from Cajuns hunting coons out in the swamp. Or maybe it was the choppy sounds of the Cajun's go-devil engines that made the hogs nervous. Either way, the hogs were extremely edgy and totally unpredictable.

A full moon illuminated the roadway so Buchanan killed his headlights. He slowed to a crawl, listening to the racket coming from the swamp and savoring the aroma of various kinds of wild game cooking on campfires. Bacon dominated the tantalizing mix. He noticed a wisp of smoke creeping across the roadway through a low spot in the levee. When he reached it, he pulled to the side of the road. He let the smoke engulf the Caddy. He knew the aroma of the wild pork would hang in his clothes for hours. But he didn't mind, he liked the smell of it. After a minute or so he decided he'd wasted all the time he could afford, pulled back into the roadway, and began to accelerate. He switched his headlights back on and noticed the hogs were gone. Two more bends in the road and he pulled up short in front of a lighted brick marquee that read *The Louisiana State Penitentiary*. He got out of the Caddy and walked to the gate. The Warden, Daniel Bruney, was standing at the gate, waiting to meet him. Buchanan looked at the brick marquee then back at Bruney.

"My name ain't there cause I ain't so sure I want this job," said Bruney.

"I certainly understand that," said Buchanan. "My man been told he was leaving?"

"He was told you were coming for him. I'm not sure he heard. He just lays there, his eyes fixed on the ceiling, looking like he's in a catatonic state."

"You can't ever tell what the man's thinking."

"I agree with that," said Bruney. "Let's go get him."

The two men turned and started across the prison yard. The Gun Bulls, who were strategically stationed at each gate, nodded as they passed. Once inside the Penitentiary they walked straight to death row and entered a long straight passageway which was totally devoid of décor. After two more abrupt turns and they arrived at their destination. The guard standing at the door to the condemned man's cell stood aside. Bruney nodded and the guard tripped the latch and shoved the door open. Mkombazi had thrown his mattress on the stone floor and was lying on a metal rack mounted in the far corner of the cell. He was still staring intently at the ceiling.

"Mkombazi!" said Buchanan. He got no response.

Buchanan looked at Bruney, shook his head then looked back at the black man lying on the rack.

"Mkombazi," repeated Buchanan. "Look at me."

The black man rolled his head to the side, made eye contact with Buchanan and said, "The man said you were coming for me."

"Get up," said Buchanan. "Your son needs you."

"How so?" asked Mkombazi…the stark reality of his changing circumstances beginning to sink in. Buchanan didn't say.

Mkombazi immediately sat up, swung his legs around, and planted both feet on the floor. Bruney stepped forward and reached out, thinking he needed help to stand. The Warden was wrong. Mkombazi pushed his hand away and stood as though his legs were spring loaded. He yawned and stretched and looked at Buchanan.

Then he said, "We go."

# CHAPTER EIGHTY-FIVE

The guard, who was still standing in the door way, was confused by the entire situation.

Bruney said, "Make a hole," and the guard stepped aside.

Buchanan gave Mkonbazi a shove in the direction of the doorway and the three men slipped past the guard and started down the corridor. Bruney led the way with Buchanan bringing up the rear.

As they neared the end of the corridor Buchanan asked, "Can we get him hosed down? He smells like shit."

"Sure," said Bruney, "when we get out in the yard."

When they got to the yard Mkonbazi was told to strip down then stand against a wall. He did as he was directed and Bruney blasted him with a hose. While they were in the corridor Buchanan had told Mkombazi he had something for him to wear in the trunk of the car he'd come in. When he was done getting hosed down Mkombazi used his clothes to dry himself then left them lying in a pile next to the wall. The Gun Bulls were a bit taken aback to see a buck naked man approaching the front gate. But they let him pass. Bruney and Buchanan walked him to the convertible and Buchanan opened the trunk. Mkombazi opened the suitcase then began examining the feminine apparel in the suitcase. He looked at Buchanan and smiled.

"Look in the backpack," said Buchanan.

He picked up the backpack, unzipped it, and found a pair of a pair of boxer shorts, some pants and a tee shirt inside.

"Suit up," said Bruney.

"There are no shoes." said Mkombazi.

"Suit up," repeated Buchanan. "We'll get you some shoes on the way to New Orleans."

Mkombazi looked back at the two Gun Bulls standing at the gate. Then he turned his back to the *Bulls* donned the clothes and presented himself for inspection.

Buchanan told Mkombazi to get in the car. He told Bruney he'd call him when he got to New Orleans. Then he and Mkombazi got in the Caddy and they left.

# CHAPTER EIGHTY-SIX

Keats crossed Lake Pontchartrain at dawn. The sun had not yet made an appearance, but there was ample light; enough light that the airboats crisscrossing back and forth under the causeway bridge could easily be seen. Keats looked to his left and toward the southeast. He could see the New Orleans skyline. It was as pretty as a picture.

"Why are the boats stopping at those houses?" asked Himaya.

"They're buying beer and bait and ice," answered Keats.

"I'm hungry," said Himaya.

"We'll eat in a little bit," said Keats. "Don't worry, you won't starve."

They breezed past two NOPD cruisers painting the traffic with radar detectors. The sight of the cruisers took Keats breath away. He checked his speed and he was relieved to see he was five miles under the limit. He changed lanes, moving two lanes to the right. That would get him downtown. He looked ahead then in his rearview mirror. He was happy to see the traffic congestion was relatively moderate this morning so he'd have ample time to do what he needed to do before breakfast. He thought about breakfast. An image of the Café Du Monde immediately popped into Keats mind's eye.

He looked at Himaya and asked, "You ever tasted powered sugar?"

"No," said Himaya. "Is it good?"

"You betcha," said Keats.

"What did you say?" asked Himaya.

"Powdered sugar tastes good," said Keats.

As they drove past the Cajun Dome, Keats changed lanes again. After a quarter of a mile they exited the freeway, stopped at a red light then turned left onto Tchoupitoulas Street. Six blocks later they crossed Canal. Canal Street is the main street that runs straight through New Orleans proper and dead ends at the Mississippi River. Keats zig-zagged onto Chartres Street then onto Decatur; drove past the Café Du Monde and parked riverside next to the French Market. He killed the engine and told Himaya they were going to buy him some new clothes when the Market opened. The vendors were just arriving and getting organized so he told Himaya he'd have to wait in the vehicle for a few minutes. Keats could see Himaya was getting antsy so he told him he could get out. Told him he could look around till the vendors were ready to open up shop if he agreed not to pester the vendors. Himaya agreed then they both got out and crossed the street.

Himaya was like a kid in a candy shop. At first he wanted to buy everything he touched. But then that changed when an elderly black man arrived and began to lay out his wares. He sold authentic African attire. Himaya was taken by what the old man was wearing which consisted of an earthy-colored collarless robe, sandstone beads, white pants that were a bit short, sandals woven from hemp, and a cap that matched the robe, everything typical of the black culture of New Orleans. Himaya told the old man he liked what he was wearing and the old guy produced an identical set. Himaya immediately stripped to his boxers and donned his new apparel. Keats gave him a once over, approved, and tried to pay the old man. But the old man refused payment. He said to see the joy in his young friends face was payment enough. They argued, but the old man prevailed. Himaya bowed to the old man, thanked him, and they left for the Café Du Monde on foot.

En route they walked through a part of the French Market where vendors were preparing to sell a myriad of Caribbean spices. The aroma of those spices mingled with bacon grease and browning flour was absolutely titillating. Keats had to damn near drag Himaya through that part of the Market. Finally they reached the cross street, made their exit then walked past the St. Louis Hotel. The rotunda in the ancient hotel had been the site of the most infamous of the slave auction blocks prior to the Civil War. But the Civil War had abruptly ended that. Keats noticed there was graffiti spray painted on the sidewalk running adjacent to the hotel. He paused and read it. It read, *"I can hear the blood of your brother crying to me."* Keats recognized it for what it was. It was a quote from the book of Genesis. Himaya paid it no attention. They moved on.

The sidewalk was coming alive; artists displaying their latest works and setting up easels; street musicians unloading guitars, amplifiers and speakers, preparing to hawk their talents, hoping to one day be discovered. The hustle and bustle was a little much for Himaya so Keats ushered him across the street and they stepped on to the sidewalk in front of the Margaritaville Bar and Grill. The Bar was already open and in full swing. Matter of fact, "Wasting Away in Margaritaville" was pulsing into the street.

Finally, at exactly 8:30 a.m., they re-crossed the street and walked into the Café Du Monde.

# CHAPTER EIGHTY-SEVEN

Buchanan and an elderly white man were sitting inside the Café Du Monde. They were alone, sitting at a table adjacent to Decatur Street. Himaya recognized Buchanan immediately, gathered his robe around him and walked directly to the table where the two men were seated.

"Where's my father?" asked Himaya.

"He's at the Double Tree Hotel," said Buchanan. "He's taking a shower."

Buchanan motioned to a young man sitting by himself at an adjacent table. Evidently the young man had been briefed regarding what he was to do, because he immediately got up and walked to Buchanan's table and told Himaya he needed to come with him. Told him he would take him to his father. Himaya followed the young man out of the Café.

Keats had a questioning look on his face. "He's taking him to the River Walk Mall first," said Buchanan. "There's a small Café Du Monde vendor in the Mall. He'll buy him a bag of beignets and some coffee then take him to a suite on the top floor at the Hotel. And that's where he'll stay." Buchanan took a quick look at everyone sitting inside the Café then leaned forward, lowered his voice and said, "Sit down, Keats."

Keats took a seat. The elderly man shoved a bag of beignets in Keats direction. Keats pulled one out of the bag, knocked a little powdered sugar off and began to eat it. While he ate Buchanan got up, went to the counter and purchased three cups of fresh coffee. He returned to the table and set a cup in front of each of the other two men. Then he sat back down and took a long pull on his coffee.

"This is the Sergeant Major," said Buchanan.

Keats fingers were coated with powdered sugar so he didn't attempt a handshake. He and the Sergeant Major simply traded nods.

The Sergeant Major said, "Relax and enjoy your breakfast, Dr. Keats. We're in a *stand down posture* right now. Buchanan has dealt our adversaries quite a blow. They're attempting to regroup at the moment. The reason we know this is because Buchanan has a mole inside his organization. His forte is crypto surveillance. The dumb son-of-a-bitch doesn't know everything he is doing on the internet is being monitored. Doesn't know he's being used to track our adversaries' movements. So relax, *mon ami*. Everything is under control."

"What's that supposed to mean?" asked Keats.

"*Mon ami* means *my friend* in French," said the Sergeant Major.

"That's not what I'm asking. The *so relax* part…what is that supposed to mean?"

"That means you can let your hair down," said the Sergeant Major. He lowered his voice and added, "Alrik Dedricksen was their team leader. Dedricksen's dead. There is no heir apparent. Ramon Ibarra is trying to put the pieces together right now. And that's gonna take him a while. In the meantime we can relax a little. Do some strategic planning."

Keats looked at Buchanan. He asked, "What about Angie?"

"What about her?"

"Is she alright?"

"She's just fine. She's here in New Orleans."

Keats took another slug of his coffee and snagged another beignet.

# CHAPTER EIGHTY-EIGHT

"I'm in a convertible," said Buchanan. "Good for two passengers only. Why don't I ditch the convertible and we'll take one of the two SUV's across town. Sergeant Major...what are you driving?"

"You don't want to ride in my vehicle," said the Sergeant Major.

Buchanan didn't ask why. He knew why. He simply said, "Then we'll take Keats Ford Excursion. There's more leg room and ample cargo space." He looked in Keats direction and said, "Finish your coffee, Keats." Keats took a slug and set his cup on the table.

"I'll park the convertible in the parking garage across the street from Harrah's and you can pick me up at the turnaround on Poydras," said Buchanan. He looked at the other two men and asked, "Sound good?"

"Good enough," said the Sergeant Major. Keats had taken another bite of beignet. Had a mouthful and didn't answer.

Buchanan got up and left.

"You know where he's talking about?" asked the Sergeant Major.

"Uh-huh," said Keats. Nodding his head.

"Good," said Sergeant Major. "I'll meet you there." Then he got up and left.

Keats dug another beignet out of the bag then got up and got a refill on his coffee. Then he returned to the table and sat back down. A young man sitting at an adjacent table got up and walked to the table where Keats was seated.

He said, "Time to leave."

"Who the hell are you?" asked Keats.

"Your guide," said the young man. "Let's go."

Keats shook his head and said, "I ain't going anywhere with you."

"Oh yes you are."

"Why?"

"Because that's what Buchanan expects you to do."

Nodding again, Keats said, "Uh-huh."

Keats pushed away from the table and stood. The young man squared off. He decided he'd better go with him and they walked out of the Café together.

# CHAPTER EIGHTY-NINE

There were a lot of pedestrians on Decatur Street, a hell of a lot of them were there to panhandle. But nobody asked either one of them for anything. Keats assumed it was the young man…it was the look on his face. Maybe the panhandlers knew him, maybe they didn't. But they sure as hell weren't going to mess with him.

"I'm parked next to the levee," said Keats.

"I know," said the young man.

"What is it you don't know," asked Keats. The young man didn't respond.

"Who the hell are you?" asked Keats. Again, he got no answer.

They entered the French Market on the food vender end, where most vendors were cutting up vegetables or browning flour, preparing to make a roux. One extremely fat guy was standing over a griddle frying thick strips of bacon. Sweat was dripping off his forehead and dropping onto griddle. Every time a drop hit the griddle it would sizzle. It was nasty. Keats couldn't watch.

They passed a table covered with men's straw hats then turned right, cut between the two buildings and crossed the street. The Creole Queen, paddle-wheeler in the middle of the Mississippi River, was passing and the pilot blew the whistle. The sound was shrill and damn near deafening. Both men scrambled to get inside the Excursion. Keats put the key in the ignition, turned it, shifted into drive and pulled into the street.

"The young man said, "You can make a u-turn on the far end of the Market.

"I know," said Keats.

Thirty seconds later and they were back on Decatur Street.

# CHAPTER NINETY

When they got to Canal Street, they had to stop and wait on a Street Car to pass. Keats had stopped in the middle of the crosswalk and pedestrians were crossing in front of and behind the Excursion. One of them shook a finger at him. As soon as he got an opening he crossed to the esplanade in the center of the street, paused then turned left. He moved one lane to the right then pulled into the drive-through at Harrah's. Buchanan crossed behind the Excursion and slid into the back seat behind the driver. The Sergeant Major opened the door behind the passenger seat and got in.

"Let's go," said Buchanan.

They crossed Convention Boulevard, made the circle then merged with the northbound traffic.

"You're gonna stay on Canal Street 'til it dead ends at City Park Avenue," said Buchanan.

"Then where?" asked Keats.

"Right now don't worry about it," said Buchanan, "you just drive."

Five minutes later he said, "Take a right on Canal Boulevard."

Then they drove through a low rent residential neighborhood. Most houses were still in the same condition Hurricane Katrina had left them in. But they were definitely not vacant. They'd become homeless refugee camps. And the natives were restless. Keats accelerated to the extent that he could.

Finally, Buchanan said, "At the end of the block make a right then slow down."

That put them on Lakeshore Drive. Lakeshore runs along the northern shore of Lake Pontchartrain. Keats could see a Marina in the distance. It turned out to be a carbon copy of the Marina in Kemah. It was also named *South Shore Harbor Marina*.

And the Catch-o-the-Day was moored in a slip. He looked, but he didn't see the Stryder. Buchanan noticed.

He said, "The other boat is there. It's parked inside one of the covered slips. It's in need of a few repairs."

"I don't see anyone on board the *Catch*." said Keats. "Where are the women?"

"They're at the Doubletree," said Buchanan. Then he said, "You're gonna come to a bar before long…it's called *Harry's*. When you get there, make the block then park in the alley behind the bar."

There was no way to miss *Harry's bar*, there was a life size fiberglass statue of Harry Connick, Jr. standing next to the entrance. And there were posters, most of which had fallen victim to graffiti mongers. But the building was in good repair. Keats looked back at Buchanan.

Buchanan was grinning. He said, "The bar belongs to a woman named Harriet. Harriet's a big woman…has absolutely no need of a bouncer." He motioned ahead. "Turn right here," he said.

Keats made the turn, circled the block then drove into the alley and parked. Buchanan and the Sergeant Major got out and went in the back door of the bar. In about thirty seconds they came out. They had a third man with them. He was staggering and stumbling and his hands were tied behind his back. Buchanan opened the rear lift gate of the Excursion and he and the Sergeant Major shoved the man inside. Then they slammed the lift gate shut. While they were doing that, *Keats' guide,* was reconfiguring the seating arrangements. He was climbing into the second row of seats, where the Sergeant had been sitting. Then he produced a handgun. He turned around and stuck the handgun in the new passenger's face. Keats could tell the young man meant business and kept his mouth shut.

"I like Harry Connick's music," said the Sergeant Major. "But why does she have to play it so loud?"

"Because she's in love with Harry," said Buchanan.

"Bet you're gonna tell me everybody in the bar is *backin' it up*," said Keats.

The young man holding the handgun laughed out loud.

# CHAPTER NINETY-ONE

They returned to the Marina and parked next to one of the covered boat slips; one of the slips that was completely enclosed. Two men came out of the back door. One was carrying a gurney. The other one opened the lift gate on the Excursion, dragged the man out of the boat slip enclosure and lowered him to the pavement. They explained, this was the man the women had taken prisoner at Kemah. Then they put him on the gurney. He struggled with them and one of the men tazed him.

"What are they going to do with him," asked Keats.

"Ultimately?" said Buchanan. "They probably gonna kill him."

"Just like that?"

"Just like that," said Buchanan. "Look. Nobody has to kill anybody…unless it's a matter of life and death. And if that's the case, then you do it. *Comprende?*"

"I guess so. So now, what do we do?"

"We drive to the Double Tree. That's where Angie is…and the others. You're in the driver's seat, Keats. Drive."

Keats nodded, backed up and left the Marina.

The suite was on the top floor of the Double Tree. They went inside as soon as they got there. The suite was fundamentally a carbon copy of the one in Kemah. But there was more glass. As a matter of fact there was a panoramic view of the entire city of New Orleans. From the windows you could see the bridge to Algiers, the Historic District, the Warehouse District, and Lake Pontchartrain. The satellite surveillance equipment was roughly equivalent to that in Kemah. But there were considerably more computer stations scattered around the room.

"Where are the women?" asked Keats.

"I don't know," said Buchanan. "Check the bedrooms."

Keats checked one bedroom after another.

"They ain't here," he said.

Buchanan said, "Don't worry about it. They will be."

Keats thought about what had happened when they'd gotten to the Hotel. When they'd arrived, the young man who'd left the Café Du Monde with Himaya had met them in the parking garage. He had Himaya with him and told him to sit in the passenger seat. Then he'd gotten behind the steering wheel. The other young man, the one who'd been holding the prisoner at gunpoint, remained in the Excursion, sitting where he'd been sitting.

Buchanan interrupted Keats thoughts. He asked, "You see an elderly black man in any of the bedrooms?"

"Nope," said Keats. "No one here but us three."

"Good," said Buchanan. "Come over here and sit next to me." Keats complied. "Take that pencil and paper and write this number down."

Buchanan was staring at a number on the screen of one of the computer monitors. He read a number off the screen. The Sergeant Major was looking at the satellite surveillance monitors. There was nothing happening on the monitors. He appeared to be examining how they'd been mounted.

"You own this suite?" asked the Sergeant Major.

"No. The Department of Homeland Security does."

Buchanan picked up his cell phone. He looked at the number Keats had recorded on the piece of paper and punched it in. It rang for quite a while before somebody answered.

"I need to speak to *Father Joe*."

Whoever was on the other end must have told him *Father Joe* couldn't come to the phone because he said, "Tell him to come inside and answer the phone. Tell him it's Buchanan."

There was a short wait. Then Buchanan said, "Thanks for coming to the phone, Joseph. I'll require a sniper, two spotters, and two or three men who aren't afraid of heights." He paused, listened for a moment then said, "That's right. That's where you send them. And I need them here as soon as possible." Then he terminated the call.

"If you need a nap, go take it now," said Buchanan.

"Take a nap?" exclaimed Keats. "I don't think so. You mind telling me what's going on?"

"Wait until the others get here," said Buchanan. That way I won't have to repeat myself."

The Sergeant Major said, "Come over here, Keats." The Sergeant Major had walked across the room and was standing at one of the windows. Keats joined him at the window. "See that bridge? That's where the sniper is going to be, him and one of the *spotters*." He pointed at the roof of the vacant World Trade Center building at the end of Canal Street and said, "That's where the other *spotter* will be."

Keats was satisfied.

# CHAPTER NINETY-TWO

There was a lot more that Keats wanted to know, but he decided he'd wait. He walked to the conference table and took a seat and within thirty seconds he was asleep.

Half an hour later Buchanan rapped on the table with his knuckles and woke him up. There were six young men now seated at the table. All six looked to be in their early thirties. All six looked hard as nails.

"Who's the sniper?" asked Buchanan. "One of the young men raised a finger. "Spotters?" Two more fingers went up. "Any of you afraid of heights?" All said *no*. "You other three are the *climbers*...right?" All three nodded *yes*. All of you get up and come to the window with me...you too Keats."

You three," said Buchanan, pointing at the three *climbers*, "Are going to hang painters' canvas in the superstructure of that bridge. Once you get that done, the *sniper* and one of the *spotters* will set up on the bridge." Then he pointed at the World Trade Center Building and said, "The other *spotter* and *the sniper* will be stationed on top of that building. The three of you can decide who does what." Then he pointed a finger towards Federal City and said, "Your target will be on the waterfront in Federal City." He locked eyes with the *sniper* and asked, "You ever shoot anybody at that distance?" The young man nodded, *yes*. "Good," said Buchanan. "When it's done the bodies or targets or whatever you want to call them will be removed from the scene by boat. More than likely the Coastguard will handle that." He looked around the table. Every face looked dead serious. He added, "Our adversaries are being tracked. They're on the run right now. You have a little time on your hands so I'm going to give you the afternoon off. I assume you all have secret clearances. Would I be right about that?" Every head in the room nodded in the affirmative. "Then hear this...stay out of the tiddy bars. Disclose nothing of what's been said to anyone and don't discuss this among yourselves." Again, there were multiple nods. "Be back in this room by zero six hundred tomorrow morning for a briefing." He took a second look at the others then said, "You're all dismissed. All but you, Keats."

# CHAPTER NINETY-THREE

### The Next Day, 9:00 AM

One of the *spotters* had loaned Keats a spotting scope and Keats was standing at the window on the east side of the suite watching the men hang the painter's canvas in the bridge's superstructure. They'd started working early that morning and now it looked like they were done. Keats had never before in his entire life seen such agile individuals. And they'd done a perfect job. The enclosure, which was designed to contain paint over-spray, would more than adequately conceal the *sniper*. As a matter of fact, all three men were inside the enclosure at that moment, and Keats couldn't tell it.

He walked across the room and took a look at the World Trade Center Building. He said, "You said the *spotter* would be setting up this morning. I'm looking at the roof now. I don't see him."

Buchanan said, "Look at the apparatus on the east side of the roof. That's a flat-roof scupper. The *spotter* is inside the scupper. He's monitoring the activity on the bridge right now, watching for intruders or anyone else who might be taking an undue interest in what's going on overhead."

"What happens if he spots trouble?"

"There's a young man inside the van they came in. He's carrying safety observer's credentials. He and the *spotter* have SAT phones. Third man will tell him when and if he's to intervene. This is not their *first rodeo,* Keats...relax."

"What's on our agenda today?" asked Keats.

"We meet again, mid-morning, all but the men on the bridge, the two *spotters,* and the *sniper.*"

"Will the women be there?"

"They're making preparation to get underway day after tomorrow. They won't be here. Look, don't worry about the women. You'll be with them when they leave."

"Are we going to get anything to eat this morning?" asked Keats. He hesitated then asked, "What about some more beignets? You said they sell them in the Mall."

"Beignets it is," said Buchanan. He added, "Let's go."

# CHAPTER NINETY-FOUR

Buchanan called Hobbs and had him meet them at the Mall. After breakfast they headed back to the parking garage at Harrah's and retrieved the Excursion. They drove through the Warehouse District, stopped and visited the World War II Museum then drove through the Historic District to Magazine Street. They parked, got out, sat outside at a sidewalk café, and shared a pitcher of Abita Beer. After two pitchers, they drove to the French Market where Buchanan talked to the man who'd sold the African apparel to Himaya. He said Himaya had returned and purchased similar clothing for his father. He told Buchanan they'd asked him if he knew anyone who'd take them in for a few days and he'd given them his address. Buchanan thanked him, made him take several hundred dollars then the three men headed for the Acme Oyster House on foot. The Oyster House, which is located on Iberville Street, was packed so they waited outside and watched the pole dancers coming and going from the tiddy bar across the street. Finally they got a table. By then it was about 4:00 pm and as soon as they were seated Buchanan ordered more Abita Beer. After a feast consisting of Char grilled Oysters, Crawfish Etoufee, Chicken and Andouille Sausage Gumbo, Jambalaya, and sweet Potato Fries, they returned to the Double Tree. Keats went to one of the bedrooms, laid down, and passed out. The two old men sat at the conference table, talked about old times, and *strategized*.

# CHAPTER NINETY-FIVE

## The Next Day, Zero Six Hundred Hours

Buchanan began the meeting promptly at six am. Buchanan sat at the end of the conference table. An unidentified middle age man sat at the other. Buchanan introduced him as a CIA Special Ops Officer, but didn't give him a name. Hobbs Sr. and the woman who'd left the San Luis Pass Bay House with Elizabeth Davenport two days earlier, were sitting next to each other. Keats was sitting next to the younger Hobbs and Denise (Reba) was on Hobb's other side. Two young men sat across from them, one Keats knew the other he didn't.

Buchanan picked up his SAT phone and made a call. He switched the phone to speaker mode and set the phone on the table. A young man answered the phone, and at Buchanan's direction, transferred the call. Nathaniel Davenport picked up. He was cordial, but unusually guarded. Buchanan asked him half a dozen questions. Davenport was evasive. Buchanan terminated the call.

Buchanan looked at the Special Ops Officer and said, "He dies tonight with a pulmonary embolism."

The Special Ops Officer said, "I'll handle it. Personally." Then he got up and left.

Buchanan briefed everyone regarding what was going to happen at dusk the next day. Then everyone but Keats and the older Hobbs got up and left.

Buchanan said, "Let's go."

All three men rode the elevator to street level, walked across the street, spent about an hour at the poker tables in Harrah's, retrieved the Excursion from the parking garage, and drove to the South Shore Harbor Marina.

When they got there Keats spent two hours looking at the technology on board the Catch. Angie was his tutor. The other two women watched while they worked.

Buchanan and Hobbs were pleased with what they saw. "You're a fast learner Keats," said Buchanan. "You watch everything these women do. They all have a different way of solving the same problems. Down the road we'll talk about that. For now…wrap it up…we're outta here."

Ten minutes later they were on the road again.

During the night Reba and Ramon exchanged text messages while Buchanan and Hobbs looked on. She'd described the vehicle she'd be driving and the route she'd be taking. She didn't ask any questions and Ibarra didn't expound on anything. Buchanan found it interesting that he never mentioned Dedriksen or any of the other hit squad members, the ones he and Hobbs had killed at the Atchafalaya Swamp Welcome Center. The texting ended abruptly.

"How do you feel about everything?" asked Buchanan.

"I'm scared shitless," said Reba.

Buchanan said, "You better be. That son-of-a-bitch is gonna kill you if he smells a rat."

# CHAPTER NINETY-SIX

### Dusk—The Same Day

Buchanan, Hobbs Sr. and Keats were standing at the window on the east end of the suite. The lights in the suite were out and all three men were wearing night vision goggles.

"There're men on the roof," said Keats.

Buchanan said, "They're Navy Seals. The Team Leader is in the street. Looks like homeless rabble, don't he."

"You have Navy Seals on the payroll?" asked Keats.

"No," replied Buchanan. "The Seal Team is part of a joint effort between the Coast Guard and the Seals."

They watched for another second or two then Keats asked, "Reba know?"

"She knows there'll be back-up. She just doesn't know what kind."

"That street sweeper part of the deal," asked Keats.

"Uh-huh."

"No stone left unturned," said Buchanan.

Keats looked back at the top of the building and asked, "How'd they get on the roof?"

"They used the scaffolding on the other side of the building...that and some grappling hooks. Heads up...Reba's down at the corner."

Reba had taken a taxi to Federal City. The driver dropped her off on Patterson Drive, about two blocks down the street from the US Coast Guard Sector of New Orleans. They watched Reba pay the driver. They watched the taxi drive off, watched Reba walk the last two blocks, watched her start pacing when she got there. Finally a tall cargo van pulled up at the curb. Three men got out and approached Reba. The first man to reach her took her by the arm and guided her to the door on the southwest end of the Office Building. Reba appeared to punch in her access code. It didn't appear to work. She turned and looked back at the suite on the top floor of the Double Tree. The man standing next to Reba also turned and looked at the Hotel.

Buchanan did a double take. He said, "That's Ramon Ibarra. Kill the son-of-a-bitch. Kill all four, right now." He was speaking into the SAT phone.

Keats head jerked around, looking toward the top of the World Trade Center. He watched four flashes. Each flash was separated from the others by mere fractions of a second.

Buchanan said, "Done. Now call the Coast Guard."

# EPILOGUE

## Early the Next Morning

The SAT phone sounded off. Buchanan turned, walked to the conference table, talking as he walked. He sat down and listened then said, "It's me." He listened for maybe ten more seconds then he said, "Explain that." His brow furrowed as he said it. "Wait one," is what he said next then, "Let me put this on speaker phone." Hobbs and Keats joined him at the table. Buchanan said, "So where is he right now?"

The person on the other end said, "We watched him book an international flight out of Merida this morning using his laptop. We know it was him, because he used his cell phone to check flight schedules. The voice print matches Ramon's. The reliability factor on that is ninety-nine point nine per cent. I hate to tell you this, but he may fly into the Louis Armstrong International Airport in New Orleans by midday tomorrow."

"So who the hell did we kill?" asked Buchanan.

"Raul Ibarra. Raul is Ramon's twin brother. We know this because the reverse facial imaging matches that of Raul not Ramon."

"Thanks for the heads up," said Buchanan. "Stay off the phone. I may need to call you back in a few minutes." Then he terminated the call.

"We have anyone in that region, Sergeant Major?"

"Manny's there," said the Sergeant Major.

"You know how to contact him?"

The Sergeant Major nodded then scrawled something on the piece of paper lying on the table. Buchanan looked at what he'd written, recognized the number then used the SAT phone to make another call. Someone picked up almost immediately. The response of the other individual made Buchanan grin.

"You got a way to get to Puerto Merida tonight?" asked Buchanan. He listened then said, "I think the CIA keeps two Blackhawks on Montana de Cusuco. You think they'd be willing to get you there?" The other individual's answer elicited more grinning from Buchanan. "That's a bunch of bullshit," said Buchanan. "I believe that about as much as I believe your *rapture of the deep* story." Then Buchanan stopped grinning. He listened for another moment or two then terminated the call. "Gentlemen," said Buchanan. "Manny said he's ready to be *resurrected*. I need to call Angelique'. She needs to know there's about to be a change of plans."

"Angelique', things have changed," said Buchanan. "Ramon Ibarra isn't dead. The man we killed was his twin brother, Raul. Forget what we've talked about. You're not sailing to Key West tomorrow…you're sailing to Isla Mujeres off the coast of Quintana Roo. When you get there you're gonna find a resort called the El Milagro Beach Hotel and Marina. You're gonna leave the *Catch* moored at the Resort's Marina then check into the Hotel. I'll make all the arrangements. Call me when you get there and get settled in a room. Got any questions?" He listened then said, "You, Keats, and the other two women." He listened a little longer then said, "I don't know whether the *Stryder* is going, or not. I'll tell you when that's decided. Got any more questions?" Obviously she had none, because he hung up.

"When do we leave?" asked Keats.

"Now," said Buchanan.

"What about you? What are you gonna do after I'm gone?"

"I'm gonna intercept Ramon."

"In a crowded airport, how will you avoid collateral damage?"

Hobbs was still sitting at the table. He said, with a grin, "We're going to invite him to a private party."

Printed in the United States
By Bookmasters